KONG UNBOUND

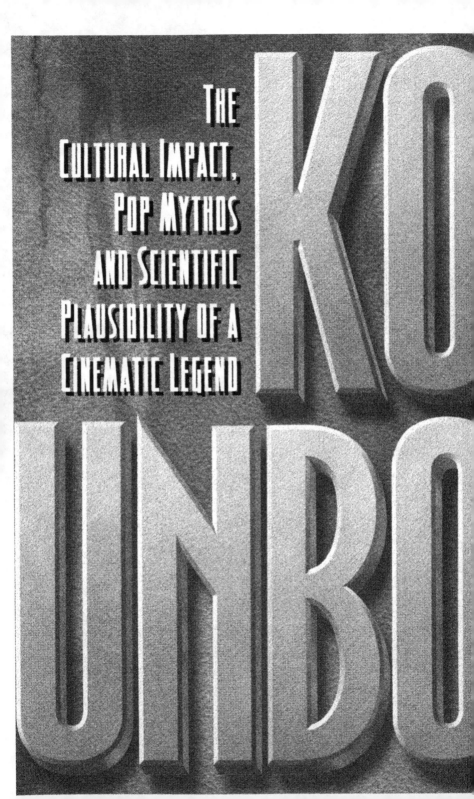

The
Cultural Impact,
Pop Mythos
and Scientific
Plausibility of a
Cinematic Legend

KO
UNBO

KAREN HABER,
EDITOR

A BYRON
PREISS BOOK

POCKET BOOKS
New York London Toronto Sydney

An Original Publication of POCKET BOOKS

POCKET BOOKS, a division of Simon & Schuster, Inc.
1230 Avenue of the Americas, New York, NY 10020

TABLE OF CONTENTS

PREFACE

RAY HARRYHAUSEN

SO MUCH has been written about the original film, *King Kong*, that it is difficult to add anything new to his legend.

To me, it was the greatest fantasy film ever made and still holds up as a splendid piece of entertainment. It was not only the technical virtuosity of Willis O'Brien and his crew but the structure of the story as well. Merian C. Cooper, Willis O'Brien, Ruth Rose, James Creelman, and Ernest Schoedsack managed to take moviegoers by the hand from the mundane world of the Depression into the most outrageous fantasy adventure of all time. Many of the scenes were inspired by the aborted project *Creation*, which was headed by O'Brien at the RKO studio, before the reign of Merian C. Cooper.

Technicians are seldom recognized as contributors to the overall screen story. In my own case, with films I have worked on, I have contributed to many scenes and sequences in the script through the process of the so-called "sweat box" meetings where the producer, the writer, and I would analyze and suggest scenes or sequences that would improve the story line. I would make detailed drawings of how I saw the sequence and submit them at the story conference. It was then the writer's job to integrate them in a logical way. O'Brien went through a similar process on *Kong*. These ideas were then credited to the screenwriter. When working on *Mighty Joe Young*, O'Brien would make drawings of new ideas that would then enhance the story line. This seems to be the nature of creating a good fantasy film.

Merian C. Cooper's original idea about the exploits of a giant gorilla was finally realized when he took over the job of heading the RKO Studios in the 1930s. RKO Radio Pictures became the cauldron where the perfect homunculus, King Kong, was born. Kong and his prehistoric companions were not brought to life by occult means of the ancient alchemists, but by the rather time-consuming process of stop-motion photography. The unique Wagnerian film score written by Max Steiner boosted the film into another, almost operatic dimension. I have a notion the ancient experimenters in the field of alchemy would be more than pleased with the results.

Ray Harryhausen
London, April 2005

FOREWORD:
KONG REVERIE
RAY BRADBURY

'M HERE to praise *Kong* because it influenced me for most of my life, and when Dino De Laurentiis' man in the ape suit appeared, my rage could not be concealed. Instead of a virgin beauty, they depicted an unclad lady of the night with not a single virtue as cover-up. I dubbed it "The Turkey That Attacked New York."

When I was sixteen, my dream was to re-film *Kong*, providing it with color, which had just appeared at that time; I wanted to see those lovely monsters portrayed in vivid hues. Beyond that, there is no reason to change the perfection of Merian C. Cooper's screenplay.

Kong's perfection is its expectations, its feelings of apprehension from the very start. This peaks when during the ship's voyage Carl Denham directs Ann Darrow to stare at the empty sky and then shriek with terror. From there on, scene following scene, the film builds to the appearance of Kong himself, and then Kong dominates the action to the finale.

Willis O'Brien's animation has never been equaled. When you consider that it was created in 1932, when most modern technologies were unavailable, some of the film's scenes are totally astonishing, such as when Carl Denham's men try to cross a log bridge and Kong lifts the log and shakes the men free to fall to their deaths.

The whole thing has a perfection that I, as a screenwriter, can only admire, for I have seen the film dozens of times in the seventy years since its initial screening.

One of the great nights of my life occurred twenty years ago at the fiftieth anniversary of the premiere of *King Kong*. Ray Harryhausen, the world's greatest living animator, attended with me in a yellow Packard limousine. And these two boys—for that's what we still are—rolled up in front of Grauman's Chinese Theatre and were twelve years old again.

There in the forecourt was a huge Kong model. We leaped out of the limo and ran into Kong's embrace. At that moment Fay Wray burst from the crowd and ran to hug and kiss us. This energy and this exultation describes how *Kong* has continued to affect our lives.

With its casting, writing, and direction, you have a film that will continue to be screened to the end of this century and beyond.

The peak in our lives occurred last year when Ray Harryhausen took Fay Wray to the top of the Empire State Building and once more declared his love, and our love, for this dear woman.

Kong will prevail far into the future and I, as his defender, will be there to the last.

Ray Bradbury
Los Angeles, March 2005

INTRODUCTION: KONG TRANSCENDENT

KAREN HABER

E ENDURES.

He persists.

He is everywhere.

On the wall of my favorite pizza parlor in Berkeley, California, a bright blue neon mural depicts him clutching the Empire State Building in one hand, a big cheese slice in the other.

In a dusty parking lot on 101 South just below San Jose, a giant balloon ape holds a sign inviting shoppers to buy discount tires.

On the wall of an influential literary agent's Chelsea district office in New York City, a mural depicts a Big Ape menacing a Screaming Blonde.

Where does the 2,800-pound gorilla sit? Wherever he pleases, in the world of kitsch.

Kongabilia flourishes.

On coffee mugs. In flip books. Birthday cakes. Window decor. Halloween costumes. Inuit sculpture. Greeting cards. *New Yorker* magazine cartoons. Paintings.

King Kong has conquered and continues to dominate the world of windup toys and refrigerator magnets.

In the miniaturized world of kitsch collectibles, Kong reigns over a vast kingdom. A quick search for King Kong memorabilia for sale on e-Bay turns up 668 items, among them: cuff links, rings, T-shirts, lunchboxes, a chalk sculpture, candy wrappers, decanters, a light switch, and to double your kitsch/double your fun: the Miss Piggy–as–FayWray jigsaw puzzle, and let us not overlook the King Kong Barbie replete with "giant" ape hand. More? How about the Burger King Kong glass, monster flicker cards, model kits, posters, photo stills, comics, film cells, toys.

But Kong is bigger than the world of miniatures.

Much, much bigger.

Tribute is paid by published parodies such as Dav Pilkey's *Kat Kong*. ("It was Curiosity killed the Cat.") In animated cartoons. Comic books. Editorial cartoons. Playwright David Lindsay-Abaire was quoted in the *New York Times Magazine* musing about including King Kong in a scene for a musical he is writing on Betty Boop. Come eat at the King Kong Café on O'Farrell Street near Hyde, in San Francisco.

If you live in tropical climes, put a King Kong Fishtail Palm in your garden. Perhaps you'd like to plant a few seeds for "King Kong Coleus" at the base of the tree.

Play a round of golf with your King Kong clubs, then relax in your King Kong massage chair, as your kid romps in his King Kong Arms-and-Legs monkey suit.

Kong's appeal crosses geographic boundaries: Award-winning British illustrator Anthony Browne's 1994 take on *King Kong*, published in the United Kingdom, is a highly desired collectible. Japanese kitsch celebrates King Kong in every medium imaginable.

Yes, Kong has triumphed over the ages. He is a Kong for all seasons, all media.

Artist Joe DeVito (with Brad Strickland) has resuscitated him in a new tale of adventures on Skull Island, and a soon-to-be-published interpretation of the original novel, Merian C. Cooper's *King Kong: A Novel*.

Of course, the original Kong medium, film, provides

plenty of tribute, beginning with the faithful new version of the movie by Academy Award–winning director Peter Jackson, soon to knuckle-walk its way across a movie screen near you, trailing a flood of new Kong-themed toys and other "collectibilia" in its wake.

Many moments in cinematic history pay homage to the vision of Wallace and Cooper, O'Brien and Schoedsack, in sequels, imitations, and/or comedic inversions. How many of you recall the sly homage paid by *The Rocky Horror Picture Show*, or *Yellow Submarine*? So, yes, the Big Ape has legs, long ones. And you can buy them—with arms to match—if you, your spouse, or your kids feel a burning desire to ook-ook around the house in simian splendor.

Face it: Kong is a pop culture colossus who bestrides our cultural narrative. He's been around for almost 80 years, both monster and punch line, sight gag and nightmare.

What began as the most elaborate animated fantasy in the history of cinema has avoided being shelved as one more quaint artifact and, instead, has lodged in our collective imagination, become part of the story that we tell ourselves about twentieth-century America. He's funny, he's scary, he's innocent, he's ravenous, he's rampaging. He wants what he wants. He's sort of like us, isn't he?

Is the giant gorilla projected upon the silver screen also a projection of our own all-too-human desires? (If only we could all be rulers of a paradise on Earth, where our frightened subjects worshipped us. If only we could run amok whenever we wished, squashing natives underfoot, interfering with the evening commute, climbing buildings . . .)

Envisioned as a terror-inducing monster, Kong has instead become an enduring folk hero. Some of the

credit is due to his creator, Willis O'Brien, who "human-
ized" Kong with great facial expressiveness and body
language. Kong was much less a monster by the end of
the film and much more an innocent ripped from his
native, unspoiled environment and victimized by the
horrors of modern civilization to which he'd been
brought in chains.

Paradoxically, Kong is the most thoroughly realized character in the movie. Initially presented as a terrible and terrifying monster, he reveals depths of curiosity,
passion, compassion. The other characters—Denham,
Ann, Driscoll—maintain their cardboard personae: the
greedy Entrepreneur, the hysterical Victim, the love-
struck Hero—while only Kong fully lives and breathes
seven decades after he made his cinematic debut. He has
entered the popular consciousness of our culture, become
a reference point, a symbol and an icon.

Born of a smaller, more culturally primitive and
restrictive time, Kong was intended as a thrill ride, a freak
show, a monster to go "boo!" in the darkness of movie
theaters. The original movie is a charming artifact much
in the way that player pianos and coin-operated banks are
amusing relics from primitive America. (Early
Americana—which is Kong to a "k.") It provides a
poignant look backwards at a now-foreign world.

Despite the movie's shortcomings, its myth has
persisted. It's transcended its crude original imaginings,
its now-offensive cultural stereotypes, its mindless violence, its obvious rape analogies, and made the long journey into the light of another age.

I will forever be grateful to Kong for confirming
that one didn't have to relinquish silliness upon attaining
adulthood. My personal history with Kong began when I
visited the offices of MAD Magazine in New York City
circa 1968. My stepfather worked on the same floor as the

MAD offices and had struck up a friendship with artist Sergio Aragonés and other folks associated with the publication. Being an odd girl given to comic-book and science-fiction reading, I badly wanted to meet the maniacs at MAD and was given a special tour of the place. I was particularly amused to see the giant face of King Kong filling the window behind the desk of publisher William Gaines. (Up to that point, I'd always suspected that adults were silly, but here was solid proof.) I had never seen the movie, but I knew who Kong was. Everybody knew who Kong was.

Q: Why did Kong climb to the top of the Empire State Building?

A: Because he couldn't fit in the elevator.

Q: How did King Kong become a punch line to a joke?

A: It was the only way to conquer him

How do we diminish our foes if we can't kill them? Make a joke out of them. We whittled Kong down to size by co-opting his image. Used him for advertisements ("Ape-solutely the best pizza you'll ever eat."). Made a sight gag out of him in decanters and lunchboxes and drinking glasses until he was a familiar member of the family. Kong as whoopee cushion. If you laugh at the monster, he loses his power.

Was it necessary to defang the Big Ape? Was he such a potent manifestation of our collective fears of the unknown that the only solution was to tame and trivialize the monster? Humor is a powerful weapon: if we're laughing, how afraid can we be? The question is, why are we laughing?

Don't underestimate the incongruity of the image of that giant ape clinging to the spire of the Empire State Building.

KONG UNBOUND

For starters, there's the size issue. The juxtaposition of extremes, large and small, can often elicit a giggle. (I speak here from personal experience: years ago, when I walked down the hallway in the dorm with my boyfriend, the difference in our sizes, 5' and 6'4", would leave my dorm mates lying on the floor, gasping with laughter.)

Add the factor of surprise: that face, that GIANT face, peering avidly in the window. There's something oddly hilarious about Kong staring into the apartment where Ann and Jack are discussing how relieved they are to be safe. Of course, one of the contributing factors to the joke is that they're not safe at all. They're oblivious. The discontinuity/disconnect between what they're saying and what is really happening may trigger the giggle. How can those ninnies not see that giant ape in the window? We see him before they do. We're sitting in the audience in the dark, screaming, "For the love of God, look out the window!"

But really, why should they? As far as Ann Darrow and Jack Driscoll were concerned, they were safe, home free. You could no more expect them to look out the window than to expect the filmmakers to recognize that the story they had conceived and depicted as a screen-borne thrill-ride would come to be seen by later more sophisticated generations as a wheezing antique, reflecting the values of its time that have become so outmoded. By the social mores of 2005, *King Kong* is rife with racism, sexism, and probably two or three more "isms" I can't think of right now.

A snapshot of world events leading up to 1933, the year in which the movie first opened, might give us some perspective on that distant era.

In 1928, five years before Kong, the first complete "talking picture," *The Lights of New York*, opened. (*The*

Jazz Singer, with partial synchronized sound, debuted the year before.)

In 1929, the United States stock market crashed in the last week of October, triggering the Great Depression, during which the gross national product (GNP) sank from $103,828,000,000 to $55,760,000,000 over 12 months. People jumped out of windows, lost their jobs, joined soup lines, surrendered hope.

In 1931, the Empire State Building was completed and dedicated in New York City.

In 1932, Franklin Delano Roosevelt was elected president.

On January 30, 1933, Adolf Hitler was appointed Chancellor of Germany. By July, he had ordered the suppression of all other political parties but the Nazis, and begun a policy of boycotting Jewish businesses. The first concentration camp, Dachau, opened.

Franklin Delano Roosevelt was inaugurated as president. In his inaugural speech was the phrase "The only thing we have to fear is fear itself." FDR quickly introduced the New Deal, economic and social reforms intended to combat the effects of the Depression.

King Kong opened. It would do $650,000 worth of business.

Six years later, in 1939, *Gone With the Wind* premiered in the movie theaters.

In 1941, *Citizen Kane* was released. Japan attacked Pearl Harbor and the United States entered World War II. That same year, less than a decade after *King Kong* opened, research began on the Manhattan Project that would lead to the development of the atomic bomb.

It was the worst of times, an era of desperation, of grinding poverty, hunger, and hopelessness, as world events darkened. No wonder movies were so popular: any cheap escape from the mean streets was welcome diversion. The movie industry thrived during the Depression. As President Roosevelt was to comment: "When the spirit of the people is lower than at any other time during this Depression, it is a splendid thing that for just 15 cents an American can go to a movie . . . and forget his troubles."

The Great Depression changed the film industry. Horror and gangster films—fantasies—and musicals—more frothy fantasy—became the order of the day. People wanted relief, wanted escape. If the rich were to be depicted, let them be shown either down on their luck, forced to find their way amidst the plucky "common" folk, or else in screwball comedies wherein dizzy heiresses are redeemed by the love and common sense of average Joes.

Films were churned out: *We're in the Money* (1933), *Gold Diggers of 1933* (1933), *It Happened One Night* (1934), *My Man Godfrey* (1936).

King Kong is undeniably of its era; it reflects the hunger and desperation of Depression-era America: beaten but brassy, with a lingering Jazz Age echo in the rhythms of speech. It also reflects hope: that there's a way out of this mess, somehow. The character of Denham embodies the generation of European immigrants' sons who were determined to make it in the face of the odds. He embodies, as well, that particular kind of American "can-do" spirit that was the antidote to the Depression blues. (Of course, he also embodied the kind of P. T. Barnum bluster and contempt for the audience that came to give showmanship a bad name.)

The film reflects the social stereotypes of the time: woman as helpless object, to be exploited, acted upon, victimized, and, ultimately, saved.

Man—white man—as objectifier, exploiter, the one who acts, the one who saves.

Man—nonwhite—is the bit player, the cook, the native, collateral victim.

Nature was there to be conquered and exploited. Why not take a chance on finding a unique "monster," conquering it, kidnapping it, and bringing it home for the amusement of the masses?

In this respect, *King Kong* was less a reflection of modernity than a throwback to the recent romantic past, to the Victorian Age when "scientific" expeditions and their discoveries were all the rage. *King Kong* as a story and spectacle had much more to do with the nineteenth century and romantic tales of Lost Worlds than with the twentieth century and its worship of the machine. It is, perhaps, an irony that this most romantic of monster movies was made possible by sparkling new technology: the stop-motion animation techniques being pioneered by O'Brien.

Stop-motion animation had been around since 1897. Various filmmakers had experimented with it in the early years of the twentieth century. But not until 1915 did Willis H. O'Brien figure out that filming progressively positioned armatured models would enable him to animate them. By 1925, he had created the dinosaur animation for the seminal *The Lost World*.

O'Brien was working on footage for a movie to be titled Creation when a shakeup in management at RKO brought about the termination of that project. Although this was, initially, bad news for O'Brien, it also brought Merian C. Cooper, a producer, on board as an assistant to the newly appointed David O. Selznick.

Cooper, a former soldier of fortune, pilot, and documentary maker, had dreamed of a movie in which a giant ape fought off biplanes from the Empire State Building.

Cooper brought with him his colleague Ernest

KONG UNBOUND

Schoedsack and with the help of several writers, this was the formative creative team that brought *King Kong* to life.

It's a testimony to the genius of Willis O'Brien that the images of dinosaurs on Skull Island has had such lasting impact.

To return to the social and economic milieu in which *Kong* was made: perhaps *Kong* became a way to take on that huge and frightening monster, the Great Depression. At least give the audiences a tangible terrible monster, and slay it.

The movie doesn't skirt the issue of the Depression. Ann Darrow is first seen stealing an apple out of desperate hunger. Carl Denham's planning a movie spectacular as a way to fill his empty pockets. In fact, the movie was made for $650,000, and grossed $5,000,000 during its first run, not bad for Depression-era income.

Kong has transcended the original intent of his creators and been adopted into our collective cultural reference library. Despite the best efforts of the merchants, Kong retained enough vestigial power to stay on the cultural radar. He settled into the background of pop culture, percolating away, occasionally engendering a cheesy sequel or spin-off film.

As of this writing there were 56,614 results for "King Kong" on Amazon.com, among them the Modern Library Classics edition of the original novel with an introduction by Greg Bear.

As of this writing, there were 5,440,000 results on Google for "King Kong," including www.kongisking.net.

And now comes Peter Jackson's homage to the legend.

When King Kong toppled from the Empire State Building's spire, that should have been the end for the big ape.

22

But somehow Kong proved unslayable, as the contributors to this volume more or less testify.

As Ray Bradbury observes Kong—and Fay Wray—transcend the ages.

And stop-motion animation master Ray Harryhausen takes us for a quick walk down memory lane.

Award-winning artist and creative force William Joyce shares a *Kong* bull session with fellow Kong-a-philes Maurice Sendak and Michael Chabon.

Science fiction legend Jack Williamson contemplates the enduring myth of Beauty and the Beast, and how Kong fits into that dra- matic template.

Award-winning artist William Stout, recounts how his obsessive love affair with Kong and all things dinosaur began.

Television ("The Trouble With Tribbles") and fiction writer David Gerrold asks the tough "after-the-movie" questions, and even attempts some answers.

Science fiction Grandmaster Robert Silverberg recalls the impact that *King Kong* had upon him as a young boy when he first saw the film, and the lasting fascination of those amazing dinosaurs.

Mystery/science fiction writer/movie buff Richard A. Lupoff discusses some of the nuts-and-bolts aspects of the making of *Kong*, and how it compared with other movies of its time.

Prolific storyteller and artist Harry Harrison gives us a glimpse of the world that Kong was born into.

Nebula-winner Esther M. Friesner does a triple-lutz on the phrase "Beauty killed the Beast."

Science fiction/mystery/thriller writer, pulp magazine collector, and movie maven Frank M. Robinson recalls the spell *King Kong* cast upon a young boy from an orphanage in Chicago.

KONG UNBOUND

Best-selling writer, world-traveler, and adventurer Alan Dean Foster recalls how *Kong* influenced him in his career choices, and weighs in on the side of the dinosaurs.

Acclaimed writer's writer Howard Waldrop provides a breathless alternate-reality view of Ann Darrow's life after *Kong*, and her hitherto unknown connection to *Mighty Joe Young*.

Once and future cyberpunk Pat Cadigan considers the deeper behavioral implications of *Kong* as a rape fantasy.

Science fiction and comics writer Paul Di Filippo pursues the notion of *Kong* as a mirror of society's cruelty and racism.

Award-winning British science-fiction author Christopher Priest considers the life and times of actress Fay Wray.

Award-winning illustrator and artist Joe DeVito meditates upon how *Kong* literally influenced the path of his life, and how he came to develop the book *KONG: King of Skull Island*.

To return to that giant image of Kong in the window at *MAD Magazine* for a moment: No matter how I begged, cajoled, or carried on, my parents refused to buy me a Kong for my own window. I pouted for several weeks.

Just now, I took a look at the vintage model of the Empire State Building that I keep on my desk as a paperweight. It looks lonely.

I think, perhaps, it needs a big ape on its spire. He endures, a Kong for all ages.

Tall, hairy, triumphant.

Kong Is Us

Richard A. Lupoff

KING KONG has been around longer than I have, part of that world of black-and-white movie horrors that started with Nosferatu and included Frankenstein's creature and Count Dracula and the Mummy, and would soon include Curt Siodmak's version of the werewolf legend, the Wolf Man, and eventually the *Creature from the Black Lagoon*.

It took a while until I was ready to enjoy the chills that those monsters provided. But in that pre-video, television-barely-out-of-its-infancy era, you weren't likely to see vintage films unless you haunted midnight revivals at art houses or made it your business to join some high-tone film society.

I wasn't high tone.

But I found myself sitting in one of the cheap seats of the Fillmore East on New York's Lower East Side on May 7, 1970. The headline band was due to perform. The auditorium was dark, and filled with a multitude of mostly drug-dazed music lovers.

The old movie screen that was used in those days for abstract light shows in which colors blended and morphed behind acid rock performers on this occasion blazed into a glorious chiaroscuro image of the Empire State Building surmounted by a gigantic ape dangling a screaming blond beauty from one huge hand.

Antique biplanes buzzed the monster, machine guns blazing. The ape, puzzled, put the woman down, studied his bleeding torso, then tumbled eighty-six stories to the bustling street below.

Cut to a street scene. An elegantly dressed man stands beside the unmoving giant, conversing with a police lieutenant.

"Well, Denham, the airplanes got him," says the lieutenant.

"Oh, no," Carl Denham replies, "it wasn't the airplanes. It was Beauty killed the Beast."

At which point the lights came up and the music began. The musicians were Grace Slick, Paul Kantner, Jack Casady, Jorma Kaukonen, and Joey Covington. They were the then-current lineup of the Jefferson Airplane. The event is preserved for posterity as the opening track of one of their albums. I believe it's *Bless Its Pointy Little Head*, but I'm not a discographer and you'll have to check with an expert to see if I'm right.

But enough ex-druggie-hippy-burnout nostalgia. The lovely blonde was Ann Darrow, played by Fay Wray; the civilian was Carl Denham, played by Robert Armstrong; and the giant ape was of course King Kong, played by an eighteen-inch-tall model built by Willis O'Brien.

King Kong was released in 1933 to an enthusiastic reception. I won't go into the storyline—everybody knows that by now. The question is, Why did Kong become a cultural icon, and why is he more popular today, three-quarters of a century after that first release, than ever before?

If you think about those popular monsters—Frankenstein's creature, Dracula, the Mummy, the Wolf Man, the Creature from the Black Lagoon, and Kong—you'll notice a common characteristic. They're all-well, wait a minute, you think about it first and in a little while I'll come back and tell you what I see in common for all those monsters and we'll see if we agree.

First, though, I'm assuming that you've actually

seen the 1933 masterpiece and not had to settle for any of its many sequels, remakes, spin-offs, and imitations. It's okay if you've seen *Son of Kong* or *Mighty Joe Young* or the Dino De Laurentiis 1976 version featuring the World Trade Center in the role of the Empire State Building or even the Japanese *King Kong vs. Godzilla*. It's okay and you needn't feel guilty even if you actually enjoyed those other films. But the one and only real *King Kong* is the 1933 version produced and directed by Ernest Schoedsack and Merian C. Cooper.

It's a movie that almost didn't get made, and when it did get made it was largely slapped together out of used and recycled materials and pre-shot footage. It was allegedly conceived by Edgar Wallace, the great English thriller writer whose prolific output ran to some 95 novels—at least that's my count—plus hundreds of short stories, military histories, plays, movies, and several volumes of verse. He even ghosted an autobiography for Evelyn Nesbit Thaw, "the girl in the red velvet swing," and if you don't know who she was you're in for a treat. (All of this done when he was not busy with his duties as a soldier, cop, merchant seaman, milkman, racecourse tout, drama critic, newspaper editor, and Chairman of the Board of the British Lion Film Corporation.)

Hollywood legend, and I don't doubt it, holds that Wallace had barely started work on the story that would eventually become *King Kong* when he died on February 19, 1932. He was fifty-six years old.

Special-effects genius Willis O'Brien had been working on a silent film called *Creation* as early as 1927. His method was to build flexible models of his creatures and move them painstakingly, frame by frame, while shooting them. *Creation* was never completed, perhaps because of Depression-era budget cuts, but O'Brien still had his models. The battle-to-the-death between Kong and the *Tyrannosaurus rex* that made it into *King Kong* was filmed before the movie was ever green-lighted and used in the pitch session at RKO.

The jungle sets had been built for *The Most Dangerous Game* (1932) and the great ancient wall on Skull Island was left over from Cecil B. DeMille's *The King of Kings* (1927).

How much Edgar Wallace contributed to *King Kong* is subject to debate. Maybe nothing at all. Maybe just the sketchiest of ideas. The plotline contains elements lifted from here and there, cobbled together and brilliantly filmed.

For example: *The Shadow* pulp magazine had made its debut in April 1931. If you've never read the very first Shadow story, you might want to give it a try. It's been reprinted plenty of times. It opens in New York with a despondent Harry Vincent, broke and hungry, a victim of the Depression, about to hurl himself off a bridge, thereby ending it all.

A taxicab pulls up and the driver talks Vincent into coming with him. Turns out that the driver is one of the Shadow's operatives. He recruits Vincent into the Shadow's mysterious organization and the story moves on from there.

A year later, in Chapter 2 of the novel *King Kong*, a failed actress, Ann Darrow, wanders the streets of Manhattan, broke and hungry, a victim of the Depression. Movie mogul Carl Denham appears and recruits her into a mysterious project of his own and the story moves from there.

Coincidence?

I think not.

Of course, in other ways the two stories are not at all similar. *King Kong* owes more to the South Seas tradition of Joseph Conrad, Somerset Maugham, T. S.

Stribling, the unjustly forgotten tale-spinner John Russell, and Edgar Wallace himself. Even more, there is the lost race, lost civilization, "white adventurer" tradition constructed by Rudyard Kipling, Kipling's compatriot and friend Rider Haggard, Arthur Conan Doyle (think Professor Challenger not Sherlock Holmes), and of course that champion of all jungle adventure writers, Edgar Rice Burroughs.

Burroughs's *Tarzan of the Apes* had hit the screen as early as 1918 and was an instant moneymaker. The first talking Tarzan was Johnny Weissmuller, and if you're familiar only with his late Tarzan films in which the budget shrank as Weissmuller's waistline expanded, you ought to make it a point to see his earliest *Tarzans*. The first of these, a huge hit in its day and in fact a minor classic, was released in 1932.

Hmm.

Nineteen thirty-two.

Here's another oddity/coincidence to chew on. *King Kong* hit movie screens in 1933, but if you happen to pick up a copy of the original *King Kong* novel—or novelization—and you peek at the copyright indicia, you'll see that the book was copyright 1932. The author is Delos W. Lovelace. Not exactly a household name today, but Lovelace was no slouch. His short stories had appeared in periodicals ranging from *The American Magazine* and *The Popular Magazine* to *The Saturday Evening Post*.

Lovelace must have had access to the *Kong* script pretty early in order to get that book written and published before the film was ever released. Do you think he had some influence on the storyline? Hard to tell. He refers to Kong's home as Skull Mountain Island. In *King Kong* the island is never named. In the sequel *Son of Kong* it's called simply Skull Island, and that's the name that everybody has used since 1933.

Another intriguing aspect of *King Kong* is the multiple versions of the movie that people have seen over the years. The Internet Movie Data Base, bless its wondrous heart, says this about those different "texts":

"The original version was released four times between 1933 and 1952, and each release saw the cutting of additional scenes. Though many of the outtakes—including the censored sequence in which Kong peels off Fay Wray's clothes—were restored in 1971, one cut scene has never been found. It is the scene in which Kong shakes four sailors off a log bridge, causing them to fall into a ravine where they are eaten alive by giant spiders. When the movie—with spider sequence intact—was previewed in San Bernardino, California, in late January 1933, members of the audience screamed and either left the theater or talked about the grisly sequence throughout the remainder of the film. Said the film's producer, Merian C. Cooper, "It stopped the picture cold, so the next day back at the studio, I took it out myself."

Both the censored "undressing" scene and the spider scene are included in Lovelace's novelization.

Okay, you've been very patient about my question. What do all those classic monsters—Frankenstein's creature, Dracula, the Mummy, the Wolf Man, the Creature from the Black Lagoon, and King Kong—have in common?

Answer: They're all human, or human-like, but they're all deformed in one way or another. Let's check out a few details.

Karloff's scarred face, rivets in the neck, lumbering walk, and mute efforts to communicate, all mark him as a damaged human being. There is real pathos to Frankenstein's creature. You can see Karloff trying desperately to express himself, to establish a decent link with humanity. Your heart goes out to him.

KONG UNBOUND

Lugosi's Dracula is powerful and elegant. We'll overlook his difficulties with pronunciation. Despite his strength and his widely acclaimed sex appeal, he is vulnerable to sunlight and to crucifixes, can't bear to look in a mirror, and has to sleep in a coffin. More to the point, he knows that he has lost his soul. There's an inner anguish to him. "There are worse things than death," he confesses, and he knows what they are.

The Mummy is Karloff again, and what a pathetic, shambling creature he is! You remember that he tried to preserve the life of his beloved and to follow her down the ages. A warped version of *Romeo and Juliet*. But the priests of Egypt caught him, cut out his tongue, and wrapped him up for a millennia-long sleep. When he awoke he was mute, crippled, and doomed.

The Wolf Man? Chaney, Junior? Folklorists will tell you that there is little resemblance between this fellow and the werewolf of legend. Curt Siodmak claimed that he made up the stuff about becoming a werewolf from the bite of a werewolf, the pentagram in the palm, the silver bullet, and the famous line delivered by the great Maria Ouspenskaya: "Even man who is pure of heart . . ." But if you've ever seen the 1941 film, you'll understand the angst of Lawrence Stewart Talbot. He doesn't want to be a werewolf, he doesn't want to kill people, and he suffers in body and soul from his monthly transformation.

As for the Creature from the Black Lagoon, the last addition to the ranks of these classic monsters, he's actually the least human—or humanlike—of the group. He isn't even a mammal, but some sort of mutant fish. And yet he's human enough to fall in love with Julie Adams when he sees her flashing by in her form fitting white swimsuit.

Captured by humans, dragged from his natural habitat, thrown into a world he cannot remotely understand—our sympathy is far more with the Gill-man than with the researchers and explorers who want to study him.

And then there's Kong himself. And that's where those excisions in the various releases of the film come into play. If you were around in 1933 and saw the film in its original form . . . No, scrub that. I don't think it's likely that you were, or did. Let me start that idea once again.

If you've seen a fully restored print of *King Kong*, or what passes for one in view of the seemingly irredeemably lost giant spider sequence, you see Kong as a pretty nasty fellow. Back on Skull Island you saw him pick up natives and crunch them like ripe cherries. He treats some of the Denham expedition the same way.

Later in the Skull Island sequence—which in fact is the heart of the film, the memorable New York events seem almost to be a tacked-on afterthought—Kong steps on a native and squashes him into the earth as if he were a cockroach. It's pretty alarming stuff. And when Kong does wind up in New York and makes good his escape from the theater where he was on exhibit, he resumes his old human-munching ways.

This isn't cannibalism, of course. Kong isn't human. Still, from the viewpoint of a human audience it's all pretty alarming. Think of a cow watching a commercial for a steakhouse if cows could understand commercials.

Kong isn't human, just as the Gill-man isn't human, but he does fit into the template of the human figure. So, for that matter, do all of these monsters, whether originally human (Frankenstein's creature, Dracula, the Wolf Man, the Mummy) or not (the Gill-man, King Kong). Nothing utterly inhuman here. No Tarantula, no Jaws, no Blob.

KONG UNBOUND

For a monster to have real staying power, we have to be able to identify with him, at least a little bit. Think Norman Bates.

But just as the child-drowning scene had to be removed from *Frankenstein*, the people-crunching scenes had to come out of *King Kong*. The reason was the same. The monster had to be made an object of pity, not solely (if at all) of fear and loathing. We don't like our bad guys to be totally bad. Even Hannibal Lecter, certainly the greatest film monster of the modern era, has an almost irresistible charm. Oh, sure, just give him a chance and he'll cook your liver for dinner and savor it with a nice Chianti and fava beans. But wouldn't you just love to sit down and chat with him, maybe even invite him over for dinner some Sunday—providing you could be sure he would behave himself?

There's a wondrous appeal to monsters, especially to monsters in some form that suggests humanity. The late Julius Schwartz, longtime comic book editor, once told me about an oddity in comic book sales. Whenever he featured a gorilla on the cover of a comic book, sales jumped. He didn't know why, he said, but that had been his experience.

Schwartz worked for DC Comics for decades and was one of their most successful editors. He shepherded the revival of superheroes in the 1960s, a decade after they had all but disappeared in favor of cowboys and soldiers and love-smitten teenagers, and just about saved what looked like a dying industry.

One of his most intriguing rescues was a long-running backup feature called "Congo Bill." You don't have to remember Congo Bill, the name pretty well tells the story: White explorer clad in pith helmet and jodhpurs tramps around the jungles of Africa getting into and out of scrapes. Congo Bill was never very successful, and when DC was ready to scrap the character altogether, Schwartz gave him a Hulk-like transformation. Bill morphed into—Congorilla!

Okay, he's gone now, but the ape transplant gave old Bill a new lease on life.

Poe used an orangutan rather than a gorilla in "The Murders in the Rue Morgue," but the idea was the same. Stuart Teitler, the legendary book scout and scholar, told me that he supported himself for many years as a procurer and dealer in rare books. One of his prime customers was a collector who specialized in volumes with pictorial covers featuring gorillas harassing nubile maidens.

Kong ahoy!

One reason for the success of *King Kong* is the fact that it was the product of seasoned professionals. We sometimes like to think of fresh-faced and talented youth springing on the world with brilliant, original works. I won't say that this never happens, but far more often the best work is the work of veterans. Such was certainly the case with *Kong*.

I already mentioned Edgar Wallace, although in all likelihood his contribution to *King Kong* was minimal if not nonexistent. The two geniuses behind the film were Ernest Schoedsack and Merian C. Cooper. You can actually get a peek at these fellows in the fighter-plane attack near the end of the film. Cooper is the pilot of the plane that kills Kong. Schoedsack is the machine gunner.

This is no mere Hitchcockian cameo, included with a wink and a nod at the knowledgeable viewer. Schoedsack and Cooper were both aviators, real ones. In fact, they first met, circa 1920, in the course of their aerial adventures. And thereby hangs still another tale. It involves Poland, and that's no joke.

As early as 1795 Poland had been carved up by its

neighbors, with parts being absorbed into neighboring empires. The Poles didn't care much for this treatment, but they weren't able to do much about it until World War I, or more properly the end of that war. Germany was humbled, the Russian Empire had collapsed and been replaced by the Bolsheviks, and the Austro-Hungarian Empire was dismembered.

Poland was reborn, but the new Poland, feeling its oats, made territorial demands that its neighbors disliked. In 1919 the Russians invaded, starting a nasty little war that has been largely forgotten by most of the world. An international volunteer group was formed under the leadership of two American aviators, Cedric E. Fauntleroy and Merian C. Cooper. Yes, that Merian C. Cooper.

Using a motley collection of leftover World War I aircraft, they created the Kosciuszko Squadron, a vital part of the Polish Air Force. Their favorite tactic was to fly over Russian lines and dive on ground units, strafing them from the rear with machine gun fire. The Russians, not surprisingly, fired back. They managed to knock down several Polish planes, including the one piloted by Merian Cooper.

The Russian general Semyon Budionny had placed a 500,000-ruble reward on Cooper's head, but Cooper doffed his officer's uniform, convinced his Russian captors that he was a corporal, and after several months in a Russian prison camp, was released.

One of the other members of the Kosciuszko Squadron was a daring aviator named—okay, you're ahead of me, aren't you—Ernest B. Schoedsack. The two fliers became close pals. When the Russian-Polish War ended in 1921, the two Americans wound up in Hollywood, and a dozen years later they not only produced and directed *King Kong*, they got to portray a fighter pilot and his gunner.

Is this too good to be true, or what? But don't take my word for it. Check it out on the Internet, or better yet, get a copy of *Kosciuszko, We Are Here!*, the story of American pilots in the Polish-Soviet War, by Janusz Cisek.

Willis O'Brien was the model maker and special-effects wizard credited with the creation of Kong himself. O'Brien had been making films—as writer, director, actor, and anything else you can think of—since 1915. His first two shorts were *Morpheus Mike* and—get ready for this—*The Dinosaur and the Missing Link*. He always had a penchant for antediluvian critters. In 1916 he made *Prehistoric Poultry* and another anticipatory gem, *R.F.D. 10,000 B.C.* The next year it was *Curious Pets of Our Ancestors*. In 1925, *The Lost World*, Arthur Conan Doyle's great dino-epic. In 1931, the famous, abortive, *Creation*. O'Brien had put in four years on that one, working on it between other projects.

By 1933 O'Brien was more than ready to proceed with *King Kong*.

Schoedsack and Cooper's boss, Executive Producer David O. Selznick, had been making films since 1923, starting with a boxing documentary about challenger Luis Firpo called *Will He Conquer Dempsey?* (Following one of the most violent and fast-paced exchanges in ring history, the Manassa Mauler knocked out the Argentine Angel in two rounds.) Selznick went on to make some 83 movies, the most famous being *Gone With the Wind* (1939). His last was *A Farewell to Arms* (1957).

Music for *King Kong* was composed by Max Steiner. Kong was Steiner's twenty-fourth film, in a career that included some 81 movies.

You're getting the point now, of course. *Kong* was no fluke. These were talented, experienced professionals who knew exactly what they were doing.

What about the cast?

Robert Armstrong, the intrepid filmmaker Carl Denham, appeared in 128 motion pictures, starting with *The Main Event* in 1928. *Kong* was his thirty-third movie. He also did a lot of television work later in his career, including several guest roles opposite Raymond Burr in the classic *Perry Mason* series.

Bruce Cabot, the handsome young ship's officer, Jack Driscoll, was the newcomer of the group. He'd made his screen debut in a 1931 serial, *Heroes of the Flames*. *Kong* was his seventh movie out of a career that eventually spanned 96, plus the usual television work.

Frank Reicher, the ship's captain, had an incredible career including 229 films, starting with *The Case of Becky* in 1915. *Kong* was Reicher's thirty-fourth film. His last was *Superman and the Mole Men* in 1951.

I've saved the lovely Fay Wray for last. The fresh-faced, virginal Fay Wray. The lost, hungry waif, Ann Darrow, whose accidental encounter with Carl Denham led her to the perils of Skull Island, the palm of Kong's great hand, the top of the Empire State Building, and ultimately the arms of Jack Driscoll. Hair so fair, skin so pale, features so innocent, ah, young Fay Wray.

Actually Wray made her screen debut in 1923 at the age of 16 in a comedy short called *Gasoline Love*. She may have been the original blond goddess, preceding even the legendary Jean Harlow by some five years. Rumor has it that her blond hair was only a wig, but then Hollywood is all about make-believe anyway, isn't it? By the time Wray appeared in *King Kong* she was a veteran. *Kong* was her fiftieth film in ten years. She worked steadily for another quarter century, bowing out in 1958 with a role in the memorable *Dragstrip Riot*, then unretiring in 1980 for a parting role in *Gideon's Trumpet*, playing opposite Henry Fonda.

It was obvious after the success of *King Kong* that the public had taken to the big ape. RKO was eager to rush a sequel to the screen. Hollywood legend has it that the studio had been in deep financial trouble before *Kong* came along. No surprise. The Depression had been sinking businesses for four years by 1933, and Franklin Roosevelt's New Deal would take a couple of years, at least, to get off the ground.

The big question for Selznick and his colleagues was, What could RKO use as a follow-up for *King Kong*? Not a tough decision. The choice was *Son of Kong*. The next question was, What kind of big ape? Would it be the ferocious, destructive, anthropophagous (and suggestively libidinous) King Kong of the original version? Or would it be the warm-and-fuzzy Kong that remained after the excisions in *King Kong* had been made?

Clearly, the studio decided on the warm and fuzzy ape, and so Ernest Schoedsack was tasked to direct the sequel. Robert Armstrong and Frank Reicher were back. Fay Wray, alas, was not, but the attractive and talented Helen Mack made a good female lead. The film did not score very well with the critics or the ticket-buying public, although it is by no means utterly worthless.

It does, in fact, revisit one of the more intriguing questions left behind by *King Kong*. Was Kong the sole surviving example of his type? Delos Lovelace's book suggests that Kong was immortal. Well, okay, he gets riddled with machine gun bullets and falls eighty-six floors to a hard landing. That kills him pretty dead. But short of such a violent episode, he might have lived for a very long time prior to 1933, and if Carl Denham and associates had not captured him and dragged him away from Skull Island he might have lived for a long time after 1933.

Still, who were his parents? Did he have any siblings? What about cousins? How many giant apes does it take to make a breeding population?

And what about the dinosaurs and the giant serpent who appeared on Skull Island? As far as I could tell from either the film or the book, there was just one example of each species. What the heck is going on? Are we talking spontaneous generation of life? If not, we're going to need a breeding population for each and every species.

As for the son of Kong—I must admit, I saw only part of this picture, late one night when I was having trouble sleeping, so my knowledge of the film is fragmentary at best; unless we're talking an early experiment in cloning, there had to be a Mama Kong somewhere on the island.

And what about those natives? In the movie they're more or less a given. In Lovelace's book, there is an intriguing suggestion that they are the fallen descendants of a once mighty and highly advanced civilization that thrived on Skull Mountain Island. What went wrong, what reduced these once great people to their present sad state, is not explained. But the idea is straight out of Kipling and Haggard by way of Edgar Rice Burroughs and the endless lost colonies and isolated minikingdoms with which Burroughs dotted Africa.

I'd really like to know more about those Skull Islanders and their ancestral civilization, but nobody seems able to enlighten me.

The actors who played those natives, by all appearances, were (to use the accepted term, circa 1933) Negroes. Lovelace in his book does make reference to racial superiority, although he doesn't dwell on it at length. Schoedsack and Cooper go even lighter on this, which is not to say that they trumpet racial equality or the cultural relativism that political correctness dictates in our own era.

At least they didn't dress up a gang of white extras and daub them with lampblack to create the islanders. In fact, two of the islanders actually get cast credit. The native chieftain was played by Noble Johnson; and the witch king, by Steve Clemento. In an era when it was all but impossible for African Americans to find work in movies, Johnson logged no fewer than 134 film credits between 1915 and 1966 and Clemento appeared in 60 films between 1917 and 1942.

Of course Ernest Schoedsack wasn't through with giant apes after *Son of Kong*. Sixteen years later he revisited the theme still again, with *Mighty Joe Young*. The plot was a close analogue of *King Kong* with a young and nubile Terry Moore playing the Ann Darrow role. This time her name was Jill Young and she had been raised in a "sister-and-brother" relationship with a baby ape: Mr. Joseph Young. The Jack Driscoll role, or at least a rough analogue of it, now changed to Gregg, was played by Ben Johnson. And of course the warm-and-fuzzy giant ape had triumphed utterly over the dangerous man-eater of Skull Island.

Merian C. Cooper still got screen credit, and good old Robert Armstrong was back, playing Carl Denham, except for a name change to O'Hara.

Nor was that the end. The 1949 *Mighty Joe Young* was itself remade in 1998. Ann Darrow/Jill Young was now played by Charlize Theron, soon to emerge as a major screen presence and Oscar winner. Gregg and O'Hara merged into Greg O'Hara, played by Bill Paxton. And if Ernest Schoedsack had at last been freed by death from his seemingly unbreakable association with giant apes, even death did not prevent Merian C. Cooper from receiving screen credit as writer.

It was a long run, from 1933 to 1998, from *King Kong* to the second *Mighty Joe Young*, with detours to

KONG UNBOUND

Japan's Toho Studio, to the drawing boards of animation studios, to comic books and endless adaptations, imitations, clones, and cultural references. Nor, of course, is the end yet in sight. Another *Kong* is visited upon us in this blessed year of 2005, nor is there any chance that the 2005 Kong will be the last giant ape we encounter. Not by a long shot.

What does it all mean? Ah, what does it all mean? I think it's pretty obvious that we see something of ourselves in Kong, and something of Kong in ourselves. That great, human-like, innocent, helpless, loving, destructive beast. Attacked, imprisoned, love-smitten, exploited. He is nature. He is us.

He cannot escape, ultimately, nor can we.

Kong!

Kong!

Kong!

Kong!

Kong!

Fay Wray, the Pulp Tradition, and the Moral Minority

Christopher Priest

HREE CONNECTED elements help explain the particular impact of *King Kong*: the personality and image of Fay Wray, the background to the way in which the script was written, and the economic, social and, moral climate in which the film was made and sold.

Fay Wray, the iconic female star of *King Kong*, moved to California in 1919 while still a child. She had been born Vina Fay Wray in 1907 in Alberta, Canada, but her father moved the family to the United States in search of work, settling first in Arizona, then in Salt Lake City. The influenza pandemic in 1918–1919 caused the death of her older sister Vaida, and Fay, thought to be of more fragile health than her sister, was sent to live with a family friend called William Mortensen in Los Angeles.

With Mortensen's support she began working as a Hollywood extra while still in high school, and by the time she was 19 she had appeared in more than twenty movies. All her appearances were in comedy shorts, playing bit parts or in crowd scenes. This was almost at the end of the silent era of movies. Her first real part was in a short comedy called *Gasoline Love*, in 1923.

After a few more similar small parts, in 1926 she obtained a six-month contract with the Hal Roach Studio by walking brazenly one day into Roach's studio and asking for work. Roach was amused rather than annoyed, and signed her for a series of two- and four-reel comedy Westerns. While working for Roach she developed and polished the technique of playing the damsel in distress, which in any event was the common lot of many young actresses in the silent era. She made at least two films written and directed by a young and then-unknown Stan Laurel. At the end of her contract with Roach she made more Westerns for Universal Studio, almost invariably cast as a supporting character.

So far, nothing in her career distinguished Fay Wray from any of the dozens of other young actresses trying to find fame in Hollywood. Her big break came when she was spotted by the expatriate German director, Erich von Stroheim, who cast her in the lead of a serious drama called *The Wedding March*. She was still only 19 at the time.

Stroheim said, with some prescience, "As soon as I had spoken with Fay Wray for a few minutes I knew I had found the right girl. Fay has spirituality, but she also has that very real sex appeal that takes hold of the hearts of men."

In *The Wedding March* (released in 1928, one of the last major silent dramas) Fay Wray played opposite von Stroheim, who cast himself in the leading role of an Austrian prince. Wray played Mitzi, a crippled Viennese harpist, who falls in love with the prince. Although the romance blossoms, Mitzi is made to marry a rich and lustful butcher, who treats her with great brutishness.

Although the Beauty and the Beast theme was and still is a Hollywood staple, *The Wedding March* was Fay Wray's first venture into this familiar territory. It would not even be worth remarking on if she had not later made *King Kong*.

A second and perhaps more interesting result of working with von Stroheim was what she learned from him about lighting and makeup. Stroheim was a naturalistic director, and as well as using immensely

KONG UNBOUND

detailed sets he lit every scene in a way that modern cinematographers take for granted, but which in the late 1920s was considered radical. His actors barely needed makeup. Wray herself later described in her autobiography the impact this had on her appearance, and also on her attitude to makeup:

"A luminous lighting made me look almost blond. A kind of shimmering tone was an enhancement so great I saw myself transformed by the photography. Gone, gone the contrasty black-and-white face of the girl in the little Westerns. Magic had happened! So, then, I would not have to use make-up; I would do these things for myself." (When the time came to film *King Kong* Fay Wray wore a blond wig over her natural dark-brown hair, and used little makeup. This paleness undoubtedly enhanced her image of vulnerability.)

Wray's career took a significant step forward as a result of *The Wedding March* (and its sequel, *The Honeymoon*, 1928, which was shot back-to-back with it). It was her first undoubted starring role, and when in later years the negative of the film was discovered and a restored print was struck, Wray flew to London to be present at the inaugural performance. She then declared *The Wedding March* to be the favorite of all her films. She was always much more ambivalent about *King Kong*.

The Paramount studio distributed von Stroheim's film, and as a result took over Wray's contract from Universal. They decided to relaunch her career, drawing comparisons with Lillian Gish. Wray soon started working with good directors (including William A. Wellman, Josef von Sternberg, and Frank Capra) and leading men such as Gary Cooper. She made at least four films with Cooper over the next five years, including a WWI drama called *The Legion of the Condemned*.

Legion was cowritten by the screenwriter John

Monk Saunders. Fay Wray fell in love with him and they married. (Saunders turned out to be a violent alcoholic and compulsive womanizer, and although they had a daughter together Wray divorced him before the end of the 1930s. Saunders committed suicide in 1940.)

Fay Wray was one of the relatively few performers of that era who transferred successfully from silent movies to the talkies. Indeed, her transition to sound was sensational. Famous in *King Kong* for her ear-shattering screams, Fay Wray made a number of extreme thrillers (the phrase horror film had not been coined in her day) where her habitual role as the endangered, put-upon young woman gave her much practice in screaming. At least two of these thrillers pre-date *King Kong*: Michael Curtiz's *Doctor X*, 1932, and Ernest B. Schoedsack's *The Most Dangerous Game*, also 1932. In the last-named film, Fay Wray and her co-star Joel McCrea were pursued through a tropical jungle, a set that was being used at the same time in *King Kong*, where similar chase scenes took place. Schoedsack was of course also co-director of *King Kong*, and in fact there is overlap between the two movies. Robert Armstrong, who plays Carl Denham in *King Kong*, was another of Wray's co-stars in *Dangerous Game*.

Nor are these the only films of that period. Wray was soon one of the busiest actors in Hollywood: in the three years leading up to *King Kong*, she was the leading lady in about twenty-five films.

This then is the background from which Fay Wray emerged, to take her most famous role. She was already a star, already a noted beauty, and had already shown herself to be adept at female-in-distress roles.

In 1931, John Monk Saunders published a novel called *Single Lady*, giving his central character some of Fay Wray's personality. Although it was filmed soon after as *The Last Flight*, another actress, Helen Chandler, was given the central role. However, a musical version was produced, and when it played on Broadway under the title *Nikki*, Fay Wray took the main part. She was performing in this when she was noticed by the film director Merian C. Cooper.

In a quote reported many times, Merian Cooper told Wray that he wanted to cast her opposite "the tallest, darkest leading man in Hollywood." Wray guessed that he meant an actor such as Clark Gable or the then up-and-coming Cary Grant, but of course Cooper was referring to the 18-inch model made of steel, rubber, cotton, and rabbit fur that became the eponymous giant ape. Fay Wray's response to the reality of this hyperbolic promise is not recorded, but you can't help feeling that it must have come as something of a disappointment, at least at first. No one, not even Merian Cooper himself, could have known at that time what the movie of *King Kong* was to turn out to be.

Nor could Wray herself have foreseen how the elements of her particular acting background would blend into the part of Ann Darrow, the object of Kong's bestial affections.

The main credit for *King Kong's* screenplay is to Edgar Wallace, the prolific British thriller writer, hired by the production company to add a certain prestige to the project. In fact, Wallace died within a couple of days of starting work and it is unclear how much of the final film is his. In all probability, none of it at all. Even the title he was working with, *The Beast*, was changed.

From the outset, the film was the brainchild of Cooper, who was to be co-director of the film (with Ernest Schoedsack). They drew up the outline of what they intended, which was to use real animals photographically enhanced for the main action. When Cooper saw the stop-frame animation work of Willis O'Brien he realized that was a better technique for what he had in mind. He handed his notes (and presumably whatever Wallace had left behind) to a screenwriter named James Ashmore Creelman. Creelman came up with a script that in general terms told the story in the way we know it today, but which Cooper judged to be unsatisfactory. He wanted the dialogue to be plainer, more down-to-earth, providing a stark contrast with the fantastical elements that would be on the screen.

Once again another writer was put to work: this was Ruth Rose, who was in reality Schoedsack's wife. Her screenplay is the final one, as used in the film. It is interesting, in fact, that so much of the script should have been written by a woman, when you consider the amount of misogyny there is throughout the story.

In the meantime, this was the period in Hollywood of transition from silent movies to talkies, and the shadow of the Depression was deepening. Hollywood has always been about making money, but it was never truer than at this time. For the previous quarter-century, the studios had made their money from silent films, but with the coming of sound, there was a sense that they were going to have to rethink many of the assumptions they had had until then. In 1932, when *King Kong* was in the writing and planning stage, the need to make money would have been of paramount concern.

The films that Hollywood was producing at this time were of course nothing like modern output. Although there was a star system, and huge sums of money were lavished on many productions, the actual stories, the scripts, were for the most part conservative. Many writers who had grown up in the world of formula fiction for the pulp magazines moved to Hollywood in the hope of bettering themselves. Those who managed to break in found themselves writing much the same kind of material, if more lucratively. Writers were employed directly by the studios, and worked in tiny offices within the studio lots. Scripts were assigned to writers, who often had to pick up the work already started by another, while their own projects could be taken away and given to someone else. Writers frequently worked on three or more different stories at once, usually without credit and certainly without a percentage of the box office.

Although none of this is strictly true of *King Kong* (it's difficult to imagine the director's wife being made to sweat it out in a writer's cubicle), this is the climate in which the screenplay was developed. Stories had to be clear, uncomplicated, and direct. Action and adventure were to predominate. Characters had to be stereotyped. There is no subplot in *King Kong*, no subtlety of motive, no plot-twists or surprise developments in the story. The screenplay is merely a straightforward exposition of the idea.

Early in *King Kong* there is a scene set aboard the *Venture*, the ship that will take everyone on the expedition to find Kong. A theatrical agent called Weston has come aboard, just before the ship is due to sail. He tells Carl Denham, the film director and leader of the expedition, that he can't find a female actor (a "girl") to play the lead part in the proposed film. This is the key exchange between the two men, as it is played in the film:

WESTON
It can't be done, Denham.

DENHAM
What? It's got to be done.
(Weston shakes his head in silence)
Now look here, Weston. Somebody's interfered with

every girl I've tried to hire. And now all the agents in town have shut down on me. All but you.

You know I'm square.

Denham has been told, presumably by his financial backers, that his next film requires a love interest, a girl with a pretty face. Against his better judgement he has instructed Weston to find him an actress.

Two suspicions that people have about Denham are implied throughout this scene. The first is that the young woman would be placed in physical danger if she went on location to make the film. The second is that Denham might be procuring her for sexual reasons, if only inadvertently: she would be the sole woman on board the ship, otherwise crewed by many tough-looking and presumably sexually aggressive males.

Denham of course denies all this and asserts that an actress would be safe with him. At the end of the exchange, Denham decides he can't leave the problem to be solved by other people, and sets off from the ship intending to find someone by his own efforts. His departing remark is, "I'm going to go out and get a girl for my picture—if I have to marry one!"

Again, there is a hint that sexual coercion will have to be used, not something that would arise, presumably, if Denham was looking for a male actor.

Ruth Rose's shooting script puts different emphasis in the exchange between Weston and Denham, and includes a revealing extra detail. This is how she wrote it:

WESTON
It can't be done, Denham.

DENHAM
What? It's got to be done.

> (Weston shakes his head in silence)
> Look here, Weston. The Actor's Equity and the Hays
> outfit have interfered with every girl I've tried to hire;
> now every agent in town has shut down on me.
> All but you. You know I'm square.

Whenever you are able to compare a shooting script with the finished product that appears on the screen, dozens of tiny textual differences become apparent. These occur almost inevitably in many films: the director or the actors elide lines of dialogue, or make sudden improvisations, or simply get the lines wrong. No one (other than the writer, one assumes) either notices or cares.

In this case, though, it seems to me that the omission is fairly significant, and the result of a decision by either the director or the studio to leave it out, rather than an ad hoc alteration on the day of shooting.

"Actor's Equity" (Ruth Rose's punctuation) is an obvious reference to the actors' union, then as now a formidable presence in Hollywood. If Denham and his film existed in the real world, the Actors' Equity Association would certainly take a dim view of him trying to hire a young actress and transport her halfway around the world to make a big-game movie that appears not to have a proper script. The view would be even dimmer if they realized he was planning to pluck some homeless young woman from the streets and give her a starring role in a new movie.

It would be unlikely, though, that this remark about the union in a piece of dialogue would ruffle anyone's feathers.

The mention of "the Hays outfit" is a different matter. This is a reference to the MPPDA, the Motion Pictures Producers and Distributors Association, otherwise known as the Hays Office. For all filmmakers of the time it was a controversial subject. It is no surprise that the remark was quietly removed from the screenplay, since it might well have drawn wrath. Fay Wray's role in *King Kong* provides an interesting insight into the Hays Code.

After a series of scandals in Hollywood in the early 1920s, the studios had banded together to form the MPPDA (later abridged to Motion Picture Association of America, or MPAA). Initially, this was set up as a PR operation, to portray and foster a positive image of the movie industry. The MPPDA was headed by William Hays, who had previously worked for the Republican Party as campaign manager for President Harding.

At the time there was growing concern about censorship in many areas of the United States. The more popular moviegoing became with the public, the more the moralists—religious groups, educational organizations, etc.—saw films as a threat to their values. Several state legislatures were under pressure to pass legislation that would strictly censor what was shown. Obviously, piecemeal censorship across forty-eight states would have made film distribution almost unworkable. Hays ran well-planned campaigns in a number of states, using the resources of the MPPDA as well as his own GOP connections, and after a state referendum in Massachusetts rejected the legislation by a two-to-one margin the battle was effectively won.

For a few years after this victory, Hays played a double game. On the one hand he was working to defend the movie industry against the continuing complaints of the moral guardians, while on the other he was trying to exercise his own moral authority over Hollywood. From time to time he would issue lists of "Do's and Don'ts" but no one took much notice.

KONG UNBOUND

In 1930, as the introduction of sound brought fresh complaints from the moral watchdogs, he published the first of his now notorious Production Codes, known forever after as the Hays Code. At first, the Hays Code had the opposite effect. The Depression was biting, and the studios were casting around to find what was certain to make money: the answer was of course the two hardy perennials, sex and violence.

The Code also lacked the force of law. Its only power resided in the implicit threat of what might happen without it. For many, this seemed a vague concern.

By 1934, the MPAA felt that the Code needed strengthening, revised rules were published, and a certificate of approval was required before a film could be released. Joseph Breen was appointed head of the new Production Code Administration. Under Breen, application and enforcement of the Production Code was unbending. A period of about thirty years followed, during which American filmmakers struggled with dozens of rules about what could and could not be shown. All that was in the future when *King Kong* was made. Released in 1933, the film falls squarely in the period now known as "pre-code." The description is a little misleading, because the 1930 version of the Hays Code was in place, but largely ignored. "Pre-code" really refers to the period before it was enforced.

Certain films of that period helped bring about the enforcement. Perhaps the best known is *Tarzan and His Mate* (1934). This is the film in which Maureen O'Sullivan went through most of the story wearing a flimsy tabard-like garment, and that included in its first version a four-minute scene of Ms. O'Sullivan apparently swimming in the nude. (In fact, the naked bather was a body double called Josephine McKim, who had won an Olympic swimming gold for the United States in 1928.)

By modern standards the film is tame stuff, and as in so many other cases you can't help wondering with hindsight what all the fuss was about. The German film *Extase* (1932) contained a similarly harmless nude scene with Hedy Lamarr, although in fact it never reached American screens. It was confiscated by U.S. Customs–the mere fact of its existence was enough to send the moral watchdogs into a spin.

But then there was *King Kong*.

It's instructive to see just how far Cooper and Schoedsack went in defying the Hays Code. Playing devil's advocate, here are the relevant provisions of the 1930 Code. The description that follows the provision is what the film actually shows and the interpretation the Hays Office would probably have put on the material.

Under the heading of Article II, Sex:

2.b. Scenes of Passion. Excessive and lustful kissing, lustful embraces, suggestive postures and gestures, are not to be shown. Ann Darrow is twice shown in a suggestive posture, an abandoned attitude, lying supine, through fear or exhaustion.

4. Sex perversion or any inference to it is forbidden. Bestiality (sexual contact between animal and human being) could clearly be categorized as a perversion. In the scene where Kong strips Ann Darrow of some of her clothes, Kong deliberately sniffs his fingers after touching her, underlining his animalistic nature.

5. White slavery shall not be treated. Although *King Kong* contains no scenes which might be mistaken for white slavery in the sense it was usually meant in the 1930s, it does nonetheless contain many of the underlying elements: the concept of a vulnerable young woman from a civilized country being put at the mercy of some alien or uncontrollable presence, who intends to make use of her for whatever purpose he wishes.

Under the heading of Article VI, Costume:

2. Undressing scenes should be avoided, and never used save where essential to the plot. Although Ann Darrow never purposely undresses, after Kong has torn off many of her clothes she does spend much of the second act of the film with what remains of them hanging away revealingly.

3. Indecent or undue exposure is forbidden. See above. After Kong has torn Ann Darrow's clothes she is in a state of semi-nudity. There are several short scenes where she is swimming, running, and so on, in which her body is fleetingly revealed. In addition, there is a scene early in the film where Ann Darrow undertakes a screen test for Carl Denham, in which she wears a see-through dress. The sexual effect of this garment is underlined by a cutaway shot to members of the ship's crew ogling her lasciviously.

Under the heading of Article VIII, Religion:

3. Ceremonies of any definite religion should be carefully and respectfully handled. The villagers on Skull Island are depicted as having built some kind of totemic religion around the presence of Kong on their island. They use a giant gong to announce or summon him, they perform propitiatory dances, they make human sacrifices, and so on. Whether this constitutes a definite religion or not is a bit unclear, but it is certainly shown to be central to their way of life. This is not respectfully handled. The villagers are depicted as uncivilized savages, coping with the dangers of Kong in only the most basic ways (throwing spears, running away, etc.).

Under the heading of Article XII, Repellent Subjects:

5. Apparent cruelty to children or animals. At least one child is shown to be put in danger in the scene in which Kong is rampaging through the village. As for

cruelty to animals, the entire film is in essence about the discovery of a large animal living in the wild. This animal is hunted, chased, attacked with spears, shot at with rifles, knocked unconscious with gas bombs, shackled, displayed for the entertainment of others while in captivity, and finally killed with aerial machine guns.

6. The sale of women, or a woman selling her virtue. Ann Darrow is captured, violently abducted, and finally offered as a human sacrifice to propitiate Kong.

The second half of the 1930 Hays Code contains probably the most controversial material, as it presents its reasons for the prohibitions. It justifies itself by way of argument: a discussion of various subjects including the meaning and effect of art, the motive of the artist, family values, respect for the police, the reaction of adults to films, the sexual responses of audiences to actions they might see on the screen, the absolute necessity of taking religion seriously, and much else.

Amid this pious nonsense there are further observations that have a bearing on the way *King Kong* was flouting the rules:

Impure love must not be presented as attractive and beautiful.

The whole thrust of the story of *King Kong* is that the giant ape falls in love with Ann Darrow, and it is her beauty that leads to his downfall. This is stated on an epigraph screen card at the beginning of the film, and it is restated in the last words of the film, spoken by Carl Denham. However, Kong is a giant animal, an immense ape or a huge gorilla. No animal is surely capable of appreciation of human beauty in any way that might be comprehensible to that human, and therefore its love is impure. *King Kong* certainly attempts to portray bestial love as attractive and beautiful.

It must not be presented in such a way to arouse passion or morbid curiosity on the part of the audience.

As the film is obviously intended as entertainment, and is not at all a serious discourse on bestiality, the actions of Kong toward Ann Darrow must be seen in anthropomorphic terms by the film's human audience. In other words, when Ann Darrow is stripped of her clothes by Kong, the titillation of the audience is in human terms: an attractive young woman, held against her will, is seen having her clothes torn from her. It is a male rape fantasy, in other words. The intention of the filmmakers is clearly to arouse passion or morbid curiosity on the part of the audience.

Nudity or semi-nudity used simply to put a "punch" into a picture comes under the heading of immoral actions. It is immoral in its effect on the average audience. On this subject the Code adds: Nudity can never be permitted as being necessary for the plot. Semi-nudity must not result in undue or indecent exposures.

Ann Darrow is semi-nude for a large part of the second act of the film, and there are several glimpses of her body. There is in fact no reason for this that could be justified by the plot, other than to titillate the audience.

King Kong duly came in for moralistic criticism on its first release, but it was a huge popular success and it has gone on pleasing audiences ever since. It was the first "talkie" in movie history to be rereleased, and on that occasion (after the Hays Code had been strengthened) certain cuts were made. Clearly, the sort of points made above reflected the feelings in the Hays Office. In particular, the scene when Kong removes some of Ann Darrow's clothes was cut, as was some of the footage of Kong rampaging through the village.

Those cuts have been restored in recent times, and the DVD versions currently on sale appear to consist of the complete film as originally released. (*Tarzan and His Mate* suffered a similar fate, incidentally. The nude bathing scene was cut out in its entirety soon after the film was completed, and some extra footage was shot to replace the more revealing moments of Ms. O'Sullivan's skimpy costume. The original footage has been restored recently.)

The performance of Fay Wray as Ann Darrow made her a major star, or at least a star of *King Kong*. Although renowned throughout the world, never again was she to find a role with which she became so identified.

The film survives because of its unique niche in film history: it was the first American major special effects movie, presenting a considerable novelty and a racy story to the audiences for which it was intended. For audiences who have discovered the film in the seventy-plus years since it was made, *King Kong* still offers novelty, in spite of the immeasurable improvements since in animation, animatronics, and other special effects. It is now a period piece, but it remains an amusing and fitfully entertaining one.

The film is certainly not a great one because of Fay Wray's performance. When given a dramatic scene to play, she is unconvincing and under-directed. There is perhaps only one scene in the entire film that can be judged as drama pure and simple, and that is the one she plays with Robert Armstrong in the diner. Carl Denham has taken Ann Darrow there to tell her what he wants from her. Their exchange is excruciating: when Denham tells her his name and asks him if she's ever heard of him she says, "Yes, yes, you make moving pictures in jungles and places." Given that it's not one of the greatest lines of dialogue ever written, the actress enunciates the words with all the emphasis of a shopping list. (Armstrong is no

help: his performance throughout *King Kong* is amateur-
ish and ill at ease.)

However, when called upon to run through
undergrowth, fall over behind tree trunks, be tied to a
platform as a sacrifice, be carried around, scream, swim,
lose clothes, she is as competent in the role as any other
young actress of that era might have been. Her slightly
bruised good looks and fair appearance added to the aura
of vulnerability the film contrived around her, but did not
improve her acting.

Fay Wray benefited more than anyone else in the
film from the screenplay. Because it has the same trashy
appeal as the pulp fiction with which it shares a tradition,
she was called upon to do little more than be a damsel in
distress. *King Kong* is a story told in a straightforward and
undemanding manner, with no plot development or
sophistication, and no efforts to fill out the characters
except in the most unsubtle way. This simplistic charm
also lies in its opportunistic flouting of the Hays Code. In
both of these, Fay Wray was seen at her best.

The Magic and Mystery of Kong

of Kong

Robert Silverberg

HE FIRST time I saw *King Kong*—and the second time, too, because I was so enthralled that I stayed to see it again the same afternoon— was eleven years old, and the film was having its third re-release, not long after World War II. It was already legendary, and I had been hearing about it from older boys for years. A lost island in the Pacific! Real live dinosaurs! A giant gorilla!

And also—I didn't need Freud to tell me that sexual curiosity begins before puberty—a beautiful actress, said to be very scantily clad!

So I went, one Saturday afternoon in 1946, to the Crown Theater on Empire Boulevard in long-ago Brooklyn, and got my dime's worth and then some. The scenes that were most revealing of Fay Wray's delectable form had been somewhat expurgated in that print, but I didn't know that then, and the ones that survived struck my uncritical pre-adolescent eye as sufficiently hot stuff. And the important thing was that there was Kong himself, as big and ferocious as advertised, and there were the dinosaurs—the dinosaurs! The ancient bones made flesh before my bedazzled young eyes. So of course I had to see it all again immediately, and stayed for that day's second show. This required me to sit through the intervening film, which was the feeble sequel, *Son of Kong*.

Even then I was able to tell that the hastily made *Son of* wasn't a patch on the original. Little Kong was a cute monster, and cute monsters weren't what I was looking for that day. So I waited it out, impatiently wriggling

and squirming all the way, and finally Skull Island disappeared in a climactic burst of volcanic fury, the screen
briefly went blank, and then the ominous, brooding intro-
ductory music of the real movie, that sinister three-note
Kong theme, resounded through the theater for the second
time that afternoon. Of course, a lot more wriggling and
squirming was ahead for me before the payoff arrived,
because I knew now that I was going to have to sit through
those interminable forty-five minutes of buildup before
Kong himself, wild-eyed and toothy, would come rampaging through the forest toward the gate in the great wall. I
wasn't capable of understanding, back there in 1946, the
artistic value of that lengthy buildup of mood and character. Remember, I was only eleven years old, and I hadn't
come to the theater that day for mood or character. I
wanted the filmmaker to cut right to the monsters.

It bothered me that he had wasted a full half of
the movie on what I regarded as irrelevant preliminaries.

Years later, I would come to appreciate the merit
of the bleak Hopperesque atmospherics of the film's earliest scenes in Depression-era New York City, but *King
Kong* was just thirteen years old at the time of my first
viewing of it, and if I wanted to see what Depression-era
New York City looked like, I didn't need to go to the
movies. I simply needed to leave the theater and glance
around me at the drab black-and-white world I inhabited,
not yet transformed into the technicolor post-war
America of split-level houses and long, sleek automobiles.

As for the sea voyage, with its careful building of
suspense and its Conradian evocation of tramp-steamer
life, that meant nothing to me either, then. My hunger to
see those dinosaurs thundering around the island had created an adequate sense of suspense in me already, and as
for the Conradian maritime atmosphere, the name and
works of Joseph Conrad were unknown to me then—my

first reading of such stories as "The Secret Sharer" and "Youth" and "Typhoon" was still four or five years in the future—but I had already had ample exposure to the gritty texture of maritime life in such movies of the thirties as *The Sea Wolf* and *Mutiny on the Bounty*. And Bruce Cabot's interminable, inarticulate shipboard courtship of Fay Wray was the sort of gooey, mushy stuff that gave me, and all the other little boys in the audience around me, a bad case of the fidgets. (Were there any girls in that audience that Saturday afternoon? I doubt it very much. Girls had their movies, and we had ours, and this wasn't one of theirs.)

Eventually, though, the long prologue came to its end and we were passing into that realm of ocean fog that marked the boundary between the world of waking reality and the nightmare world of *King Kong*. And then we had our first glimpse of craggy, foreboding Skull Island, and then at long last we were standing once again with Carl Denham and his crew on the shore of Skull Island, the drums were beating, the fur-clad dancers were dancing the frenzied ape-dance, and the gate in the wall was about to open. And I settled back happily in my seat, knowing what to expect but loving the prospect of experiencing it all once more, just as today I return to some familiar work of art—*The Marriage of Figaro*, let's say, or Beethoven's Ninth, or Picasso's "Demoiselles d'Avignon"—not in any expectation of surprise, but with the happy expectation of renewed satisfaction.

And thus it came to pass. Kong, looming above the treetops and looking more terrifying than he will at any later point in the film, comes roaring up toward the wall. Fay Wray—Ann Darrow, that is—screams that wondrous scream, already rehearsed at Denham's behest aboard the ship, that we will hear so often in the hour to come. Kong, dazzled by her beauty, stares at her in tender and befuddled fascination, releases her from the posts to which she was bound, and runs off into the mysterious jungle with her. Jack Driscoll—Cabot—cries out that she must be rescued, and with Denham and his men gives chase.

At once they are plunged into a dark, Dantesque otherworld choked with alien-looking vegetation. Swirling Paleozoic mists close in around them. And then, the *Stegosaurus* emerges from the underbrush, flicking its spiked tail from side to side. It charges! It is felled by a gas grenade! It twitches the fearsome tail in its death-throes! Yes! Yes! The whole thing is happening again! The long neck of the *Brontosaurus* will rise slowly from the muddy lagoon! The fearsome *Tyrannosaurus* will appear, and Kong will give battle! The *Plesiosaurus*! The giant iguanalike creatureThe *Pteranodon*! Ann and Jack, dangling on their vine as Kong reels them in! The plunge from the cliff into the sea! The rescue of Ann! The fury of Kong, his smashing of the gate, his onslaught against the native village!

And at last the captive Kong, treacherously ensnared and brought back to New York as a pitiful theatrical exhibit, bursting loose one final time, charging about in Manhattan, smashing up the elevated train tracks, plucking the wrong girl from her hotel room and discarding her, finding the right girl, climbing with her to the very summit of the newly constructed Empire State Building, symbol of all that is vast and majestic about New York City—bringing us at last to the awesome climax, the tiny planes buzzing around the enraged monster at the top of the skyscraper, the tragedy of the lovesick beast now consummated in a hail of bullets—I confess that that final scene of Kong's martyrdom, which adults find so poignant, was lost on me at the time, just as the movie's long moody introduction had been. It was exciting, sure, to watch that battle in the sky, and Kong's antics a thousand feet above the pavement gave me a nice acrophobic tingle, but at eleven I had scant sympathy for the great ape's thwarted emotional fixations, and I saw his climbing of the Empire State Building not as tragic defiance of the incomprehensible urban world but just as a silly strategic mistake. (If he had headed out across the Hudson River to New Jersey and points west it would have made a lot more sense to me.) And I had come mainly for the experience of seeing dinosaurs and Mesozoic jungles, after all, not a big ape's goofy, one-sided love story.

Only after later, post-pubescent viewings of the movie did I come to perceive the poignancy of Kong's love-induced martyrdom, which, as we can see from the way the film is framed by the faux Arabian proverb that introduces it ("And the prophet said, 'And lo, the beast looked upon the face of beauty. And it stayed its hand from killing. And from that day, it was as one dead.'") and Denham's somber epitaph for Kong ("It was beauty killed the beast.") at the end, was meant by the creators of *King Kong* to be the thematic mainspring of its dramatic action.

Thematic mainsprings meant nothing to me in 1946; dinosaurs meant a great deal.

Still and all, it had been a thoroughly worthwhile afternoon at the movies—a journey into fantasy that I knew already would mark me for life. Of course, sticking around to see the second show was destined to have some negative consequences that, had I been older and wiser, I might have foreseen. It meant that I got home a little after six that afternoon, three hours or so later than expected. Six o'clock in my household was dinnertime on Saturday, and my father was waiting for me outside the house with wrath in his eye. The wrath of my father was no trivial thing. Not only had I caused apprehension by failing to return home at the usual time, but I had delayed my family's dinner. There were some difficult moments for me that evening. It was, shall we say, a turbulent hour or two. I have long since blocked the specific details—this was, after all, close to sixty years ago—but the general outline of what ensued would not be hard for me to reconstruct.

No matter. My father forgave me eventually, because he always did, and in any case he knew how obsessed I was (is there any little boy who isn't?) with dinosaurs. Though my interest in dinosaurs is considerably less obsessive now than when I was eleven, my fascination with *King Kong* remains ever green.

On that day in 1946 I knew that I was going to see it again and again in the years that followed, and, in fact, I have, beginning with the next theatrical re-release five or six years later, and then in a later re-release in which the expurgated scenes showing a few provocative glimpses of Fay Wray's lissome figure and some gory chomping of villagers by the infuriated Kong were restored to the print. I went to see the unfortunate 1976 remake, too, and when video recorders became available I bought a cassette of the original film, which I still watch from time to time. After those many viewings *King Kong* still remains, for me, the most powerful and fascinating of all fantasy movies, head and shoulders above all the rest.

For me as a small boy, *King Kong* was all about the dinosaurs; but I came to realize long ago that the reconstructed saurians, cleverly done though they were, were actually only an incidental aspect of this film's strange and lasting appeal. I think I understand, by now, where the power of this movie, its enduring magic and mystery, resides. And certainly the compelling hold on me that it continues to exercise has very little to do with the realism of its portrayal of prehistoric life. Realism is not the commodity that *King Kong* has to offer. The thing that it offers is, indeed, quite the opposite of realism. Certainly the central scenes of the movie do recapture, for imaginative eleven-year-old boys who have spent too much time peering up at the skeletons of the fossil dinosaurs on the fourth floor of the American Museum of Natural History in New York, the feel and imagery of the prehistoric world. These scenes put us down in that same Mesozoic of the mind that we have already created for ourselves out of those reassembled bones and the murals on the museum wall: the steamy jungle of unfamiliar tropical plants, the incomprehensibly huge reptiles, the sense of the Earth of a hundred million years ago as being virtually another planet.

All that is very exciting, sure. But as I've said, the dinosaurs don't really occupy a place at the true heart of the film. They're just decorations, props, part of the scenery, rather than the essential item that the movie delivers, and that is why *Kong* is superior as a work of art to all other dinosaur movies from the archaic *The Lost World* of 1925 to *Jurassic Park* and its various sequels of modern times. There are just five or six saurians in the whole movie, and, despite the care that the animators took in simulating their real-life appearance, this is no earnest documentary on dinosaurs: scientific plausibility is, throughout the movie, always secondary to dramatic effect, and when it must be scrapped entirely for the sake of such effects, the moviemakers—Merian C. Cooper and Ernest V. Schoedsack—cheerfully and unhesitatingly throw it overboard.

For one thing, the population of dinosaurs that Cooper and Schoedsack chose to bring to cinematic life for us never existed as contemporaries at any single moment of the past. *Brontosaurus* (which we now are instructed we must call "*Apatosaurus*," a name that doesn't roll easily off the tongue of anyone who learned his dinosaurs back in the 1940s, and which I prefer to ignore) was a creature of the middle and upper Jurassic Period, flourishing some 150 million years ago. *Stegosaurus*, of the formidable spiny tail and odd triangular plates of armor along its back, was roughly contemporaneous with *Brontosaurus*, and so was the *Plesiosaurus*, which is the critter with the serpentine neck that comes close to throttling Kong in his own mountaintop den. (Viewers often mistake this beast for some sort of giant snake, but if one watches the battle closely, as I have done so many times, one sees the little legs that identify it as a plesiosaur.)

But *Triceratops*, which figured in the original screenplay and in Delos W. Lovelace's official 1932 novelization of that screenplay but wound up on the cutting-room floor, didn't evolve until the late Cretaceous, near the close of the saurian era and perhaps thirty or forty million years after *Brontosaurus* and *Stegosaurus* became extinct. Thirty or forty million years is no inconsiderable gap. A *Triceratops* would have been nearly as much out of place in the world of *Brontosaurus* as it would be in ours. The *Pteranodon*, the winged reptile that nearly succeeds in flying off with Ann in its clutches, dates from the Cretaceous also.

Then, too, there's the feisty bipedal carnivore with which, as Ann looks on in shock and horror, Kong has a nasty and ultimately triumphant wrestling match nearly five minutes long. Some commentators on the film have called this one an *Allosaurus*, an animal which would have been contemporary with the *Brontosaurus* and the *Stegosaurus* (as I recall, the American Museum of Natural History has mounted one in a pose that shows it feeding on the carcass of a *Brontosaurus*); but the monster in the movie has the vestigial forearms of the somewhat similar *Tyrannosaurus*, a much later dinosaur, which was larger and even more fierce-looking. Andrew Boone, who wrote a piece on the dinosaurs of *King Kong* for a 1933 issue of *Popular Science Monthly*, thought it was a *Tyrannosaurus*. So do I. (The Lovelace novelization sidesteps the issue by referring to the creature simply as a "meat-eater"; but that scene is told from the viewpoint of Ann Darrow, and she, never having been a small boy, would not have been likely to be able to identify specific dinosaurs as readily as any small boy of that era could have done.) Since *Tyrannosaurus*, too, was a denizen of the Cretaceous, it has no business hanging out with such Jurassic creatures as *Brontosaurus* and *Stegosaurus*.

As for the final monster, the one that comes slithering up a vine in an attempt to attack Jack Driscoll, it is not one that I can identify at all. To me it looks like a giant iguana, and perhaps that's what Cooper and Schoedsack intended it to be. Iguanas did exist in Cretaceous times; but whether this is one, and whether they ever got this big, I am unable to say. I suppose it's beside the point, really, that the giant reptiles of *King Kong* come from widely differing eras of the past, since the premise of the movie is that the whole bunch of them have (inexplicably) survived into modern times on Skull Island, and it's just as easy to believe in the survival of Jurassic dinosaurs as it is of Cretaceous ones, all mixed up merrily together on their remote isle regardless of era of origin, if one can believe in the survival of any dinosaurs at all.

The real issue for sticklers for scientific accuracy is that in most cases the dinosaurs we are shown don't behave as those dinosaurs actually did when first they walked the earth. Consider the *Brontosaurus* (or *Apatosaurus*, if that is what we must call it now). There can be no doubt that in its own day it was a vegetarian.

The design of its body admits of no other dietary habit. It was a ponderous four-legged animal, not likely to move very quickly on land and certainly not built for hunting live prey. It had no fangs; it had no claws. Its teeth were weak wobbly pegs, not at all suitable for the rending and tearing of flesh. Like the equally vegetarian hippopotamus, one of the bulkiest animals of our own era, a *Brontosaurus* could doubtless do a great deal of damage to unwary humans who blundered into its path, but chasing them through a swamp to gobble them down, as the *Brontosaurus* does in *King Kong*, would not be a part of its nutritional program. *Stegosaurus*, too, was a vegetarian, though perhaps the reason why it launches that furious charge against Denham and his men had more to do with annoyance over their invasion of its turf than with appetite. Perhaps.

The voracious *Pteranodon* that scoops up Ann and attempts to make off with her is another fantasy-creature. Though the biggest *Pteranodons* did have wing-spreads of 25 feet or so, as the one in the movie does, their bodies were small and light and flimsy, and their wings were less efficient in design than those of modern birds, which is perhaps one reason why birds are everywhere in our world and flying dinosaurs are unknown. So it is improbable that even the largest of *Pteranodons* would have been able to lift a woman of Ann Darrow's weight, 110 pounds or so, into the air.

Nor would it have had much use for her even if it had succeeded in absconding with her, because *Pteranodons* had no teeth, so the mainstay of their diet must have been insects gulped down in flight, or perhaps, fish scooped from the water as a pelican does.

That *Plesiosaurus* that wraps itself python-fashion around Kong's neck in that picturesque cavern high up on the side of Skull Mountain is depicted realistically enough—but *Plesiosaurs* were marine animals, dominant creatures of the Jurassic and Cretaceous seas. Whether they ever came up on land is doubtful; but even if they did, how did this one ever hoist itself up through the jungle to take up residence in a mountain pool?

Even the *Tyrannosaurus*, everybody's nightmare dragon of the saurian crowd, may be acting out of character in *King Kong*, if modern paleontological thought is correct. Though it goes after Kong with great vim and vigor and obvious intent to kill, the preferred theory nowadays was that *Tyrannosaurus* was a scavenger, feeding on carrion, rather than a hunter. Certainly those tiny forearms don't seem to be the weapons of an efficient killer.

The biggest improbability of all is Kong himself. Nowhere does the fossil record provide us with apes his size, or anything even approaching his size. Not that we have any clear idea of how big Kong actually is; in his first appearance, turning up at the village gate to collect his new bride, he seems to be forty or fifty feet tall, but in the final scenes, both when he is shown chained on the theater stage and when he attacks the elevated train in the streets of Manhattan, he appears no more than half that size. Elsewhere in the movie—when he is tossing Denham's men off their log, for instance—we might guess his height at only fifteen or eighteen feet. These all too visible fluctuations are, I suspect, the result of the relatively crude special-effects techniques of the day, though some may have been due to deliberate choices by the director: in that opening scene the immensity of Kong's glowering head, looming over the terrified Ann, creates an unforgettable visual impact, but in later scenes it may have been necessary to diminish Kong's apparent size in order to fit all of him into a close-up action scene involving the human characters.

Regardless, though, of whether Kong was fifteen feet tall or fifty, paleontologists have never found the fossil remains of any prehistoric apes that even approach such dimensions. Kong is depicted as a super-gorilla, down to the habit of triumphant chestpounding. But modern gorillas, though massive in bulk, rarely reach a height of much more than five feet. (They are also fairly gentle creatures except when seriously provoked, and their diet is strictly vegetarian.) Some fossil traces of large gorilla-like primates of earlier times have been found, but these are mostly fragmentary—a jawbone here, a skullcap there—and even the biggest of these creatures probably stood no taller than six or seven feet.

No two-legged Kong-sized animal could ever have existed under the gravitational conditions of Earth, anyway: its bones would not be strong enough to support such a vast mass, nor would a heart proportional to the creature's size be capable of pumping blood through its huge body. These difficulties are irrelevant in the case of immense water-dwelling creatures like today's whales, for whom the force of gravity is not a problem. But the biggest land animal that ever existed was *Baluchitherium*, the enormous rhinoceros-like creature that roamed Central Asia ten or twenty million years ago, and though it was twenty-five feet in length and stood sixteen feet high at the shoulders, an awesome thing indeed, it was not of Kongian mass.

Kong is just an invention–nothing more than a fantasy creature, born of Merian Cooper's desire to make a movie about a ferocious, horrifying beast of colossal size that becomes emotionally involved with a pretty young woman. Cooper, an aviator, explorer, and maker of documentary films set in exotic places like Persia and Siam, had become interested in gorillas during the course of his travels, and then in Komodo dragons, the giant lizards of the East Indies. The notion of pitting a gorilla against a Komodo dragon in a movie began to attract Cooper around 1929. But, as he wrote many years later, "I always believed in personalizing and focusing attention on one main character, and from the very beginning I intended to make it the Gigantic Gorilla, no matter what else I su rounded him with."

Then, having heard that RKO Films had been toying with the idea of a movie involving animated dinosaurs, and in fact had already shot some experimental scenes using dinosaur models, Cooper dropped the Komodo dragons from the scenario and suggested to David O. Selznick, the head of RKO, that they make a film together in which his giant gorilla encounters dinosaurs: "My idea then is to not only use the prehistoric animals for their novelty value, but also to take them out of their present character of just big beasts running around and make them into a ferocious menace. The most important thing, however, is that one animal should have a really big character part in the movie. I suggest a prehistoric giant Gorilla, fifty times as strong as a man—a creature of nightmare horror and drama." A creature of nightmare horror.

Here we have the key to understanding the power that the movie that Cooper and Schoedsack ultimately made exerts. It is a lively and imaginative adventure story, yes, full of action and suspense and excitement, and a tale of a tragic love (as well as one of a more conventional kind), and it brings off some interesting special effects with great vigor and force. But first and foremost it is the cinematic record of a dream—a nightmare. It brings us by a series of evolving stages out of a familiar urban environment through a barrier of mist and fog into a strange primeval place where the laws of everyday reality are suspended; it exposes us to terrors and perils unknown to the daytime world; it puts us vicariously through experiences of a sort we would never expect to undergo in our quotidian existences. The film has the force and authenticity of the most vivid of dreams; and, like all dreams, it reaches us on subliminal levels where such matters as scientific plausibility are unimportant and irrelevant.

In the closing years of the eighteenth century the English poet Samuel Taylor Coleridge produced two magnificent works that, like *King Kong*, operate on us like dreams made tangible: "The Rime of the Ancient Mariner" and "Kubla Khan." The latter poem, which Coleridge left unfinished, is not only dream-like in its content but also, if we are to believe Coleridge's own statement, in its origin, for he tells us that he fell asleep in his chair while reading an account of the palace of Kubla Khan, the Mongol Emperor of China in the thirteenth century, and had the entire poem unfold itself to his sleeping mind. Upon awakening he began at once to set it down on paper and was able to transcribe the work that we have; but, alas, he was interrupted, as he tells us, "by a person on business from Porlock, and detained by him above an hour," after which the rest of the poem had passed from his mind "like the images on the surface of a stream into which a stone has been cast."

More than a century later a British literary critic, John Livingston Lowes, became fascinated by the process by which something Coleridge had been reading had touched off a lengthy work of such great strangeness and beauty, and set out to investigate, in detail, the entire body of reading from which Coleridge had generated the unforgettable images of his two great poems. The result, published in 1927, is one of the definitive analyses of the creative process: *The Road to Xanadu*, a study in literary detection that has never been surpassed.

KONG UNBOUND

Lowes discovered that between 1795 and 1798, the period during which "The Ancient Mariner" and "Kubla Khan" were being hatched, Coleridge had kept detailed records of everything he had read, and had made notes, also, of stray images and facts that he had found in the curious assortment of books he had been studying. Coleridge's notebooks, Lowes wrote, were a chaotic hodgepodge of miscellanea, "like nothing else in the world so much as a jungle, illuminated eerily with patches of phosphorescent light, and peopled with uncanny life and strange exotic flowers." But in them he saw not only "a document in the psychology of genius" but "a key to the secrets of art in the making." And he plunged in, following Coleridge's track through hundreds of obscure and esoteric books in search of the jumbled, disconnected bits of fact and in some cases the actual fragmentary phrases out of which Coleridge had distilled that pair of wondrous poems, so that he could demonstrate "how those shining shapes arose from chaos." The book that resulted remains fresh and vital to this day, and well repays reading by anyone interested in the genesis of art.

The way Lowes traced the sources of "The Ancient Mariner" and "Kubla Khan" to a thousand places, the writings of the naturalist William Bartram, the journals of the great sea-captain James Cook, the scientist Joseph Priestley's treatise on optics, and a horde of other books, is not something I need to rehearse here. Suffice this passage to show his method: "Those, then, at last, are the raw materials. The result is all of them and none of them—it is a new creation.

"The fishes which Father Bourzes saw in tropical seas and Bartram in a little lake in Florida, and the luminous blue and green protozoa which Captain Cook observed in the Pacific, and the many-hued

ribbon-like creatures that Sir Richard Hawkins marveled at off the Azores, and Dampier's water-snakes
in the South Seas, and Leemius's coiling, rearing
marine serpents of the North, and Falconer's gam-
bolling porpoises and dolphins—all of them or some
of them—have leaped together like scattered dust at
the trumpet of the resurrection, and been fused by a
flash of imaginative vision into the elfin creatures of
a hoary deep that never was and that will always be."

Merian Cooper did not keep notebooks of
Coleridgean detail. But before his death in 1973 he provided extensive evidence of the materials out of which he
and his Hollywood collaborators wove the dark dream
that is King Kong. The starting point was that vision of a
film in which a giant gorilla does battle with the dragon-
lizards of Komodo Island, which swiftly gave way to one
employing not real lizards but fantasy-dinosaurs that had
miraculously survived on a little-known island in the
South Seas. Using that much, he was able to interest
RKO in the general idea of the movie.

The next thread seems to have been the ancient
legend of Beauty and the Beast, which scholars have
traced back to Greco-Roman times, but which Cooper
probably found in Charles Perrault's 1697 collection of
Mother Goose fables, or in the 1744 Contes Moreaux of
Mme. de Villeneuve, the best-known of many retellings
of the fairy tale of a lonely monster transformed into a
handsome prince by the love of a beautiful maiden.
Cooper could not, of course, use the story in that form:
his monster's love could never be consummated, nor
could the maiden's willing kiss magically turn Kong
into a matinee idol, and so the ending of the film
would necessarily have to be a tragic one. Toward that
end, Cooper invented the "Arabian proverb" that
served as the picture's epigraph—it is found in the

treatment for the film that he wrote in 1930—and employed the beauty-and-the-beast theme as the structural armature for the story he intended to tell.

Certain French scholars have suggested that another of the shaping sources of *King Kong* was Jonathan Swift's *Gulliver's Travels*, specifically the section in which Gulliver, finding himself in the land of Brobdingnag where everything is of gigantic size, is seized and carried off by a pet monkey of Kongian proportions who apparently mistakes the little human for an infant of her own species. The resemblance between Gulliver's frightening adventure in the monkey's grasp and Ann Darrow's similar captivity in Kong's great paw is certainly a close one; but Cooper, in a 1964 interview, asserted that the Swift book had played no part in the planning of *Kong*. He did vaguely remember some details of Gulliver's first voyage, the one to Lilliput, but none at all of the later chapter dealing with the giants of Brobdingnag. Though a plausible thematic connection, the Gulliver link must be discarded.

The search for sources now turns to other people. Moviemaking is a collaborative art; and so, while John Livingston Lowes had needed to investigate only the mind of Coleridge in seeking the sources out of which "The Ancient Mariner" and "Kubla Khan" were concocted, the search for the origins of *King Kong* involves many individuals other than Merian Cooper. The thriller writer Edgar Wallace, forgotten now but as popular an author as Stephen King or Tom Clancy in his day, was the next contributor.

Wallace, who was then under contract to RKO as a screenwriter, was given Cooper's treatment and turned it into a 110-page screenplay, unfinished at the time of his death in February, 1932. It varies in many details from the screenplay of the ultimate movie (which was primarily the work of Ruth Rose, the wife of Cooper's cinematic collaborator Ernest Schoedsack, working not from Wallace's draft but from one by a screenwriter named James Creelman) but in broad outline is the same story. (Cooper said, in a memo of July 1932 to Selznick, "The present script of *Kong*, as far as I can recall, hasn't one single idea suggested by Edgar Wallace. If there are any, they are of the slightest." But this sweeping statement is contradicted by the evidence of Wallace's own script, which still exists, and must have been part of a struggle over the credits for the movie.)

In the Wallace scenario most of the characters have different names—not a significant point—and the lengthy opening sequences of the final movie are omitted, so that it goes almost immediately to Kong's island. Denham is an explorer searching for wild animals to bring back for a circus, Ann ("Shirley" in the Wallace draft) is not offered to Kong by a Kong-worshipping native tribe but is simply seized by him as a tough member of Denham's own crew is attempting to rape her, and the climactic scene of Kong's escape from public exhibition takes place not in a Broadway theater but at a circus performance in Madison Square Garden. But the heart of Wallace's screenplay deals with the Kong-Shirley "romance" and with the monstrous inhabitants of what Wallace called Vapour Island on account of its steaming volcanoes, and these scenes are the familiar ones of the final movie, the *Brontosaurus* chase, the swooping *Pteranodon*, and so forth.

For these, Wallace, though he based his scenario on Cooper's outline, almost certainly drew upon a film directly ancestral to *King Kong*, the 1925 *The Lost World*, and on the Arthur Conan Doyle novel of 1912 from which it was adapted. That much of the plot of *King Kong* is derived from *The Lost World*, book and movie, is beyond question. The lost world of Doyle's book is an all but inaccessible plateau somewhere in South America, where an eccentric scientist, a man as stubborn and indomitable as Cooper's Carl Denham, has discovered that prehistoric animals still survive. An expedition is launched; the explorers undergo horrific adventures involving menacing dinosaurs; ultimately—in the book—a *Pterodactyl* is captured and brought back to London to be placed on public display, but escapes and flies away. (In the movie, the captive is not a small flying reptile but a tremendous *Brontosaurus*, which in the course of making its escape destroys London Bridge before swimming up the Thames toward the safety of the English Channel.)

Everyone involved with *King Kong* was familiar with the earlier movie, a huge commercial success in its day, and Edgar Wallace himself, at least, surely knew the Doyle novel as well. So it is no coincidence that both in its jungle scenes and in its denouement *King Kong* follows the model of *The Lost World*.

The Lost World, like *Kong*, unfolds by moving from the realistic to the fantastic in steady, plausible stages, so that we move along steadily from step to step and suspend our disbelief willingly when at last we enter into the ultimate display of prehistoric wonders. The reporter Malone's own romantic fantasies form the framework for the tale; the characters are accumulated in the traditional manner of the quest-adventure until the cast is complete; then the narrative proceeds unhurriedly toward the first astonishing glimpse of marvels. Again, *King Kong*'s early displays of Skull Island's unusual fauna follow the pattern set by Doyle. And, finally, the story comes to an appropriate conclusion with the clinching demonstration of the explorers' veracity: the public unveiling of Professor Challenger's *Pterodactyl* (or, in the movie, his *Brontosaurus*), and the inevitable dramatic

outcome of that bit of theater, provide the cathartic fin-
ish that such an adventure demands.

What makes the relationship between *The Lost
World* and *King Kong* more than mere speculation is the
presence of the pioneering animator Willis O'Brien as
technical director of both films. O'Brien had been doing
stop-motion animation of dinosaurs as far back as 1917,
when he worked on a five-minute short called *The
Dinosaur and the Missing Link* at Thomas Edison's film
studio: an early version of the battle between Kong and
the *Tyrannosaurus*.

The Lost World, O'Brien's first major project,
seemed almost magical to the reviewers, particularly
O'Brien's *Brontosaurus*. "How was it done?" asked the
Boston Herald. "How a naturally moving animal as big as
a ship could chase real people down a real street and
apparently break through a real bridge is too much for us.
We'd better just believe it happened."

For *King Kong*, seven years later, Willis could produce dinosaurs even more convincing than those he had
done for the earlier movie.

But his contribution to the unique texture of
Kong was not limited to the animation. The dark,
brooding look of the film that does so much to give
it its dreamlike atmosphere was O'Brien's doing. A
group of charcoal sketches that he prepared during
the course of designing the movie still survives. In
them we find, depicted with a power almost worthy
of Gustave Dore, that famed illustrator of *Dante's
Inferno*, or Max Ernst, the surrealist artist whose
strange jungle scenes reveal images never seen on
this world or any other, the peculiarly haunting character of the *Kong* world made visible—the palpable
Mesozoic humidity, the dense, mysterious tangles of
vines, the mysterious jutting tentacles reaching

toward the explorers, the titanic, overwhelming figure of Kong himself looming out of the jungle, the swooping arcs of *Pteranodon* wings cutting the air, the enraged *Tyrannosaurus* leaping high in its fury. O'Brien's sketches, somber and dark, were translated with amazing fidelity into the mise-en-scene of the film itself, which, of course, was done in black and white. (The use of color rather than black and white was, I think, responsible in part for the generally acknowledged failure of the 1976 *King Kong* remake. The later film was updated in many other ways, of course-the lost island is discovered not by a director looking to make a sensational movie, but by a team of experts from Petrox, a presumably ruthless international oil cartel, and Kong's final doomed climb takes him up the side of the World Trade Center, not the Empire State Building; and the 1976 Ann Darrow, not limited as was her predecessor to terrified passivity and a repertoire of horrific screams, shows her annoyance over being kidnapped by Kong by calling him a "goddamned male chauvinist ape."

But the second movie is never able to dip into the magic well of symbolism that powered the older, cruder film, and for that I blame the use of modern cinema technology and color photography: everything is crystal clear, right out in plain view, nothing dreamlike about it at all. And so we never believe in what we are seeing.

Though O'Brien's design for *King Kong* leaned heavily on his earlier experiences as an animator of tales of adventure among prehistoric animals, he drew also from the world of the fine arts, specifically from Arnold Boecklin's once-famous painting *The Isle of the Dead*. Boecklin, a nineteenth-century Swiss artist of the romantic school, achieved great influence in his time through paintings of mysteriously sinister landscapes with mythological overtones. *The Isle of the Dead*, of which the best-known version is in a museum in Basel, depicts with a marvelous air of strangeness a boat moving toward the shore of an eerie island that presents a forbidding face of vertical stone cliffs. Any art student in the early twentieth century would have known that painting, and clearly it was O'Brien's inspiration for the shot showing the initial approach to Skull Island through the fog. Other paintings of the same school may well have played a part in shaping the texture of the film, as did, probably, the Doré drawings for Dante and the nineteenth-century woodcuts with which such novels of Jules Verne as *Voyage to the Center of the Earth* were illustrated.

What the immediate sources of Cooper's desire to use a giant gorilla as the center of his movie were is something we will never know. But plenty of possibilities present themselves.

One likely candidate is Edgar Rice Burroughs' oft-filmed novel of 1912, *Tarzan of the Apes*: Tarzan's father is killed by a fierce anthropoid ape, which is later slain by Tarzan.

In *Stark Mad*, a 1929 Warner Brothers movie, explorers in Central America find a Mayan temple where a gigantic ape is chained to the floor.

Edgar Wallace's own 1927 novel, *The Avenger*, depicts a movie company working on location in a remote, bleak English province being harassed by a menacing orangutan, who at one point chases the female star across the countryside.

And H. Rider Haggard's adventure novel *Heu-Heu, or The Monster* (1924) features a fifteen-foot-high ape-god living on an island in the middle of a lake in a swampy African wilderness and worshipped by a local tribe. In the end it turns out, as the island is destroyed by a volcanic eruption much like the one at the end of *Son of Kong*, that the "ape" is just a costume worn by the high priest on stilts.

Thus drawing their material from a multitude of sources, Cooper, Edgar Wallace, O'Brien, Steelman, and Ruth Rose all worked together to create a film of astonishing hallucinatory power. The effect is precisely that of a dream made visible and permanently recorded on celluloid.

It is Carl Denham's dream, primarily. (Cooper unabashedly designed the character as his alter ego-adventurer, filmmaker, aviator.) His unfettered sleeping mind serves up a fantasy in which he alone has access to an isle of wonders where he will create his greatest film documentary; and then, gathering a cast of more or less willing participants and functioning mainly as an observer himself, he sweeps off to that isle, seizes its greatest prize, and returns to New York to discover that he has overreached himself and will be—figuratively—cast down from the heights, just as his hapless captive is in a more literal way. (Why does he choose to bring home a giant ape to exhibit, when a *Tyrannosaurus* would have caused a much greater sensation? In part, of course, because the *Brontosaurus* of *The Lost World* forecloses that option.

But more profound explanations can be offered. For one, Kong is a kind of god, the beast-god of Skull Island, who must be propitiated by the islanders to keep the dinosaurs at bay; capturing him, chaining him, exposing him to the view of a New York theater audience in what is clearly a crucified posture, affords a frisson that the capturing of a snarling, toothy *Tyrannosaurus* could not possibly provide. Then, too, we think of dinosaurs as cold and mindless killers; Kong is a mammal, a primate, capable of engendering a hopeless love within his breast and thereby dooming himself to the pathos of his tragic death. To the dreaming mind of Carl Denham, he, too, must have been a sort of alter ego.)

There is also a dream within the dream—for Carl Denham is dreaming Ann Darrow, but she herself is having the nightmare of all nightmares, a constant series of abductions and a close approach to the most appalling kind of rape imaginable. She is helpless and vulnerable throughout.

We see her first penniless on the New York streets; then she is swept up willy-nilly by the imperious Denham for an unspecified film project, and carried off on a sea voyage to a destination unknown even to the crew. Then Denham rehearses her for a role that involves her being menaced by some enormous monster, after which she is kidnapped by savages, who take her into the jungle and leave her, tied like a sacrificial victim, to be seized and run off with by a beast of horrendous dimensions and frightful aspect. Soon it appears that the beast's intentions are not simply to devour her but to subject her to what surely could be called a fate worse than death. (Kong, as we see him in the film, has no visible genitalia, so perhaps his interest in Ann is not sexual—one can only hope—but we can't really be sure.) Though her captor is distracted from time to time by encounters with other troublesome monsters, Ann never succeeds in escaping him for long: there is a steady series of recaptures and minor molestations, and even after her rescue and return to civilization she must be captured once more, ripped by that huge hairy paw from the safety of her own hotel room, taken to the summit of the tallest building in the world, and left perched there, in as precarious a place as any nightmare could provide, while a desperate aerial battle rages all around her.

For Ann Darrow, then, the movie is one long nightmare, and the unforgettable shrieks that Ann

KONG UNBOUND

Darrow constantly emits—who can remember any of her spoken lines, and who can forget her screams?—are clear proof of that. She is having an awful dream, though in fact she is just a character within the mind of Carl Denham, who is dreaming her. And Merian C. Cooper is dreaming him; but as we watch, the dream becomes our own.

Once we have seen it, the Cooper-Schoedsack *Kong* will never release us. It inserts itself into the region of our minds where dreams burrow and cling, and remains there forever.

King Kong:
A Parable of Progress

Jack Williamson

KING KONG left an indelible imprint when I saw it in 1933, the year it was released. Long before the 1970s, when I studied it for a film class I was teaching, it had earned recognition as a cinematic masterpiece. Even now, I find its raw power still deeply moving. Built on the pattern of the great Greek tragedies, it can be seen in many lights, perhaps best as a parable on our own uncertain future.

It's first of all a great adventure story, richly imagined, its somber tone set by the Arabian proverb that opens it: "And the prophet said, 'And lo, the beast looked upon the face of beauty. And it stayed its hand from killing. And from that day, it was as one dead."

In a searching review, Tim Dirks identifies a wealth of themes: man against nature and the struggle for survival in the jungle, unrequited love and the repression of sexual desire, the corruption of innocence by a sophisticated civilization, and the forces of economic depression. Most of them, I think, reflect the impacts of high technology on our lives and our society.

Of course, a thirty-foot giant is sheer fantasy. The force of gravity limits the possible dimensions of any animal. The strength of muscle and bone varies with the square of their thickness. The load they bear grows with the cube. Twice the thickness means four times the strength, eight times the load. The giant dinosaurs must have crowded that natural limit. Not that any such question is enough to break the film's instant appeal.

King Kong was shot during the spring and summer of 1932 in an RKO studio. RKO was near bankruptcy, the project too ambitious for the budget. With no funds for any expedition to exotic locations, the producers used the jungle sets left from *The Most Dangerous Game*. The gigantic gate had been built for Cecil B. DeMille's *The King of Kings* and would be used again for the burning of Atlanta in *Gone With the Wind*.

When filming was finished, the backers found no money for music. Co-producer and director Merian C. Cooper paid for it himself and hired Max Steiner to write the score. Talking pictures were still nearly new, and the film struck home with its sound effects. Ann Darrow (Fay Wray) repeats her ear-piercing scream again and again, as does the great ape his thundering bellow, which was made "from the reversed roar of an alligator mixed with the regular roar of a lion."

Willis O'Brien, already famed for his 1925 feature *The Lost World*, was the chief technician. Generations ahead of computer animation, his special effects are still remarkably convincing. He built a giant hand, arm, torso, and head for Kong, but most of the on-screen action was accomplished through stop-motion photography. Miniature figures were moved and shot frame by frame against backgrounds projected from the rear. The miniature Kong was only eighteen inches high. The Production Code censors cut a few of the most violent scenes out of the 1934 rerelease, though they were later restored. Kong's battle with a gigantic spider was cut, and several shots of the man-killing *Brontosaurus*; also the scenes of Kong picking clothing off Ann's unconscious body, and his acts of rage in New York when he chews a victim to death and drops a woman off a high building when he sees that she is not his beloved.

KONG UNBOUND

A fantasy is allowed one, but only one, new premise or assumption. That can be anything, possible or not, so long as the story follows a convincing chain of its logical and reasonable consequences. The gigantic ape is the premise here. To capture belief, it should offer an easy bridge into the fantasy world from the everyday here and now.

Here that bridge toward Kong and his jungle fastness begins on a dingy Hoboken dock in Depression-era New Jersey. The way should be free of any shock that might break the illusion of reality. To coax us ahead, the story should capture curiosity, wake interest, and offer escape from boring or oppressive realities. Everything to come should be planted in advance, with no unexpected rabbits left to be pulled out of a hat. If a gun is going to be fired, the audience should know it's there. That much is essential. If the story is also to offer some theme of universal wisdom, that's bacon to eat with the bread.

Kong begins with a night watchman talking about a ship ready to sail with a strange cargo. Carl Denham (Robert Armstrong) is a daring and reckless film producer setting out on a secret expedition that holds the promise of high adventure, the hope of great reward, and fears of unknown peril. He has to hide the risks from the captain and his crew. His illegal cargo includes ammunition, high explosive, and a gas bomb that could "knock out an elephant."

Story interest requires conflict and difficulty. We can feel concern for a helpless person in trouble. Denham wants an actress to play that role, but his theater agent is unwilling to send any young woman on a voyage to an unknown destination with an all-male crew. Searching on his own, he finds Ann Darrow (Fay Wray), jobless and hungry, about to be arrested for stealing an apple from a street vendor.

He rescues her. When she faints into his arms, he takes her out to eat and offers her work. She's reluctant, afraid he wants her for sex. He assures her that there will be no funny business and tempts her with the promise of money, adventure, and fame. She shakes with him and they sail next day, before he can be stopped and his weaponry seized.

On the long voyage to the South Pacific, the first mate, Jack Driscoll (Bruce Cabot), is afraid that a young and lovely and attractive woman will cause trouble from the crew. Shy and awkward with her himself, he tries to warn her: "You are all right, but, but, but women just can't help being a bother. Made that way, I guess."

She is on deck for a camera test when Denham sees her petting a pet monkey. He makes a sardonic comment. "Beauty and the Beast, eh?"

A neat anticipation of her coming encounter with the giant ape.

As Driscoll watches, Denham has her look up high, register surprise and terror at what she sees, and scream at the top of her lungs. Beginning to fall for her, he's afraid her life is in danger. When she leaves to change her costume, he demands information from Denham about where they are bound and what may lie ahead.

"Oh, you have gone soft on her, eh?" Denham scoffs at his concern. "I've got troubles enough without a love affair to complicate things. Better cut it out, Jack."

"Love affair? You think I'm going to fall for any dame?"

"I've never known it to fail: some big, hard-boiled egg gets a look at a pretty face and bang, he cracks up and goes sappy."

"Now who's going sappy? Listen, I haven't run out on ya. Have I?"

"No, you're a pretty tough guy, but if Beauty gets ya . . . Huh, I'm breaking into a song here."

"Say, what are you talking about?"

"It's the idea of my picture. The Beast was a tough guy too. He could lick the world. But when he saw Beauty, she got him. He went soft. He forgot his wisdom and the little fellas socked him. Think it over, Jack."

A hint of a theme that could make the game worth the candle.

As they near their mysterious mid-ocean destination, Denham unfolds a crude map of Skull Island. He says it was made by the master of a Norwegian bark, who learned about it when he picked up a canoe full of natives who had been blown out to sea. Named for a skull-shaped mountain peak, it has a long peninsula separated from the mainland by a towering wall built by a lost civilization. They keep the wall repaired.

"Because they need it." Denham says they fear something on the other side. Something "neither Beast nor man. Something monstrous. All powerful. Still living. Holding the island in the grip of deadly fear . . . I tell you there's something in the island that no white man has ever seen."

Denham plans to crank the camera himself when they find it. He had one picture spoiled when his cameraman lost his nerve and ran from a charging rhino. In another screen test, he tells Ann how to react.

"You're looking down. When I start to crank, you look up slowly. You're quite calm. You don't expect to see a thing. Then you just follow my directions." He starts cranking the camera. "Now look higher. Still higher. Now you see it. You're amazed. You can't believe it. Your eyes open wider. It's horrible, Ann, but you can't look away. There's no chance for you. No escape. You're helpless. There's just one chance, if you can scream. But your throat's paralyzed. Try to scream, Ann. Try. Perhaps if you didn't see it you could scream. Throw your arms across your eyes and scream, Ann. Scream for your life!!!"

At last, sailing through dense fog and a gap in a dangerous reef, they reach Skull Island and drop anchor off the peninsula. A dense fog shrouds the island. They land a party when it clears. They hear drums, pass an empty village, and find the natives chanting "Kong, Kong!" outside a massive gate in that frowning wall. A girl dressed in flowers and feathers is being offered as a bride to Kong.

The chief sees Ann, offers six women for her, and turns hostile when they refuse to trade. They retreat to the ship, Driscoll angry at Denham for putting Ann in danger. Stammering clumsily, he reveals his feeling for her.

"When I think what might have happened to you today, if anything had happened . . . I'm scared for you. I'm sort of, well I'm scared of you too. Ann, uh, I, uh, uh, uh, say, I guess I love you . . . Say, Ann, I don't suppose, uh, I mean, well you don't feel anything like that about me, do you?"

She lets him kiss her.

That night they see lights ashore and hear drums again. The natives slip out in a canoe, get aboard the ship, and kidnap Ann. When they miss her next morning, the Chinese cook finds a bracelet the natives have dropped. A rescue party lands too late to save her. The gate is closed again. Inside it, she is bound between two great pillars, sobbing in helpless terror. The chief offers prayers and has a huge gong struck to let Kong know the sacrifice is waiting. The natives retreat and slide a huge bolt (an obvious phallic symbol) to seal the gate again.

KONG UNBOUND

From the top of the wall, they watch Kong come crashing and roaring out of the jungle. Ann struggles in vain to escape and screams, a star in the terror scene she rehearsed with Denham. Leaning close to leer at her, Kong bares his hideous fangs, beats his breast, and roars again, the ultimate image of primal violence until but her beauty overcomes the beast in him. Trapped in impossible passion, he carries her back into the jungle.

Driscoll leads the rescuers setting out to follow her, leaving Denham and his group to guard the gate. Skull Island is the elemental jungle world. Sheer cliffs, yawning canyons, and dark forests are choked with hanging vines and veiled in thick fogs, all guarded by an army of enormous dinosaurs.

Untamed nature at its wildest, its convincing illusion all created with no computer animation by O'Brien and his experts working far ahead of their time. The rescuers battle a *Stegosaurus* that seems immune to rifle fire, and knock it out with a gas bomb. A raging *Brontosaurus* kills several men before the survivors escape and overtake Kong, the reigning spirit of his primordial universe.

Hearing them coming, he puts Ann in the fork of a tree and lumbers to meet them at the brink of a chasm they are trying to cross on a fallen log. He picks up the log and shakes off the men clinging to it. Driscoll has crossed ahead. He hides in a cave and stabs a giant finger with his knife when Kong gropes for him.

A gigantic lizard climbs a hanging vine to attack him from the pit below. He cuts the vine to let it fall. Kong tries again to reach him but turns when he hears Ann screaming in terror. A gigantic *Tyrannosaurus* is coming out of the jungle beyond her. Fighting to defend her, Kong boxes and wrestles with it in a spectacular stop-motion sequence.

They knock down the dead tree where Ann is sitting. It falls, pinning her under it. They fight until at last Kong kills the dinosaur by tearing its great jaws apart and beats his breast in triumph. He frees her from under the fallen tree and carries her farther into the jungle.

Meanwhile, Denham has overtaken Driscoll. He agrees to go back for gas bombs, while Driscoll follows Kong and Ann, promising to signal when he locates them. Back at the village Denham tells the crew, "Keep your eyes peeled. We leave at dawn, whether we get a signal from Driscoll or not."

Kong carries Ann to his den in a cave on top of the mountain, foreshadowing his spectacular climb with her up the Empire State Building. A giant lizard-like reptile follows them out of a pool they have passed. She sees it and screams for help. He comes to her aid. It attacks him. It coils around his neck, choking off his breath. At last, after a desperate battle, he kills it.

He carries her to a higher ledge and roars his triumph once more, a sound so fearsome that she passes out. Examining her unconscious body, he picks off some of her clothing. When she wakes and struggles to escape, he strokes her tenderly and then sniffs his fingers, totally captivated by her beauty and even her scent.

Climbing to the cave, Driscoll dislodges a boulder. Kong hears it and goes to listen, leaving Ann on a ledge outside. He rushes back to rescue her from a huge pterodactyl diving to snatch her up. While he fights and finally kills the winged monster, Driscoll climbs a vine to reach her. He starts back down the vine with her hanging to his back. Kong grabs the vine to haul them back. They fall off into the river that flows below the mountain.

With Kong in pursuit, they are swept down the river and get back to the wall. The survivors are anxious

to leave the island. Denham stops them. "Wait a minute
. . . We came here to make a motion picture and we've
found something worth more than all the movies in the
world . . . We've got those gas bombs. If we can capture
him alive."

Driscoll objects that Kong is on his mountain,
out of reach.

"Yeah, if he stays there." Denham looks at Ann.
"But we've got something he wants."

Kong has followed her. He breaks though the gate
and wreaks his fury on the village, uprooting a tree for a
club to swat the defenders and biting off one victim's
head. As he charges toward the beach, Denham knocks
him out with a gas bomb and orders the crew to secure
him with anchor chains and build a raft to float him out
to the ship.

An action story often ends with what A. J.
Budrys calls a validation, a sequel to the main action
that dramatizes its consequences and its significance. Kong has been conquered and the validation
begins here.

The captain doubts that any chain will ever
hold Kong.

"We'll give him more than chains." Denham is
arrogant in his triumph. "He's always been king of the
world. But we'll teach him fear. We'll be millionaires,
boys, I'll share it all with you. Why in a few months it will
be up in lights on Broadway. 'Kong, the Eighth Wonder of
the World.' "

The scene changes to a vast New York auditorium
where spectators are waiting to see "Carl Denham's Great
Monster." Backstage, he briefs newsmen on Ann Darrow
as "the Beauty who conquered the Beast." When the curtain rises, Kong is chained to a great metal frame shaped
to resemble a cross. He sees Ann standing with

Denham. As the flashbulbs blaze, he breaks his chains. The audience stampedes. Driscoll helps Ann escape into a hotel across the street.

Kong follows. Insane with rage, he kills the driver of a car that has crashed into the hotel, climbs the building, and snatches a sleeping woman out of a window. He drops her to the street when he sees she isn't Ann, climbs higher, and thrusts his giant arm into another room to knock Driscoll out and seize Ann.

He carries her across the city, smashing trains on the way. In a sequence I'll never forget, he climbs the Empire State Building with her in his hand. Denham says they are licked, but Driscoll suggests that airplanes might fly close enough to shoot Kong down without harming her.

Fighter planes dive at him, machine guns blazing. He lays her down on a ledge, roars his defiance, and bats at the planes, knocking one into the street. Badly wounded, he picks up Ann for a last fond look, puts her back on the ledge, and strokes her gently before he loses his grip and plunges down into the street.

Driscoll climbs the dome to rescue and embrace her. Down on the pavement, Denham pushes through the police to reach Kong's lifeless body, lying crushed and sprawled in a pool of his blood. A police lieutenant comments that the airplanes got him.

"Oh, no," Denham says. "It wasn't the airplanes. It was Beauty killed the Beast."

Cooper had conceived the idea for the film and shot a test reel for a film he called *Creation* "which combined life action and animated footage of prehistoric creatures in the fashion of *The Lost World*, a silent film that had been a hit a few years earlier." He showed it to Selznick, who okayed it. Scripts were written and production began. Opening in April 1933 in two of the largest theaters in New York, the film set box office records.

On an investment of $650,000, it earned $5,000,000 in North American film rentals, saving RKO from bankruptcy. It was rereleased in 1934, some of the violence censored. Released again in 1952, with the deleted scenes restored, it was selected by *Time* as the "Movie of the Year."

What was the secret of its instant appeal? We are all of us, I think, born to face a universal conflict between raw animal instincts and the social selves we must become. Kong strikes an elemental chord. He's a powerful symbol of primal urges toward rape and violent aggression that most of us suppress and forget.

The image is stark. The great ape roars out of his jungle world, drumming his chest in defiance of civilization. We watch love for Ann transform him into a social being. At the end he gives his life for her.

The stuff of classic Greek tragedy. In the Poetics, Aristotle defines it as "the imitation of an action that is serious and as having a certain magnitude, complete in itself." The fall of the hero excites the emotions of pity and fear. The action "should be single and complete, presenting a reversal of fortune and involving persons renowned and of superior attainments."

To wake that pity and fear, the tragic hero can't be entirely either good or evil, but someone more like us, whose traits we can feel in ourselves. His downfall comes from a mistaken action that results from his tragic flaw or an error in judgment. That flaw is often hubris, an unworried pride that leads him to ignore divine warning on moral law.

The original dramas were performed as solemn religious ceremonies, the characters speaking in formal verse, but the pattern still drives the secular film. Kong has defied the ethos of our culture. Identifying with him, we pity his fall from the tower and feel a secret fear that his fate may be our own.

He belongs in the gallery of noble savages, along with Tarzan of the apes, Frankenstein's monster, Cooper's Mohicans, Huxley's Savage in *Brave New World*, and Valentine Michael Smith in Heinlein's *Stranger in a Strange Land*. The noble savage is a child of nature, born with a simple wisdom not yet spoiled by a bad society. He often enjoys half-magical powers or skills that excite our envy.

The realist may object that actual savages commonly fail to meet our standards of nobility. They are more apt to seem ignorant and superstitious, as much inclined to vice as any of us. Yet the idea has a wide appeal. We are all subject to the disciplines of society, often restless under the rules of convention and public opinion. Consciously or not, we are most of us rebel souls, yearning for powers and freedoms we imagine.

Kong is a modern martyr of an endless revolt against the rigid mind-sets of the Middle Ages, when the churchmen tried to rule the world with such thought police as the Spanish Inquisition, torturing heretics or burning them at the stake. Two influential rebels were Johann Wolfgang von Goethe and Jean-Jacques Rousseau. Goethe's Faust sells his soul to the devil for knowledge and power. A pioneer champion of the individual and the freedom of the human spirit, Rousseau touched off the Romantic Movement, a tide of change that swept away the disciples of classicism in every avenue of art and life.

There is a vast literature that invests the primitive with the innocent magic of Eden and finds it haunted by the Satan of civilization. Read *Genesis* and

The Lyrical Ballads. Read Dashiell Hammett and Raymond Chandler. Read *The Great Gatsby* and Faulkner's *The Bear.*

Does all that matter to us now? I think it does. I grew up in an age of optimism. Our world was far from perfect, but we could find hope in an avalanche of new technologies solving old problems. Steam power had replaced muscle power. Steamships and railways and then the automobile had bridged the gulf of distance. The telephone and radio were opening the information age. In the 1930s I rode Greyhound buses to visit the Century of Progress exposition in Chicago.

Continued progress has overwhelmed that optimism. Modern sanitation has let populations outrun world resources. More dramatic advances—genetic engineering, the conquest of the atom, computer technology—have given us powers that may prove too great for us to handle.

H. G. Wells, with his early science fiction, dramatized the limits to progress: in ourselves, in the world around us, in the nature of progress itself. Dr. Moreau's creatures revert when their animal instincts overcome their superficial humanity. Invading Earth to escape their dying planet, the Martians are victims of their own past progress. Eliminating hostile bacteria, they've lost their natural immunities. They simply decay.

In *The Law of Civilization and Decay*, published in 1898, Brooks Adams is more explicit about decay. Our virtues are taught by our families and our neighbors in the village. Drawn into the city by the fatal allures of civilization, we are lost in a sea of faceless strangers, that vital disciple lost. Tolstoy's Anna Karenina is a victim of the city, an innocent destroyed by the corruption of Saint Petersburg society. She dies under the wheels of a steam locomotive, a powerful symbol of his theme.

King Kong offers stark contrasts between primitive nature and the culture of progress. Skull Island against New York City Kong's passion for Ann against Denham's lust for money and fame. The ironic likeness between the *Pterodactyl* that dives at Ann and the fighter planes that shoot Kong off the tower. In Aristotle's terms, the terror we feel as he falls may be the hidden terror of our own future fate.

A Myth for All Seasons

Harry Harrison

THE YEAR was 1932 and the United States was in the depth of the Great Depression. Merian C. Cooper, an executive at the then nearly-bankrupt RKO Studios, was deciding the fate of Production 601. This was a film project that was tentatively titled *Creation*. It was to be a fantastic adventure about some submarine sailors trapped on a strange island that is teeming with hordes of ferocious prehistoric animals—inspired in no small amount by Arthur Conan Doyle's *The Lost World*, a very successful silent film starring Wallace Beery. However, the real stars of this film were not the human actors, but the prehistoric monsters. They were created by Willis H. O'Brien, assisted by a youthful Ray Harryhausen, who virtually invented stop-motion special effects for film. But after going over the figures for the new project, Cooper decided production costs would be too high, so he axed the film. Though he really did like the visual impact of prehistoric monsters. This raised interesting possibilities. What if they combined the dinosaurs with another idea then in development—that of a giant ape tearing up Manhattan? It was a pretty way out scenario—but it had possibilities . . .

As they say: the rest is history.

King Kong was the result. A classic science-fiction film that still works over seventy years later. "Why?" you may very well ask. That is a very good question.

It works because it is a downhill, continuous action adventure that never slows or stops moving. It has a plot that could have been lifted whole from any of the pulp magazines that were at their zenith of popularity at this time. And it was not only the science-fiction magazines that featured this kind of fantasy-adventure. *Argosy* and *Adventure* published their share of this sort of story, along with *The Spider*, *The Shadow*, and many others. *King Kong* is a good old-fashioned pulp story writ large, in glorious cinematic black and white. Complete with totally new special effects, chilling sound effects, and a great musical score. Most films of this period had a few bars of classical music, drumrolls, and such like. But Max Steiner wrote a score that fitted the action perfectly. An innovation at the time.

A lot has been written about *King Kong* since it was released in 1933. It still captures the imagination. There are a number of Web sites devoted to it, including one in French and another in Dutch.

This film was not intended for a close examination. It roars onto the screen, introduces the cast and the plot in lightning-quick time—then gallops headlong into an exciting adventure. And it is a visual treat; from the very first sighting of King Kong, the great ape dominates the action. It's like having a fifty-foot gorilla in your backyard . . .

I'm sorry—how high did you say he was? Fifty feet? Well, that depends; it's like saying "How long is a piece of string?" Kong's height is quite elastic. In the opening jungle scenes he is more or less 18 feet tall. This fits his height relative to the dinosaurs that he does battle with. But then things go strangely awry. We know that there never was a man in a gorilla suit playing Kong. Willis O'Brien made the King Kong model out of a metal armature, covered with trimmed rabbit fur. (Minus an anus or cleft buttocks, as well as the usual male crotch tackle—but, after all, this was in the thirties.) The 18-inch model was moved slightly, a frame or two was exposed, then it was moved again. When projected at normal speed the stop-action film had all the movement and action that a director ever required. When the stop-motion model beast is combined with the filmed Fay Wray she cowers away quite realistically from his breast-beating menace. But they had to get closer than that to convince the audience that they were actually together on the screen.

For real physical contact with the actors O'Brien made a large model of Kong's foot, as well as one of his outstretched hand. The foot was great for pounding a shrinking native into the ground. Fay Wray screamed and cowered away in his life-size palm.

Life-size? What size? If you take her height at roughly five and a half feet, his hand is more or less six feet long. Taking a gorilla's palm length in proportion to his height gives us a ratio of 11.66 to 1. So the close-up Kong is now 70 feet tall. He instantly shrinks to 18 feet in the process shot of him tearing her skirt off. (We'll look at this bit of voyeurism a bit later.) To add to the confusion, when he is chained to the metal cross onstage in New York City he is 24 feet tall—this was his height as well when he climbs the Empire State Building.

But I don't care about his height, you say. What about the story?

What about the story indeed? I regret to report that factual inconsistencies still do continue to pop up. From the first time Skull Island appears out of the unusual sea fog we have to swallow a number of inexplicable facts.

Looking at the island from the sea it appears to be some miles in length, hilly and jungle covered. Our brave adventurers prepare to land on a small peninsula of flat, cleared land that sticks out into the sea. It is cut off from the rest of the island by a high wall that contains a single, giant gate. There are no canoes or other craft on the beach. A village of native huts fills the rest of the small peninsula, leaving only enough room for a dance floor before the gate.

That's interesting.

The islanders don't fish for food because there are no boats or nets in evidence. They don't farm, because there is no land for farming, nor is there any cultivation in sight. Perhaps they live by raiding the interior of the island through the barred gate? But this is never suggested or implied; quite the opposite, in fact. That wall and gate, built by an "earlier and greater civilization," is there to lock away the natives from the island's fractious lifeforms.

So the temptation is very great to seek an explanation of their strange lifestyle. We must reject the obvious; that they live by doing the Kong dance and offering him female sacrifices. (They also have a large orchestra, presumably hidden in the huts, that plays for their dances.)

As for the food they eat, like the other actors, it must be from the studio canteen . . . No, this is too easy an out: we must search further.

It should also be noted for the record that they are Negroid, not Polynesian. This interesting fact will later be examined in greater detail. Their presence on a Pacific island is just as anthropologically mysterious as that of the dinosaurs, who should have vanished from the earth some 65 million years ago.

One is tempted to say, well, that's entertainment. It was perhaps a simpler age when the film was made and people tended not to ask embarrassing questions. The popcorn was warm, the seats comfortable, and they could escape the Great Depression immersed in a cracking good adventure.

Perhaps we can understand this world better if we understand what motivates it. If we lift the curtain a bit we find that what is stated as fact, many times during the film, is just not true.

More than once the bold adventurer/film producer, Carl Denham—played by Robert Armstrong—states clearly, without any doubt, that the dominant theme of this island adventure is about beauty and the beast. And beauty is what destroys the beast. When the photographers are ushered onstage to photograph the captive Kong and silk-clad Fay Wray, Denham tells them, "This is about beauty and the beast." In fact the film even opens with this theme, as an "Old Arabian Proverb" fills the screen: And lo, the beast looked on the face of beauty. And it stayed its hand from killing. And from that day, it was as one dead.

However, Cooper did not rely on scholarly research for this seminal quote.

He just made it up.

Then again, in the very end of the film, when they are all looking at the dead Kong after his fall from the Empire State Building, Denham drives his message home: "It was beauty killed the beast."

Was it? Let's take a look at Kong's relationship with human women. After Fay Wray is captured by the natives she is secured to two stone posts by ropes that are passed through holes in the stone, which are then tightened by sticks twisted in their ends. It is implied that the pillars were made by the same "superior civilization" that constructed the imprisoning wall and gate, which opens in front of the pillars. Since these constructions were there before the movie team arrives we can infer that this ceremony had been done before. With human sacrifices—we are not told whether male or female, though it is never questioned that the sacrifices are women. In fact this is spelled out when the cowering crew suggest that Fay Wray was taken because she is the "Golden Woman." It is also stated by one of the sailors, in the unthinking racial bias of this period, that "Blondes are scarce around here."

So our poor blonde is trapped in an ancient ritual—obviously a sacrifice of some kind. We haven't seen King Kong yet, but the omens are not good. The dancing natives wear ape suits and masks, so monkey business is obviously involved. When the gate is finally opened and the giant ape appears, we know that the real action has finally begun.

But what will Kong do? To answer this question we will have to consider what has happened in the past. The natives obviously fear Kong—so we can assume that females are sacrificed to pacify the living god. Kong would then do . . . what? We can assume that he will break the ropes and retreat into his jungle world with the sacrifice, just as he does with the Golden Woman. The gate would once more be sealed behind him and peace would return.

But what happened next behind the wall? We are not given any details, so we will have to make some assumptions. Would the sacrifice be eaten? Kong was surely equipped for the job with four very unapelike canine teeth. Later in the film he bites and kills people, but we never see him eating them. Like most primates, he appears to be an omnivore. But if he didn't eat the sacrifice, what on earth—or Skull Island—did he do with her?

Can we safely assume that sex is out? Let us examine the possibilities. Sexual attraction, for one thing. What if a normal-sized man was presented with a cowering six-inch-high female ape. What would go through his mind? A lot of things, we can safely assume. But would sexual intercourse be one of them? Highly unlikely. We are left with the possibility of consuming flesh, not consuming passion.

It might be wise if we drew the curtain on this line of speculation. Back to Fay Wray.

We know that Kong carries her back to his cliff-top lair/cave. Where, yes, he does show a certain prurient interest. He removes her skirt and bulges his eyes. Heaven knows what he sees or plans to do, because intervention by a *Pterodactyl* interrupts this tender scene. And before Kong can resume his disrobing examination, Bruce Cabot comes to the rescue and spirits Fay Wray away.

Now we must question Kong's motives. Instead of simply forgetting about the meal that got away and having the dead *Pterodactyl* for dinner, he leaves the jungle and tracks her back to the native village. We can only assume that he is after his Golden Woman, because he certainly hasn't acted like this before with his darker sacrifices. For the first time he breaks down the gate and destroys all in his path. Chews on one native, then stamps another into the ground with his massive foot. But before he can carry out whatever dastardly deed he has in mind for Fay Wray he is felled by gas bombs.

Are we supposed to assume that the beast is attracted to—or heaven forbid!—in love with beauty? It is time to look at the myth of Beauty and the Beast that this story is supposed to be about.

This seminal fairy tale is *one* of the very few where the main characters actually get to know each other before they fall in love. Sleeping Beauty falls in love after one kiss, while Cinderella swoons with love after only one evening. However, in the fairy tale Beauty spends weeks, perhaps months, with the Beast before she gets to know . . . what?—his inner self?—before falling in love with him.

Which has nothing whatever to do with the movie plotline. Yes, we are told over and over that this is the story of Beauty and the Beast. But this planted information bears no relationship to the classic fairy tale.

Discard the faulty description and examine the evidence before our eyes. Kong is interested in the sacrifice; he rips off her skirt to take a closer look. When she escapes him he goes looking for her. Why? Let us examine a few of the possibilities.

We must look closely at the science in the film *King Kong*. Perhaps the answer has to do with the physical existence of this strange world. Close observation reveals that this may not be our Earth at all— but a parallel world with completely different species of animals. The dinosaur herbivores that appear during the film all turn out to be carnivorous; a hungry *Brontosaurus* chews on the fallen sailors after Kong drops them into a valley. Then there is the constricting snake with legs, something that left no fossil record on our Earth. Is the film set in a completely different universe from the one we know?

Consider another possibility. Can we safely assume that inter-species romance is out? Love cannot be the reason. But what about sex? This is not very likely, unless there is something about the size of Kong's male organ that we do not know. We assume that we can't see it because of film censorship—when perhaps it is invisible because it is just too small to see. Lost behind his cropped rabbit fur. This opens an unhealthy path to speculation that it might be best to avoid.

Another fact we must take into consideration is that it is only Fay Wray he is looking for. We know this because, after climbing the building in New York, he pulls a woman out of her room, examines her, then drops her to her death when he discovers that she is not Fay Wray.

KONG UNBOUND

So what then is his motivation?

That Kong has many human traits is undeniable. For one thing, he is a good boxer. He doesn't just seize and rend his prey, but subdues one prehistoric animal with a good right cross, followed by two quick jabs. And he has curiosity, not just in the dress-tearing scene but in the way he moves his dead saurian prey's broken jaw back and forth. Perhaps he is philosophically pondering mortality?

What is the truth then? The romantics will say it is unrequited love. He follows her for love, takes her to him, places her carefully on a safe ledge on the top of the skyscraper before defending her by batting at the attacking airplanes. A tender tale.

Those with dirty minds might still be considering sex. It is a possibility. But until we have some physical evidence we must put it among the unproven considerations.

Eating her is out; he had more than one opportunity to take a quick bite.

Perhaps religion and myth should be considered. In the land of myth, speculation is king. Perhaps this is modern mythmaking; a moral for our time.

Here is a beast who is pronouncedly ugly. He terrorizes a community and forces them to present him with sacrifices. This has been going on for many generations and the situation appears to be mutually acceptable on both sides. The humans have a religion where they can actually look on the face of their god. And they can keep the population under control at the same time. Kong has a good time bashing the local wildlife, with an occasional ritual ceremony and snack to keep him happy. Then it all changes. He is presented with white meat instead of dark meat. He takes a more intimate look at the sacrifice, but is interrupted by a *Pterodactyl*.

The object of his interest is taken from him;he gives chase. Then the Lilliputians subdue and imprison him. But he proves to be too strong for them. He bursts his bonds and gives chase in New York City, looking for the missing sacrifice. Despite all odds he manages to find her. Then flying creatures attack. He must defend her and he dies trying.

Does he die for unrequited love?

Or does he die when the Lilliputians try to steal his dinner?

Or does he die before he can consummate his bestial lust?

Or does he die because in the end the beast always dies?

Or perhaps there is a completely different explanation.

Could this all be taking place in an alternative universe?This would explain the strange animals, including the four-legged snake. Could it also explain King Kong?

What do we really know about him? Very little. He appears to be a one-off. We see no Mrs. Kong or any little Konglets. He is the only mammal in a world populated by saurians. Could he have been placed there by the same "ancient civilization" that made this island his prison?

This raises the strong possibility that the ship carrying our heroes sailed into the fog . . . and right into an alternative universe. Where mankind originated in Africa—but stayed black. The ship's captain speaks a Polynesian language and the Skull Island inhabitants can understand him. Therefore the other Polynesians in this alternative universe must be black as well. But is there an ancient civilization that not only had architectural and wall-building skills, but were also well versed in magic?

Could this ancient civilization have also put a curse on some then-existent hero or villain? Transformed him from man to ape and sentenced him to live alone and forever on this island prison. Not quite alone, since he was supplied with the occasional female sacrifice. Imprisoned in his ape's body, he would look at the sacrifice and pine over his lost manhood. If the superior race were white as well, everything falls into place. He is a dark-skinned ape doomed to look at dark-skinned women forever. And sigh over his lost humanity.

Is this the first American science-fiction film? We find an important clue when we look at the screen credits. Edgar Wallace was one of the contributors to the original screenplay. Although he is usually considered a mystery writer, a close examination of his titles reveals that most of them would be considered science fiction today. Did he originate the idea of an alternate history? We shall never know because he died before the film was completed. It is a nice thought, though.

Everything in this alternate world appears to be working smoothly until Fay Wray arrives. Her appearance causes seismic disturbances in the Skull Island world. Suddenly all the pieces begin to fall neatly into place. It is obvious that during the countless centuries that Kong has been magically imprisoned on this remote island, his white ancestors have expanded and covered the globe. Has he been finally forgiven for his original sin? Why else would they send him the Golden Woman? He must pursue her and discover the truth.

All is explained. The strange species, his lonely existence, the natives supplied magically with food.

What we have here is a new myth of godlike revenge. Like Sisyphus pushing his boulder forever up the mountain, only to have it roll down so he has to do it again the next day. Or poor Prometheus, who stole fire from the gods. This mightily annoyed them, so he was chained to a rock and every day a vulture flew up and ate out his liver, which grew back at night. Will we ever discover what Kong's sin was that put him in a great ape's body and doomed him to suffer forever among the lowly beasts? Deprived of his humanity for eternity.

His teeth offer one clue. All primates have upper canine teeth for tearing out chunks of flesh, along with not-too-formidable incisors in the lower jaw. Baboons have great tusks suiting their partially carnivorous diet, proportionally the same size as those of a saber-toothed tiger. Our human mingy ones reflect an herbivorous past. But Kong is in a class of his own! Unlike any other animal, alive or extinct, he has long, matching canines in his lower jaw. They serve no purpose. If anything they would interfere with biting and chewing. Only magic could have blessed him with this inoperable set of gnashers; a godlike jest to make a beast of a man.

So for countless years, perhaps centuries, he has been trapped in the body of a beast. But perhaps his suffering is now to be at an end. Has he served his sentence and could now be offered salvation? Is that what the Golden Woman represents? At last he will break down the gate and escape his prison. No wonder he is so excited.

Yet in the end he dies a tragic death. Unlike Samson, who kills his tormentors when he brings the temple crashing down, Kong dies alone. Is his fall symbolic of the fall of mankind? Is this film a religious parable?

Or is it just the story of a great ape who should have stayed at home?

The Golden Woman certainly has a lot to answer for.

Kong:
The First Wonder of My World

William Stout

LOST MY cinematic virginity to a fifty-foot gorilla.

One evening in 1952, when I was three years old, my parents bundled me into my flannel peejays, popped me in the backseat of our old Ford, and drove over to the Reseda Drive-in (deep within the smoldering heart of the San Fernando Valley) to see my very first movie, a national re-release of the 1933 film *King Kong*.

Transfixed from the first frame of the film and by Max Steiner's thundering score, I quickly forgot about my popcorn as I watched the movie from the edge of that comfy backseat, my eyes as big as hubcaps. I gripped the top of my parents' car seats in sheer wonderment throughout the dinosaur sequences. This dazzling fantasy turned to terror when a gigantic face appeared at Ann Darrow's hotel window, followed by a huge furry hand reaching in from another window of the same room. It grabbed her bed, pulling it closer to the window until its massive paw could finally reach the woman and grab her—which it did, scaring the hell out of me, as it metaphorically threatened the safety and sanctity of my own bed and bedroom. Just as Kong was forever changed after his first glimpse of Ann Darrow, I was eternally transformed by those images that were forever seared into my developing brain. My obsession and love affair with King Kong—and with dinosaurs—had begun.

Years later our family got one of those heavy newfangled glowing boxes that was becoming a popular addition to many a suburban home—a television. Our first one had a screen about six inches high surrounded by a massive four-foot wooden box. In 1955 Channel 9 in Los Angeles began to trumpet the arrival of something called the *Million Dollar Movie*. The channel promised to show the same great film twice a day for an entire week, plus three times each on Saturday and Sunday. The first *Million Dollar Movie* was *King Kong*. *King Kong* turned out to be so popular that it was held over to become the second *Million Dollar Movie*. Channel 9 screened *King Kong* 32 times in two weeks! To repay their gift I never missed a showing.

In between screenings I would act out parts of the film with the other boys in the neighborhood, new Kong devotees all. My favorite game was running down the sidewalk shouting out "KONG'S COMING!," pretending that our sidewalk was a path through Kong's jungle and that the mighty great ape was so close behind us that you could smell and feel the moist heat of his banana breath.

Later that year the Eighth Wonder of the World was once again the star of the *Million Dollar Movie* and I racked up another 16 showings, bringing my viewing total of *King Kong* to 49 times—all before I was seven years old! I think it must have done damage at a genetic level.

In the Catholic Church there is a saying: "Give us your children until they are seven and they'll be ours forever." Michael Apted's "Up" documentaries (*35 Up, 42 Up*, etc.) that follow the lives of lower middle class children as they grow older in seven-year increments appear to confirm the speculative qualities of that statement in regard to childhood interests if not religion.

The fact that some fifty years later I make a huge part of my living breathing drama and life into dinosaurs and other prehistoric creatures using my words, brushes, pens, inks, and paints, I believe is a direct linear result of the spell *King Kong* cast upon me as a child.

Another artist directly affected by *King Kong* is admitted Kong fan Frank Frazetta, whose own trunks and branches laden and dripping with verdant moss recall the moist shaggy trees populating the big gorilla's lush silver screen jungle. Not coincidentally, in the 1970s Frazetta was hired to paint the well-inspired covers to a couple of King Kong paperbacks.

Now let us contemplate The Log. This iconic moss-covered fallen tree with a girth the size of a sequoia that bridges a primordial Skull Mountain jungle chasm has become the inspiration for countless exotic pictures both fantastic and scientific. The famous Kong log setting has shown up numerous times reinterpreted within the excellent paleoart reconstructions of Doug Henderson. Doug has used The Log so often and has executed it so well that I regard Henderson's artistic theme-and-variation exercises involving The Log as valid an artistic theme as Monet's water lilies or Van Gogh's sunflowers. The Log setting has been visually quoted cinematically as recently as 2004 in *Sky Captain and the World of Tomorrow*. Captain Englehorn's ship *The Venture* makes a brief sunken cameo at the bottom of the sea in that film as well. *King Kong* continues to influence and affect our culture.

The fact that I'm not shy when it comes to proclaiming *King Kong* the best movie ever made and that I don't hesitate to use Kong references in my own work (including The Log) resulted in my being hired in 1991 to illustrate two covers for the Fantagraphics five-issue comic book adaptation and serialization of *King Kong*. The other cover artists for that series were fellow Kong aficionados Dave Stevens, Mark Schultz, and E.C. Comics legend Al Williamson. Kong's tyrannosaur sparring partner repeatedly turned up in Williamson's comic book stories and sketches of the 1950s (and later). The good lizard's most dramatic appearance was his star turn as the target of Al's E. C. comic book adaptation of Ray Bradbury's science fiction classic "A Sound of Thunder" for *Weird Science-Fantasy #25*.

My fascination with *King Kong* enhanced my life in another way. *Kong* connected me with a series of links to other artists, other pleasures, other enjoyments and inspirations. I examined *Kong* later in life in an attempt to puzzle out the keys to its success and the reasons for its profound effect and influence upon me. In the act of performing my research I was introduced to the world of Willis O'Brien and cinematic special effects, and in particular stop-motion animation. A new passion for and fundamental understanding of visual effects was gathered and perceived through my investigation of the work of Willis O'Brien and his protégé, fellow stop-motion animator and my own future friend and collaborator Ray Harryhausen. When I began my own career as a designer in film my focus and specialty quite naturally became effects films, particularly in the genres of horror, adventure, and science fiction.

The fact that I've always had a passionate and visceral response to the drawings and paintings of prehistoric life by paleoart pioneeer Charles R. Knight, I'm sure comes in no small part from Knight's dominant influence on the appearance of the dinosaurs in *King Kong*. Using the justly famed paleoartist's widely reproduced reconstructions of prehistoric life as a source of reference and inspiration (in particular the Charles R. Knight murals for the American Museum of Natural History in New York and Chicago's Field Museum of Natural History), the enormously talented Marcel Delgado sculpted and detailed his three-dimensional primordial beasts for the stop-motion animation models of *Kong*.

Regarding the work of Marcel Delgado, I must take a moment, sidestep a bit and share an incredibly frustrating personal mini-tale to my fellow *Kong* nuts and collectors.

In the late 1960s I was an art student at the famed Chouinard Art Institute (the school that helped train the Walt Disney artists and that in turn was supported by Disney and transformed into CalArts as a result of the generosity of Disney's will) near downtown Los Angeles adjacent to MacArthur Park. One afternoon between classes I passed the window of an antiques shop. I slammed to a halt at the jaw-dropping sight of an exquisitely carved and detailed two-and-a-half-foot-long wooden *Triceratops* on display in the show window. I ventured inside and inquired about the sculpture. The antique dealer informed me that the dinosaur had been carved by someone named Marcel Delgado, an obscure local artist. I quietly gulped at the name and mustered the nerve to ask how much he wanted for it. "Three hundred dollars." was the reply. I was a poor art student; he might as well have told me it was three hundred thousand dollars—the result would have been the same. There was no way that I could swing that kind of dough. I admired the Delgado *Triceratops* for about a week or two every time I passed that window. Then one day it was gone, sold. To this day I have no idea as to its destiny or whereabouts.

And now, back to our show . . .

I discovered that the lush black and white jungles surrounding Skull Mountain in Production 601 (*King Kong*'s first title) were directly influenced by the superb illustrations produced by the prolific hand of Gustave Doré for *The Bible*, John Milton's *Paradise Lost*, Perrault's *Fairy Tales*, Chateaubriand's *Atala*, La Fontaine's *Fables*, and Dante's *The Divine Comedy*. As a result of searching out and obtaining those volumes I gained a new appreciation for Doré's stunning work. With Doré's rich complexity of dark-and-light systems my artistic horizons were both elevated and expanded.

The tremendous success of *King Kong* and its hard-core cultdom rightly or wrongly has indelibly linked its cast to *Kong* more than to any other film in their varied filmographies.

Carl Denham's tough show biz savvy is made palatable and even appealing by his boundless enthusiasm for his bigger-than-life entertainment projects. Actually, I think I identify with Robert Armstrong's passionate showman more than I do with Bruce Cabot's hunk hero Jack Driscoll—which probably tells you much more about me than you should know. When someone doubts the sincerity of my friendship I am still inclined to open my hands and arms, proclaiming "Bala! Bala!"

Jack Driscoll is the prototypical All-American laconic Can-Do kinda guy—the perfect man to rescue Ann Darrow from the jungles and clutches of Kong. Besides his being a good rope climber, Bruce Cabot's lack of acting experience at that point in his career (he later acquired the thespian skills to hold his own in *Cat Ballou* and a whole slew of John Wayne movies) actually enhanced his performance as the awkward Guy's Guy lover of Ann Darrow. Cabot's athleticism as Driscoll is completely natural and believable.

Fay Wray as Ann Darrow, the film's Golden Goddess, is the perfect mixture of two seemingly polar opposites: innocence and sexuality. And let there be no doubt that a good portion of the subtext of this film was about what Preston Sturges referred to as Subject A. Her pre-Code sheer form fitting gowns and general lack of costuming during the jungle sequences still stir the blood of this Beast for Kong's Beauty. Even Kong's own curiosity was piqued enough to pick away at her clothing and then sniff his fingers. Not only did Fay Wray exude sensuality, she also had the best set of tonsils in the business; her screams set the standard for all future scream queens. In fact, her *Kong* screams were used in several subsequent films as "scream loops" for other actresses.

Frank Reicher's Captain Englehorn is the film's anchor. As befitting someone whose job is to lead and command, he's the rock who keeps his cool and stands his ground when all hell is breaking loose. Reicher's pitch-perfect portrayal of the gruff captain is the finest, most natural performance in the film.

Victor Wong's Charley got such a positive response during the making of the movie that his role was constantly being rewritten and expanded in not only *King Kong* but *Son of Kong* as well. He transcends his loveable 1930s comic Chinese stereotype by allowing the gravity of Charley's inner soul to ground his character, letting the light of that soul shine through his performance. You know that he would risk his own life for Ann Darrow as unhesitantly as any other member of that tough and surly crew.

The stern native chief could easily have been another 1930s black caricature but as written by Ruth Rose and performed by Noble Johnson the chief is at turns the leader of his people, a devoutly religious man, a quick (although unsuccessful) negotiator and a very imposing and scary guy. Though never shown, it is implied that it is the chief who orders his people to assist Captain Englehorn's crew in attempting to hold back the gates against the assault of Kong, an indication that the welfare of his tribe is of more concern to him at the moment than his animosity for the ship's intruders.

I'm also fond of the easily excitable Fundamentalist witch king as played by Steve Clemente.

That little troublemaker (he seems the most likely candidate as the instigator for Ann Darrow's kidnapping) is the maniac who publicly (and rightfully, I might add) blames the disruption of the tribe's religious ceremony on the intrusion of the white interlopers. Hence, Denham and crew become responsible for the tribe's (and their own) subsequent bad juju. What I love about Clemente's performance is that his witch king seems to keenly relish the thought of finally having found a scapegoat for any of the tribe's forthcoming ills. Before Denham and company came along, anything bad befalling the tribe had to pretty much be the responsibility of the witch king himself–but not any more!

Of course the most memorable actor in the film is Willis O'Brien. Obie performed in the film under the guise of Kong. This former boxer used his pugilistic skills in staging the knock-down, drag-out fight between the giant gorilla and the tyrannosaur. Through O'Brien's skillful manipulations of a 20-inch scale model, we are all made to feel real emotion for *Kong* and see the mighty ape's death as tragic.

Looking at the O'Brien footage in the films that lead up to Kong, it is remarkable how from film to film his aesthetic and technical leaps seem exponential in quality. The demands he put upon himself and his effects crew for Kong and what they delivered were not to be rivaled for decades. The breathtaking preproduction drawings of Mario Larrinaga and Byron Crabbe set a high bar for the effects staf–a challenge that Obie's remarkable effects crew both met and exceeded.

Max Steiner's powerful *Kong* score revealed to me at a very early age that music can become or suggest or reinforce a character in a film (as dramatically and effectively demonstrated many years later by John Williams with his pulsing string bass double notes in

Jaws). Steiner's orchestrations (sometimes simple, sometimes complex, but always memorable) without exception enhance and deliver whatever mood is called for in the film. The range of music is spectacular. From the simplicity of the jungle drums and the chords leading up to "Kong's Theme" to the bright-lights-big-city Broadway fanfares for the introduction of the story's lead characters on stage in New York, Steiner never misses. Coincidentally (or perhaps not?), it was Steiner's "Tara's Theme" from *Gone With the Wind* that was used as the theme music for the *Million Dollar Movie* that premiered *King Kong* on television.

Murray Spivack was *King Kong*'s sound effects guy. He personally made all of the raspy dinosaur sounds (and then added a heavy bass effect for extra weight and drama), found and enhanced the right roars for Kong (essentially lion and tiger roars recorded during feeding time at the Selig Zoo, slowed down to lower their tone and then played backwards) and even provided the screams for the men falling into the pit from King Kong's jungle log shakedown.

CUT TO: 1983. Without hesitation I coughed up the hefty big bucks for the 50th anniversary re-creation of the premiere of *King Kong* at Grauman's Chinese Theatre as well as for the equally expensive private *Kong* VIP party afterwards. I got my photo taken clutched in Kong's giant hand, the great gorilla's face directly behind me (Jim Danforth and Bob and Kathy Burns had sculpted and fabricated a magnificent full-sized replica of the giant Kong head and shoulders—as well as adding the clutching hand—that stood in the forecourt of the Chinese Theatre at the film's original premiere). It seemed like all of my friends, acquaintances, and fellow *Kong* and movie monster fans throughout the years were there: Rick Baker, Ray Bradbury, Forrest J Ackerman, Hugh Hefner, and many more. At the party Ray Harryhausen debuted his bronze tribute sculpture of Kong fighting the T. rex. John Landis immediately snapped it up for his own King Kong collection. Vacillating between fanboy and colleague, I brought my copy of *The Making of King Kong* (by Orville Goldner and George E. Turner) and persuaded most of the party's attendees to sign it.

The author of my book's final autograph patiently sat in a corner, graciously smiling and signing for a line of *Kong* fans. When it became my turn, suddenly everyone else vanished from the room. The two of us were engulfed in a black limbo and time stood still as Fay Wray signed my book. As she handed the book back to me accompanied with her charming and still radiant smile the spell was broken and all of the partygoers suddenly reappeared. I'll never forget that eerie and magical moment.

King Kong, the first film I ever saw, remains my favorite movie of all time. Nothing else even comes close. For me, *Kong* is the perfect movie. It has all of the elements I like in a film: fantastic adventure, both sophisticated and broad humor, terrifying horror, tantalizing sexiness, exotic mystery, an intoxicating mood, that Beauty and the Beast theme, obsessive passion (both on and behind the camera), a powerful music score, biplane dogfights over the Empire State Building (with the amazing Art Deco Chrysler Building in the background), a couple of awkward romances (Kong's and Driscoll's), misty jungles–and several film canisters' worth of dinosaurs and other prehistoric beasties, scrappers every one of them. Oh, yeah—and a great, big, giant gorilla. No other film packs in as much entertainment as *King Kong*.

I think we should all choose our own epitaphs before we go. The one I've chosen is paraphrased from a Captain Englehorn line in *King Kong* when he answers a question from Jack Driscoll regarding the sanity of Carl Denham: "Not crazy—just enthusiastic."

So to Mr.'s Cooper, Schoedsack, O'Brien, Delgado, Larrinaga, Crabbe, Wallace, Steiner, Spivack, Armstrong, Cabot, Reicher, Wong, and Johnson; and to Ms.'s Rose and Wray: Thank you for the best 100 minutes ever witnessed by the world—100 minutes that changed my life forever.

P.S.: And would someone please find that damn spider pit sequence!?!

The Myth Goes Ever Downward: The Infantilization, Electrification, Mechanization, and General Diminishment of King Kong

Paul Di Filippo

"OUR CULTURE, it digests events by making lesser and lesser versions of the original. After a ship sinks or a bomb explodes—the Original Tragedy—then we have the news version, the television movie version, the talk radio versions, the blog versions, the video game, the Franklin Mint Commemorative Plate versions, the McDonald's Happy Meal version, the one-liner reference on *The Simpsons*. Echoes that fade."
—Chuck Palahniuk, "A Church of Stories"

R, as Karl Marx might've phrased it, if he'd been born in the middle of the twentieth century instead of at the dawn of the nineteenth, "The first time as tragedy, the second as farce, the third as a Renny Harlin film."

One of the qualities of a true, potent myth is its susceptibility—nay, its blatant invitation—to misprision and betrayal and even denial by perhaps well-intentioned yet deaf (but unfortunately not dumb), blind, and talentless acolytes. I am not talking about works of deliberate satire or parody here, but rather about seriously intentioned sequels and offshoots of the Original Tragedy that fumblingly recast or attempt to extend the material in such a manner as to rob it of all its archetypical force and resonance.

This inevitable devaluation of the seminal myth is seen in direct proportion, I believe, to the potency of the original. The more affecting and touching and powerful the primal vision, the more likely it is that any subsequent renditions of it will be shallow, dunderheaded, and cack-handedly produced. It is almost as if the supernal aura of the original myth, while captivating and astonishing the viewer/auditor and instilling in him or her a feverish desire to replicate the effect, also blinded the watcher and decreased his or her intelligence by half.

Another aspect of this Chinese-whisper–style meme of degradation is perhaps a subconscious desire to undercut any painful truths delivered by the myth. Confronted with harsh yet undeniable judgments on the flawed nature of mankind and the implacable laws of the universe, the average human feels a need to trivialize the message in subsequent retellings.

True, the kernel of every veracious myth is also paradoxically indestructible, and may be successfully transplanted to different soil by a respectful, insightful creator. James Joyce refashions Homer's *Odyssey*, and value is added to rather than subtracted from the myth of Ulysses's wanderings. It is quite possible for some modern writer to meaningfully restage the tragedy of Oedipus in postmodern suburbia. Thus do myths accrete substance over the millennia.

But unfortunately, in the majority of cases, new handlings of a myth merely diminish its luster.

Nowhere is this process seen more ludicrously and painfully at work than in the case of *King Kong*. (Okay, we already agreed that *Star Wars* was off the table for discussion today, right?)

The original film of *King Kong* (1933) was, and remains, one of the central myths created in the twentieth century. Its core conceits, scenes, imagery, and dialogue diffused outward everywhere into the culture, as the essays in this very volume attest. It remains as powerful a viewing experience today, some seventy years after its creation, as it was upon its first release. It's an organic work of genius.

But in between that release and the first remake in 1976 (when the whole cycle I will describe was potentially relaunched), *King Kong* suffered nothing but cinematic indignities, assaults that continued to strip away any clouds of glory that remained from the template. (The misconceived De Laurentiis remake itself, of course, is generally seen as the biggest slap in the face of the original myth, but my self-appointed remit will stop short of examining that film, preferring to concentrate on the less high-minded, cheaper, and thereby more revelatory outings that preceded it.)

In other media, of course, Kong almost immediately became a cliché and a shorthand trope for savagery-versus-civilization. The number of one-panel cartoons alone, in *Playboy* and *MAD*, to mention just two venues, that employed Kong for easy laughs is astronomical. But if his reputation could have been salvaged anywhere, it would have been in films, the medium in which Kong was born.

Yet, amazingly, no major screenwriter, director, or studio saw fit to capitalize on the classic status of Kong for over forty years. In this opening decade of the twenty-first-century when intellectual creations are market-tested, branded, accessorized, and franchised to the *nth* degree, it's somewhat startling to us to find that Kong was so underutilized for so long. But this very omission is as telling as the treatment he did receive in those few vehicles to be discussed below. For the very same reasons adduced above, silence regarding a myth can be seen as a tactic of diminishment as well.

According to my best researches, and discounting such faux Kongs as *Mighty Joe Young* (1949), the character of Kong (or his legitimate son) played a major part in only three widely seen films subsequent to the original:

The Son of Kong (also 1933)

King Kong vs. Godzilla (1962)

And *King Kong Escapes!* (1967)

(Two products of Bollywood will crop up in any investigation of *Kong* sequels: B. Mistry's *King Kong* [1962] and A. Shamsheer's *Tarzan and King Kong* [1965]. A plot description of the former reveals it to be of metaphorical import only: the title of "King Kong" is bestowed on the strongest man in a prince's kingdom. As for the latter, unavailable to me, I strongly suspect that any film that gives second billing to Kong, placing him under a human who dares to style himself "king of the apes," will not privilege or burnish the animal myth at the expense of the human one.)

Each of these films managed to undercut, suborn, transvalue, and debase the Kong legend in truly unique and awesomely bad ways until, finally, the mid-1970s myth-mongers of Hollywood had no recourse other than to attempt to hit the reset button and stage a full retelling of the original. A project not impossible or unworthy of success—this is, after all, what we hope the Peter Jackson version will accomplish—but also a project that cannot be approached in a mercenary or overly revisionary manner without dooming itself.

But before examining just how the lone authorized sequel and two Japanese spin-offs managed to reduce the magnificent, terrifying Eighth Wonder of the World to a laughingstock, it would help us to very briefly itemize just what made the original *Kong* so great. Identifying the winning archetypical, narrative, structural, and stylistic elements in the original will make their lack in the follow-ups all the more apparent.

KONG UNBOUND

The elements that made *Kong* such a classic are the same ones that contribute to the success of any film.

Writing, acting, pacing, cinematography, thematic coherence, subtext. And the ineffable synergy arising from a combination of all of the individual elements.

The main writing credits for *King Kong* are shared by director Merian C. Cooper and famed pulp novelist Edgar Wallace. Wallace died during 1932, and it's hard to quantify at this remove how much he contributed. But his involvement with the film marks the only time in the Kong canon that a seasoned prose writer—Wallace produced literally scores of books of all types—had a hand in the scripting. It seems likely that Wallace's vast writing experience and honed dramaturgical sensibilities are directly responsible for the impressive qualities of the script. The dialogue crackles, the plot is logical, and the scene-setting is economical. As always, expert writing proves invaluable.

The two leads—Fay Wray and Robert Armstrong—were both experienced professional actors prior to appearing in *Kong*. Wray had some fifty films to her credit already, while Armstrong boasted nearly thirty. Both inhabit their roles with utter believability, generating immense empathy in the viewer. Their acting is not Shakespearean, but then that is not what's required.

The film—at a mere 105 minutes, in contrast with today's bloated SF and fantasy epics—moves along with the velocity of a streamlined Art Deco railroad engine. And its delaying of Kong's entrance—he doesn't appear until some forty minutes into the story-allows for the buildup of viewer excitement and for identification with the human players.

The technical aspects of *King Kong*, among which I'll naturally include Willis O'Brien's arresting and convincing stop-motion SFX, are outstanding as well. Such episodes as the fog at sea that serves as a liminal barrier to those approaching Kong's island are beautifully filmed. The giant gates cordoning off Kong's sanctum successfully convey an air of Lovecraftian antiquity.

The explicit thematic issues are artfully arranged and objectified. A panoply of opposites forms the backbone of the film. Civilization versus savagery, old versus new, nature versus artifice, masculinity versus femininity, mass culture and mass media versus individual unfiltered experience, light versus darkness—these are just some of the dichotomies that the film explores. In addition, the heritage of Western colonialism comes in for a probing dissection, as does the global economic system.

Finally, and most critically, a certain vital subtext, obvious to me but perhaps minimized in previous discussions, rears its head most significantly. It is this particular mythological, allegorical aspect of the film that I suggest is most responsible for the subsequent wariness and clumsiness with which creators approached or failed to approach *Kong*.

King Kong is a film about racism. Specifically, the American experience of slavery and its aftermath.

Kong is the black man in America.

Kong's birthplace is Polynesia, not Africa, of course. Yet the natives to whom he is a god are plainly Negroid. One might argue with some justification that this particular racial presentation is merely a consequence of the realities of Hollywood filmmaking during the 1930s. There were hundreds of blacks easily available as extras, but not hundreds of Samoans. And one would be right, strictly on the most prosaic of levels.

Nonetheless, the visual realities on the screen potently trump any such disclaimer. Kong is worshipped by blacks, and consequently must be seen as their racial avatar and stand-in. His capture and transport in chains to the United States exactly replicates the grim historical realities of the slave trade. His rampage through New York and his execution by the forces of law recapitulate the exact same lynching that would have awaited any uppity Negro who tried to assert himself.

In the year 1910, nearly 90 percent of American blacks still lived in the South. Then, between 1913 and 1915, the bottom fell out of the cotton market, due to a variety of reasons, depriving Southern blacks of their livelihood. Thus began the great northward migration that eventually transformed cities from Boston to Chicago to New York. By 1920, the American map of racial distribution had been totally redrawn, with attendant cultural and social upheavals.

Why does Kong climb the tallest building in Manhattan, and not some random structure close by the theater from which he escapes? (The film's creators even switched Kong's roost from the originally intended Chrysler Building to the Empire State when the latter edifice passed the former in height.) In order to most vividly symbolize that Kong—and the forces and racial population he represents—threaten to dominate the entire white-man-created island, for however short a reign. The wrist shackles he wears in these final moments further cement his identification as an escaped slave.

Some thirteen years after the start of the northward migration of blacks—and all it entailed—Hollywood had found an objective correlative, a mythic vehicle to encapsulate the national uneasiness with the shifting dynamics between races. And the picture the film painted was not a flattering one to the white power structure. Unable to deal with the realities and demands of Kong once he rebels and steps outside his role of "entertainer" (Kong as Josephine Baker, as Duke Ellington, as Louis Armstrong), the whites have no plan or strategy other than to kill him.

Kong is a noble giant, his murderers desperate pygmies.

No wonder this pro–African-American myth stirred uneasiness in the audience, at the same time it captivated them.

It was time to back up and recast the tale in a way that would be more flattering to the white audience.

By all accounts, *The Son of Kong* was a hasty sequel thrown together by the same producer and director and studio to capitalize on the unexpected success of *King Kong*. The tailing-off of mythic resonance, the diminution in talent, and the skewing of the original themes were visible from the outset.

First, the lack of Edgar Wallace or some other veteran storyteller as a scripter was dire. Credit for this script goes to Ruth Rose, who had a small hand in *King Kong* and later went on to write *Mighty Joe Young*. Whatever Rose's talents, she was no Edgar Wallace. And in fact, her distinctive womanly perspective on the tale resulted in a curious feminization and infantilization of Kong, to be discussed below.

Second, the replacement of the marvelous Fay Wray by the B-grade substitute Helen Mack as the female lead could not fail to diminish the story's impact.

Third, the lack of Willis O'Brien's genius on special effects (journeyman Harry Redmond steps up to the helm) means fewer and less convincing shots of the hairy protagonist, as well as a generally lackluster supporting cast of monsters.

To step through the movie is to see all of these factors working in harness to produce a pale, revisionist remake that undermines everything the original stood for.

The film opens a month after the events of *King Kong*. Carl Denham (still vividly portrayed by the zesty

Robert Armstrong) is a prisoner in his own apartment. It is notable that he is protected from process-servers and reporters by his landlady. The once world-conquering filmmaker and explorer is now reduced to hiding behind a woman's skirts. Masculine virtues and powers are seen as inutile in the civilized world.

Note also that the first image we see of Kong is that of a poster from the ape's abortive public appearance. Kong has literally been rendered two-dimensional, the first step in reducing his legend, his potency.

At his wit's end, Denham seeks out the old skipper, Captain Englehorn (Frank Reicher), who took part in the original capture of Kong. Denham proposes that he become partners with Englehorn, throwing over all his artistic and professional ambitions to become merely a roving bum in the tramp freighter business. This diminishment of Denham parallels that of Kong. The fate of white man and black man, master and servant, is karmically linked.

Such an ironic, degraded fate for Denham might even seem thematically promising at this early point in the film. Continuing the subtext of the original, the film could have been positing a moral retribution against the white man who enslaved Kong. After all, Denham does utter such guilty phrases as "I'm sure paying for what I did to you [Kong]," and "Kong sure was a hoodoo for me." The hypothetical course of the sequel could have found Denham making moral restitution somehow for his sins against Kong, via Kong's son, in effect acknowledging the guilt of all whites toward all enslaved blacks. But such was not to be the case.

After some minor adventures overseas, Denham ends up with a female companion, Hilda (Helen Mack), and a villainous compatriot named Helstrom (John Marston). Comparison of Hilda and Ann Darrow (Fay

Wray) proves enlightening. Ann is unemployed, while Hilda has a job, albeit an insecure one. Ann's actions are dictated entirely by Denham and her lover, and by circumstance, while Hilda is self-motivated (she stows away to join Denham). And most tellingly, Ann has no visible connection to the savage world, being utterly a city girl, while Hilda is already part of the semi-barbaric Polynesian scene and, most tellingly, plays with small monkeys in a mistress/pet fashion. Hilda is aggressive and capable and enterprising, unlike Ann, and while this portrait of a competent woman is psychologically valid and intriguing, it undercuts everything about the Kong–human female dynamics that proved so affecting in the first go-round.

The relationship between Helen and Denham also undoes everything postulated about Denham in the first film. Denham was too much the preoccupied artist/showman to become romantically involved with Ann Darrow. The thrill of conquest was his drug. But in the sequel, he has dropped any such lofty ambitions and become merely a treasure-hunter and lover. Art and science have flown out the window in favor of money and sex.

After a time, Denham, Hilda, Helstrom and Englehorn are marooned on Kong's island. They penetrate to the savage interior with very little trouble and with almost no contact with the natives, thus minimizing both the verisimilitude of Kong's environment and also the Negroes' screen presence and the subsequent allegorical yoking-together of Kong and black man. And what do they find in Kong's ancient domain? A pint-sized, vest-pocket Kong. Not another lone full-sized ape or pack of mature apes that logically might have existed as part of the giant-ape breeding population, but a sourceless juvenile. And the juvenile is not master of his environment, but is stuck in quicksand.

KONG UNBOUND

Denham and Hilda rescue the putative Son of Kong, who responds not with the untamable ferocity of his dad, but with an almost simpering kowtowing. The original Kong has been reduced not only in size, but also in independence. When Denham and Hilda manage to wrap a bandage around baby Kong's finger, the viewer can no longer deny that whatever the original Kong stood for, this pale protégé represents the antithesis. As Denham literally says (after calling Son of Kong a "baby" several times), "You're not a patch on your old man."

Even the battles with other animals that Son of Kong participates in are farcical shadows of the titanic struggles that the original Kong had with a T. rex, a snake, and a *Pterodactyl*. Son of Kong gets to battle a large bear, and that's about it. And the realistic grue-someness of the O'Brien SFX (notable in the scene where the T. rex's jaw is literally ripped off) are replaced by bloodless thumpings.

This Son of Kong has absolutely no lustful chemistry with Hilda, another instance of his undeveloped, immature state. Whereas the first film symbolized the abduction and rape of a helpless white woman by a majestic and threatening male creature of blackness, this sequel portrays the mothering of a harmless pet by a dominant female.

But an even more troubling recasting of man-ape relations awaits. Like Twain's Huck and Jim, Denham and young Kong bond in a mildly homoerotic fashion. The movie concludes with the sinking of Kong's island as the result of an earthquake. Trapped on the highest pinnacle of the island, Son of Kong sacrifices his own life to save Denham's, like some kind of furry Leonardo DiCaprio. (This casual destruction of the "lost world" that gave birth to Kong might also be seen as the willful symbolic destruction of Africa.) The black man has reverted to ball-less servitude, offering up his life for the master's use.

So here we have the official extension/capstone of the Kong mythos: robbed of sexuality and menace, reduced in size and ego, infantilized, feminized, and house-broken, the Eighth Wonder of the World has been reduced to a harmless buffoon.

Is it any wonder then, after this derogatory, demeaning defanging and declawing, Kong would be rendered cinematically impotent for over thirty years, until a non-Western culture adapted him for their own uses— uses that were a further betrayal of the original?

Whatever potential vital mythic significance a giant ape could have represented in the Japanese culture—whatever analogous underclass or outcast group King Kong could have stood for to Japanese eyes—whatever deep meaning a naïve Asian director and scriptwriter might have derived from the figure of an archaic primate survivor from the depths of time—we will never now know. Certainly, Kong would have had to be repurposed for Asian values.

But it is certainly not the case that either *King Kong vs. Godzilla* or *King Kong Escapes!* chose to utilize the big ape in anything other than the most superficial of ways. And by randomly accreting incompatible traits and capacities to Kong, these films succeeded in further bastardizing Kong's emblematic meaning.

During the 1950s, SFX master Willis O'Brien tried to revive the *Kong* franchise by pitching the notion of a film to be titled *King Kong Versus Frankenstein*, with the Frankenstein monster in this case being a chimera of reanimated animal parts, instead of human. O'Brien's project was never to see the light of day, and it's doubtful if such a match-up would have fruitfully enlarged Kong's metaphorical remit. But as matters fell out, producer John

Beck offered the idea to Toho Pictures, and Godzilla became Kong's sparring partner.

Kong's potentially mighty stature, however trivialized over the years since *The Son of Kong*, can be seen in the fact that the ape receives top billing over the reptile, and is declared the eventual winner of their contest. Additionally, this third Godzilla film—featuring the first color appearance of either Kong or Godzilla—would have been the logical early place for Godzilla to meet his most stupendous rival. But despite these heartening tokens of Kong's value, the film goes on to only further diminish and confuse Kong's being.

Perhaps the biggest false step was in making the film a comedy. The sub–Groucho Marxian stylings of IchiroKo Arishima as Mr. Tako bring any drama to a halt as soon as he appears. This tendency to laugh at Kong was evident in *The Son of Kong*, but only reaches full-blown criticality here. The troubling, cathartic, multivalent tragedy of *King Kong* is as far removed from *King Kong vs. Godzilla* as the laughable man in a Kong suit is removed from O'Brien's elegant stop-motion figurines. (It is reported that SFX director Eiji Tsuburaya deliberately made the Kong suit look faintly ridiculous to counterpoint the more frightening look of Godzilla.)

As the film opens, an unholy alliance among advertisers, a publisher, and a pharmaceutical firm has drawn two bumbling reporters to Kong's island, where a berry with mysterious narcotic properties has been discovered. But the natives are reluctant to sell their crop to the First World, since they need all their harvest to distill vast quantities of narcotic juice to pacify Kong.

From the outset then, we have a portrait of Kong as an addled drug addict. Rather than a lusty demigod who needs to be propitiated with sacrificial brides, he's nothing more than a sexless rogue elephant who's gotten hooked on the fermenting fodder of the agriculturalists he lives among. And the narcotic does nothing so interesting as drive him into killer rages, but simply causes him to fall into a stupor.

The natives here are not Negroid, but rather Polynesian or Asian in physiognomy. Again, a practical outcome of the national origins of the film, but also an undeniable visual reworking of the original trope. And a wastefully disproportionate amount of screen time is devoted to their frug-style native dances and an attack on the village by a giant octopus, which Kong must battle.

Obviously, continuity with the Kong mythos established by the Radio Pictures films is out the window here, and this jettisoning of Kong's heritage, however debased, can portend no good.

During this introduction to the 1962-era Kong, we also learn that Godzilla, reawakened from glacial cold storage, has been attacking Japan. When a drugged Kong is brought to Japan, the two creatures meet in a series of battles that reprise Kong's original duel with the T. rex, but without the elemental Darwinism. (Seeing Godzilla deliver a World Wrestling Federation style jump-kick to his opponent renders issues of nobility moot.) Such a mammal-versus-reptile scenario might have preserved the lowest-level thematic values of the original, save for one thing: Kong is portrayed as deriving his power from electricity.

Yes, incredible as it may seem, this savage token of all that is natural and untechnological, this purely organic beast whose first nemesis was the completely artificial biplane, is now just some Duracell toy. The sight of Kong literally chewing on high-tension wires in order to get amped up to battle Godzilla is the biggest transvaluation of the creature in the cinematic canon to this point.

At this juncture, Kong has taken a giant step further toward being co-opted by humanity, his essential primeval character viciously undermined.

Two final observations about this film:

The frame tale of Kong's and Godzilla's exploits involves the United Nations. Kong is no longer strictly an American icon. But globalizing Kong, trying to make him mean everything to everyone on the planet, turns him into a diffuse ghost.

And lastly, a curious image occurs for the first time in this film, and then again in *King Kong Escapes!* Kong is secured with cables (shades of Gulliver being lashed by the Lilliputians) and airlifted by helicopters.

I would like to offer the notion that this is a Christ reference, deriving specifically from a very influential film of the same vintage: Fellini's *La Dolce Vita* (1960). That classic opens, of course, with the famous image of a giant statue of Christ being flown above the Roman cityscape, an image that would have been fresh in the minds of cinemagoers around the globe. The parallel between Kong's aerial travel and this image is inescapable. But more important for the Christ allusion is the splayed-out, crucified posture that Kong assumes during each airlift. To read Kong as martyred Savior is not a big jump.

Now, Kong as Christ is a further domestication of his original essence. Whatever kind of godling or demigod the original Kong represented, he was certainly not the meek and self-sacrificing Christ, no champion of humanity but rather an antagonistic cosmic force to be placated. But as Kong fights for the salvation of Tokyo, he becomes both an attack dog and a martyr, two roles 180 degrees removed from his initial presentation.

Kong as Electric Jesus. Is there any further degradation he can undergo?

Unfortunately, the answer is yes.

The spy craze was arguably at its height in 1967, the year when *King Kong Escapes!* was released. Thus we find Kong embedded in a second-rate parodic thriller, filling a role that Oddjob or Jaws or even Miss Moneypenny might have taken in a James Bond film. Again, all potentially useful continuity with *King Kong vs. Godzilla* was trashed, as the film tried instead to establish a tenuous tie-in with the Rankin/Bass TV series titled *King Kong* (1966).

The megalomaniacal Dr. Huu (Eisei Amamoto), ostensibly a power-mad genius whose plans blow up in his face with surprising frequency, is seeking to mine Element X from beneath his polar hideout, at the behest of Madame Piranha (Mie Hama), representative of some unknown cabal. (What good Element X will do anyone is never explained.) To accomplish this, the Doctor has built the most logically designed digging machine: a robotic version of King Kong, whose favored mining technique is dropping grenades from a utility belt. When this creation proves incapable of securing Element X, the only solution is to capture the real King Kong to do the digging. (What? That's not the first plan that would have leaped into your brain?)

Kong has been interacting, meanwhile, with some United Nations personnel (continuing the theme of Kong's globalization). The native inhabitants of Kong's island, by the way, have been reduced on screen to a single individual, further de-linking Kong to any racial subgroup. One of the UN crew is a woman named Lieutenant Susan Watson (Linda Miller), who acts as a kind of go-go–booted girlfriend to the ape. Susan's relations with Kong are neither those of Ann Darrow nor those of Hilda. She is not a ceremonial bride nor a smothering mother. Rather, she acts with Kong precisely as

KONG UNBOUND

Marlo Thomas did with her boyfriend Donald in *That Girl* (1966–1971): cajoling, cooing, hectoring, chastising. Kong is now a Modern Male and his love-interest a Liberated Woman. So much for eternal archetypes.

Employing various technologies reminiscent of the cheesy Supermarionation wonders of the *Thunderbirds* (1965–1966) shows, Lieutenant Watson and her adoring commander Carl Nelson (Rhodes Reason) eventually forget about Kong and go up against Dr. Huu to save the day.

Kong's role in all this *Get Smart* folderol is minimal. The main thematic usage of Kong seems intended to stage a kind of John Henry–style contest between organic Kong and Mechani-Kong. But when Kong is hypnotized by Dr. Huu and outfitted with a radio-headset and tools, the living ape in effect becomes the very thing he is supposed to stand in opposition to. And while Kong does indeed rebel and break his bondage, the ultimate lingering image of Kong is one of an enslaved and roboticized victim.

During the climax, as Kong and Mechani-Kong battle atop Tokyo Tower, Mechani-Kong holds the symbolic higher ground. Eventually, due to no action whatsoever on the part of Kong, the tower snaps and Mechani-Kong falls to its doom. At this point, the assembled soldiers and populace blithely stroll off, secure in the knowledge that a thoroughly co-opted organic Kong presents no lingering danger. His emasculation and servitude is comprehensive and unbreakable, a sharp contrast to his original untamable ferocity.

As Kong literally swims off into the sunset, never to reappear until the 1976 remake, he resembles nothing so much as a fur-covered paddle-wheel ship cruising to dry-dock oblivion.

From his earliest incarnation as the supreme ruler of an antediluvian jungle—ensnared by the wiles of his inferiors, seduced by miscegenational longings after alien beauty and gunned down by heartless firepower, defiant to the end—King Kong has traveled a pitiless road of inartistic cinematic misunderstanding and abuse. Reduced first to an apron-string–tied juvenile, then resurrected as an electrified, roboticized, lobotomized, domesticated "partner" of humanity, King Kong lost all the grandeur and magnificent rebelliousness that characterized his origins.

Is it possible to reinstate the glory that was Kong—with or without any perhaps outmoded racial undertones—when such a bad taste has been left on the collective mental palate by the three films that followed the first?

Myths die hard, if they ever truly die at all.

Kong can live again—if a creator of sufficient vision approaches his story with understanding and empathy and respect.

We live in hope. But please, please, please, don't let his girlfriend have evolved into Paris Hilton. That might provide a blow too great for even Kong to absorb.

Give Beast a Chance

Esther M. Friesner

"IT WAS Beauty killed the Beast" is a phrase that evokes many things for me, chief among them marijuana, and Vassar. I know you are all going to be surprised to hear this, given my youthful allure, but it was all the way back in the Age of Too Damn Many Lava Lamps that I attended that bastion of self-important intellectual superiority, Vassar College. You will also no doubt be shocked–shocked, do you hear—to learn that in those days, whilst in the pursuit of a second major, I found same in the Drama Department where some of my fellow students actually smoked . . . marijuana!

Yes, unthinkable as you may think it, the Noxious Weed was actually being employed by students in the Vassar College Drama Department, who thereby placed their health, their sanity, and their immortal souls in unspeakable peril, to say nothing of ruining any chance they'd ever have of rising to the highest (no pun intended, honest!) ranks of elected public office.

But damn, was it ever fun for a non-toker like myself to hang around them when they were wasted! Which they were, in significant numbers, on one particular Saturday night when dear old Muthuh Vassar treated her ungrateful brats to a free showing of that classic flick, the original 1930s vintage *King Kong*.

Thus it was that one of the most cherished memories brought away from my bright college years was that of locating my Drama Department friends after the houselights went on and having them reach up en masse to drag me across their laps while they howled in giggly grief, "It was Beauty killed the Beast!"

Which brings us to the topic of this essay, and not a moment too soon.

When I was approached to write for this collection, one of the themes on offer was "Beauty and the Beas—Must It Always End Badly?" This got me to thinking. Those of you out there who know me well—or even peripherally—will realize that the phrase "Something gets Esther to thinking" should serve as a warning to hide all sharp objects, permanent markers, and some of the larger livestock, since such cerebration may well result in the same sort of merry hijinks as ensued when Kong broke his chains in New York City and tried to catch a subway train. Literally.

Before we go any further with the whole Beauty and the Beast theme, let's return to that Vassar screening I mentioned earlier and the line that so deeply affected my herbally enhanced friends. (In their condition they probably would have reacted the same way over the words WITH ALMONDS on a Hershey bar, but work with me here.) I don't pretend to quote the Famous Last Line precisely because it's so Famous that I'll bet the rest of you are going to be just as convinced as I am that you already know it word-for-word so you don't have to look it up online. You know the one I mean, the one that the character Carl Denham says in response to the declaration that the airplanes were what put paid to poor old Kong. "Oh no, it wasn't the airplanes," says Denham. "It was Beauty killed the Beast."

Bitch, please. You're not fooling anyone but yourself. It was the airplanes. And if it wouldn't have been the airplanes, it would have been the tanks, or the machine guns, or any other armaments that the Big Apple could cough up. Forget calling out the troops, this is New York City: Even back in the 1930s, that means serious Attitude coupled with mass quantities of munitions. If Kong hadn't grabbed the lovely and perpetually screaming Ann Darrow (portrayed by Fay Wray, as only those people who've been living under a large rock their whole lives need to be told), sooner or later we'd still have had one big ape carcass stinking up the sidewalk, with a crowd of Damon Runyon types demanding the 1930s equivalent of "Who's your Daddy?" So before we get into the Beauty and the Beast thing per se, let's give a closer look-see at the Famous Last Line. Most of all, let us do what so few people tend to do in their day-to-day encounters with so-called Received Wisdom: Consider the source.

The source in this case is, as already mentioned, Carl Denham. And what does Carl Denham do for a living? He makes movies. Not films, not cinn-eh-maaaah (pronounced through a cloud of clove cigarette smoke with a languorous Eurotrash accent), but movies. You know, like with plots and stuff? He's a showman. He sells spectacle, sparkle, and splash.

He has also got the survival instincts of an outhouse rat. Picture it: He has just brought a giant prehistoric ape into the heart of New York City for the purposes of exhibiting it and making a bundle of cash thick enough to choke, well, a giant prehistoric ape. He has assured everyone who will listen that this is Perfectly Safe (which differs from "It was Beauty killed the Beast" insofar as one is a Famous Last Line and the other pertains to the realm of Famous Last Words). Yet what has happened? The giant prehistoric ape has broken his chains, rampaged through the streets of Manhattan, slaughtered innocent people, destroyed property both public and private, given Gotham subway riders something to gripe about besides a fare hike, and capped it all by plunging to his death from the top of the Empire State Building and sending New York's doughty Sanitation Engineers into major conniption fits. Have you ever tried to get giant prehistoric ape bloodstains out of concrete?

All right, so by enabling Kong's rampage Denham also helped folks remember that there are worse things than being caught in the middle of the Great Depression, but Shirley Temple provided the same level of temporary psychological uplift and she didn't have to destroy a subway train to accomplish it.

Not that she wouldn't have liked to, but there were contract issues.

Standing in the midst of the wreckage and carnage that never would have happened if he had only adopted a live-and-let-live-far-away-from-New-York-City policy with regard to giant prehistoric apes, what thoughts must have been going through Carl Denham's head? Probably two, viz:

1. There goes my security deposit.

2. I have just pissed off most of Manhattan, so if I want to continue chewing my food instead of taking nourishment through a straw, I'd damn well better come up with a diversionary tactic to save my bacon.

And while he is no doubt cudgeling his brains for just the right sort of flash and flimflam to make New Yorkers stop staring at him like he's to blame for all this (even though he is), it falls right into his lap: Love.

Actually it falls right off the Empire State Building and misses his lap by a country mile, which is a lucky thing for Denham. You can just see the little Get Out of a Crowd-Pleasing Ass-Whupin' Free lights twinkle to life above his head as he utters that Famous Line: "It was Beauty killed the Beast."

Awwwwww. No longer are the crowds fixating on

KONG UNBOUND

Kong's rampage, its aftermath, or the tax hike that no doubt must be imposed to defray cleanup costs. Instead they have been distracted by the romantic aspect of the whole disaster, the fact that big as he was and hard as he fell, King Kong died not of lead but of love. Denham has worked in the film industry long enough to know that once you drag Love onstage, Ignorania, the Muse of Willful Stupidity, is sure to follow.

If you find that hard to believe, interview a random sampling of people who saw the movie *Titanic* and ask them to pinpoint the most historically significant part of that tragedy. I'll give you a hint as to the answer you'll hear most often, and it has nothing to do with epic-scale loss of life and property: It begins with Leonardo DiCaprio and ends with glub, glub, glub.

Yes, 'tis a show biz truism old when Sophocles was young: Hose the audience with Love and all sorts of bad behavior on the part of your characters is washed away and forgotten. In *Wuthering Heights* Heathcliff and Cathy run roughshod over the lives and feelings of innocent, trusting people, but that's okay because . . . they're in loooooove. Scarlett O'Hara uses other people's vulnerabilities like toilet paper, but we still feel so sorry for her when Rhett walks out because . . . she has finally realized she loooooooves him. Romeo slays literature's numero uno Clueless Nice Guy, Paris, instead of letting Paris kill him (Didn't he remember that he'd come to Juliet's tomb to die? D'uh.) but who gets our sympathy? Romeo, because he was out of his mind with . . . loooooove.

Given all of the above, who can blame Denham for pouncing on a prime straight line like "Well, the airplanes got him" and using it to his skin-saving advantage? He didn't even have to work especially hard to come up with it, seeing as how he'd been ballyhooing the Beauty and the Beast angle of the whole Kong project since

154

before the S.S. *Venture* left the Hoboken docks at the start of the picture. Never mind that "It was Beauty killed the Beast" makes little sense in the context of the original "Beauty and the Beast" story.

And that, Gentle Reader, brings us further along the road to answering the main query upon which this essay is based, namely, Must It Always End Badly?

Short and simple answer: No.

Slightly longer simple answer: No, of course not, because the original "Beauty and the Beast" does not end badly and what were you thinking?

Short and more complicated answer: For whom? And while you're answering that, define "badly."

Much longer and much more complicated answer: The narrative template for "Beauty and the Beast," if not the tale itself, has been around for a long, long time. No one disputes the fact that many world cultures have produced variations on the story. The best-known versions in Western literature come from such eighteenth-century French writers as Madame de Villeneuve (whose 1740 telling of the tale took a whopping 362 pages), Madame le Prince de Beaumont, Madame L-héritier, and of course Charles Perrault.

Let's go through some of the basic ingredients in the story and see how *King Kong* measures up by comparison. (Those of you who are tittering like smutty-minded schoolkids at the juxtaposition of the term measures up" with King Kong, please get a life.)

Your basic Beauty and the Beast tale needs must have a Beauty (Screamy Ann) and a Beast (King Kong). So far, so good; no need for deeper analysis.

Early in the story, due to circumstances beyond her control, Beauty has to be handed over to the Beast. Ann is handed over to Kong, right enough, but that's where the similarity ends.

KONG UNBOUND

In some versions of the tale, Beauty is handed over because her merchant father has stumbled across the Beast's home and helped himself to a portion of the Beast's property. In at least one version, Beauty is partly responsible: She has asked her father to bring her back a rose from his travels and the only rose he finds in bloom is in the Beast's garden. The Beast catches Beauty's father and threatens to kill him unless he can persuade his daughter (in some cases one of his three daughters) to come live with him. When the merchant returns home and recounts what happened, Beauty willingly agrees to sacrifice herself in order to save her father.

One of the earliest sources of the tale, the myth of Cupid and Psyche, is somewhat different: The initial offense that necessitates the ensuing action is completely inadvertent. Psyche is such a great Beauty that people begin to worship her as more lovely than the goddess Venus herself. Venus accepts this with the level of self-control and perspective one has come to expect from the Greco-Roman gods, i.e. none. Even though Psyche hasn't sought this worship, Venus wants her punished, so sics her son Cupid on her with instructions to make Psyche fall in love with some lowborn, unworthy, dog-butt–ugly person. This backfires when Cupid klutzily wounds himself with his own arrow while carrying out the hit on Psyche.

Some time later, Psyche learns the eternal lesson that there is such a thing as being too gorgeous. (Very few men want the responsibility of marrying the most beautiful woman in the world; not after that Helen of Troy mishegaas.) Her parents, haunted by visions of enduring the ancient Greco-Roman version of never having the kids move out of the house, go to the local oracle for advice. They learn it has been decreed that their daughter must marry a monster (Beast) that all the world fears.

They must therefore leave her at the top of a cliff, said cliff being the Will Call window for the monster.

Even though this means that they won't have to hire a wedding caterer, Psyche's parents are loath to fulfill the oracle's directive. Psyche, however, is probably sick and tired of having to attend family events where everyone asks her "So? When are you going to get married already, a shayna maidel like you?" She goes to the cliff top willingly and is swept off to meet her destiny.

Note the use of willingly in both the mythic and traditional versions of the tale. Note it well, because in King Kong there is absolutely nothing willing about how Ann Darrow goes to meet her Beast. The natives of Skull Island offer Carl Denham six of their own maidens in exchange for Ann. When negotiations break down, they kidnap her and stake her out as their sacrifice to Kong. Unless nonstop screaming is the 1930s New York woman's way of expressing acquiescence, Ann Darrow is not conforming to the behavior of a typical Beauty.

To return to the "Beauty and the Beast" template, after agreeing to live with the Beast, Beauty is transported to his home. This is usually a palace of some sort, filled with all manner of treasures, luxuries, wonders, and magic. Beauty's every desire is fulfilled instantly by invisible servants.

In the traditional Western versions, the Beast converses with her but does not attempt physical intimacy. In the myth of Cupid and Psyche . . . Okay, he's the son of Venus: Do I have to draw you a picture? However, although Cupid consummates his relationship with Psyche, he does so entirely in the dark, and furthermore forbids her to attempt to see what he looks like. She remains under the impression that she really has been married off to a monster, or why would he lay down such rules?

KONG UNBOUND

Kong really is a monster in just about every commonly understood sense of the word. Unlike his fellow-Beasts, he does not transport his Beauty to an opulent, magical palace filled with luxuries, comforts, and invisible servants. Instead, Ann finds herself lugged into a desolate cave where the on-site amenities include intermittent dinosaur attacks.

This situation is made worse by the implied fate of Kong's previous "brides," namely that they became less helpmate than Hamburger Helper™ In some traditional versions of "Beauty and the Beast," Beauty's family presumes that the Beast is going to devour her because, hey, he's a Beast! In *King Kong* there's no need to waste time speculating on Beauty's imminent consumption; it looks like a surefire bet.

Then, just when it seems as if things could not get any worse, Ann Darrow discovers that when it comes to giant prehistoric apes, there actually is a Fate Worse Than Lunch. Many the keen-eyed *King Kong* viewer claims to have noticed that when Kong looks at Ann, he's got something a little more terrifying on his mind than dipping her in Roquefort dressing and treating her like a screaming buffalo wing. Yes, Gentle Reader, Kong is smitten. Gentlemen and giant prehistoric apes prefer blondes.

And Ann, as both a New Yorker and the only woman onboard the ship that brought Denham & Co. to Skull Island, is not entirely naïve as to what Kong is contemplating. Being staked out as a sacrifice, being dragged through a dinosaur-haunted primeval jungle, being stowed in a stanky old cave, all these pale by comparison to Kong's implied amorous intentions. Yeah, Ann, I'd scream too. Here I would like to interject a side-note on the subject of my own second thoughts regarding Kong's supposedly more-than-Platonic interest in Ann. Like many an overeducated person, I find it difficult to watch movies without jumping on board the Symbolism Express. I do not merely view, I interpret, and in this I am not alone. I admit freely that the first time I saw *King Kong*, I saw nothing dangerously sexual in his actions toward Ann. It was only after reading an article that played up the significance of said actions that I smacked my forehead and exclaimed, "How could I have been so blind? It's obvious that Kong doesn't just like Ann, he desires her. Of course! What could be a more natural drive for a 50-foot-tall prehistoric ape to have?"

Though Kong clearly does feel some affection for Ann—his tender care in placing her out of harm's way just before he plummets to his death demonstrates as much—in retrospect I would like to say that far too much misdirected Freudian freight is being dumped on the big lug. It would make for a refreshing change if, instead of regarding him as a symbol, we took him at face value; that is to say, as an animal. Once we do that, all the implications of Kong/Ann sexual attraction must fall by the wayside.

When confronted by something or someone new, including food, what will most animals do? Sniff it. Even dogs, famous for gulping first and regretting it later, will take a moment to investigate the unfamiliar fare. Further exploratory behaviors may follow. Kong is used to receiving native women as his sacrifices, and no matter how high a standard of personal hygiene those women maintain, Skull Island is not the best place on Earth to buy soap. The key fact here is a simple one: Ann doesn't just look different, she smells different from Kong's usual sacrificial snacks. Kong is big, but he's not stupid: It may look like food and it sounds ("Eeeeeeee!") like food, but it doesn't smell like food, so he'll take it To Go while he decides if it's safe to eat.

In other words, Kong's supposedly salacious actions towards Ann aren't about sex, but about self-protective curiosity. In addition to this, let us consider the *King Kong* sequel, *Son of Kong*, which provides irrefutable evidence that our boy Kong knows the difference between mate and meat. So stop screaming, Ann; he's just not that into you. Here endeth the side-note.

The conventional plot of "Beauty and the Beast" has Beauty discovering that the Beast is not as bad as everyone thinks. Although he looks monstrous, he has a tender heart and a stimulating intellect. The two of them come to enjoy each other's company and it soon becomes evident that the Beast has fallen in love with Beauty. But when push comes to cuddle, Beauty is still unable to get over her gut-level revulsion when the Beast proposes taking their relationship to the next level. ("I'm sorry, dear Beast, it's not you, it's me. It's me, throwing up a lot at the very thought of you touching me.") So although there has been none of that slowly evolving friendship and respect between Ann and Kong as between other Beauties and their Beasts, there is plenty of reluctance (to put it mildly) to go beyond the Can't We Just Be Friends? stage.

Meanwhile, back at the myth, Psyche has had no trouble getting physical with her Beast, though you'd think that after some time she'd figure out that her so-called "monster" was anything but. Even if all the lights in the bedroom are out, whatever happened to the Braille School of Applied Anatomy? Or was she wearing mittens the whole time?

As "Beauty and the Beast" progresses, Beauty reestablishes contact with the family she left behind when she came to live with the Beast. In some versions she sees a vision of her father on his deathbed, in others—including Cupid and Psyche—she is the victim of homesickness. The Beast gives her permission either to pay a short visit to her family or to have her family come visit her. In the former instance, he implores her to return to him within a short, stipulated time. In both cases, usually for selfish reasons, the family members contrive to upset the happy relationship between Beauty and the Beast. (Beauty's father doesn't want to lose his favorite child a second time, so has all the clocks in the house set back in order to deceive her. Psyche's sisters, envious of the splendor in which she lives, plant suspicions in her mind about her unseen husband so that she breaks the taboo against seeing his face, ultimately causing Cupid to fly back home to Mother.)

Beauty returns to find her Beast on the point of death because he loves her so dearly that he is literally incapable of living without her. Psyche passes through many ordeals until she is once more permitted to see her pseudo-Beast husband. In both versions, the possibility of losing the Beast forever forces the Beauties to reorder their priorities: Nothing is more important than True Love; not physical appearances, not family ties, not public opinion, N-O-T-H-I-N-G.

Having realized that she loves the Beast in spite of everything, Beauty acts to save his life, either by a declaration of her willingness to marry him as-is, by the fall of a teardrop, by a kiss, by whatever outward action signifies her inner revelation. No sooner does she do this than a marvelous transformation occurs: The Beast is a Beast no longer. By the power of Beauty's unconditional love, the spell upon him is broken and he is returned to his original form as a handsome young man/prince.

The big transformation in the myth of Cupid and Psyche is somewhat different, since the Beast was never really a Beast. Instead Psyche is transformed into a goddess so that she will be worthy of her divine spouse,

Cupid. Her husband's realm is the heart, hers is the soul.

And they lived happily ever after.

Very little of this applies to Beast Kong and Beauty Ann. Her initial reaction to Kong—sheer screaming terror—remains unchanged for the duration of the film. This Beast offers his Beauty no gallantry, no exalted conversations, no attempts to win her heart. All he does is carry her around and occasionally sniff her, but not every woman appreciates an Ivy League courtship.

Like the traditional Beauties, Ann Darrow does want to return to her "family"—in this case, Jack Driscoll, first mate of the S.S. Venture, all-purpose hero, and gosh-you're-swell love interest—but it's less a matter of visiting than escaping. Beauty and Psyche are content to remain with their Beasts. Ann just wants out. Beauty and Psyche both return voluntarily to their Beasts—in Psyche's case, she goes through several fairy-tale–style tests and ordeals to earn the right to see him once more. Ann didn't consent to go to her Beast on Skull Island and her feelings remain unchanged (and loud) in New York City when he wants her back again.

That brings us to the climax of our several stories, namely the death of the Beast. (At this point, the myth of Cupid and Psyche has to drop out of the running since the Beast element there was merely a ruse on Cupid's part.) In the traditional tales, Beauty kills the Beast only symbolically in that she transforms him from Beast to man. Yes, there are some versions where Beauty returns to find the Beast dead in his rose garden, whereupon her kiss, pledge of love, or tears simultaneously resurrect and transform him, but the fact remains that when the smoke clears, there's no dead body left onstage. It remains a symbolic death.

Ann, on the other hand, brings about Kong's 100 percent pure-dee genuine I-got-the-corpse-right-here demise. There can be no talk of symbolic deaths when you're eyeballing one doozy of an ape cadaver. Kong is not transformed into anything but landfill. Ann and Kong do not live happily ever after, unless we're talking about when *Love-Slave of Skull Island* by Ann Darrow makes it onto the Best Seller lists.

Now let's step back a pace and do the math here: In the traditional Beauty and the Beast tale, the narrative ends with everyone pretty, rich, and married. In *King Kong* it ends with New York in shambles, a dead ape, plenty of collateral fatalities, and Ann Darrow slated to wed Jack Driscoll. He's first mate on a shady ship that makes extended voyages to dangerous ports, for which he'll collect Depression era wages. So after the wedding she'll probably spend her time pining for an absent husband who'll be oceans away, risking his life for paltry pay; yeah, that's got all the earmarks of a fun marriage.

"Beauty and the Beast" does not end badly for the main players. *King Kong* does, and as if to affirm this, *Son of Kong* opens with Carl Denham dead broke as a result of the Kong fiasco. From which we may conclude that, no matter how often Denham compares the events and characters surrounding his enterprise to Beauty and the Beast, it's just not the same story. Retellings of archetypal tales do not automatically result from tossing the basic ingredients into the same container. Flour, fat, pan-drippings, and water make gravy or glop, depending on what you do with them.

Speaking as someone who watches far too many cartoons for my own good, I'd like to add that when the creators of *The Simpsons* parodied *King Kong* as "King Homer" in one of their "Treehouse of Horror" Halloween episodes, they actually got the whole "Beauty and the Beast" angle right. Marge in the Ann Darrow role is a traditional Beauty, communicating with the Beast, sympathizing with him, coming to see him as something more than a monster, and although there is no magical metamorphosis into human form for King Homer, she ends by marrying him anyway. (He devours her father, but what newlywed couple doesn't have a few issues to work out?)

The irony of it all is that, while *King Kong* can't claim true kinship to the traditional "Beauty and the Beast," nor even to the myth of Cupid and Psyche, it does have its roots in a far older tale: the story of the wild man Enkidu as recounted in the Sumerian epic of *Gilgamesh*.

Like Kong, Enkidu dwells with beasts in the wild. He is described as strong and extraordinarily hairy, also very Konglike. All attempts to capture him are fruitless until someone has the bright idea to send the harlot Shamhat to, er, talk things over with him. She is a very persuasive talker. He keeps talking with her for six days and seven nights, after which the poor guy can hardly walk straight. Then, just as Kong is transported to the Big Apple, Enkidu is taken to Uruk (a.k.a. The Big Onion) where, unlike Kong, he manages to acclimate. This is a good thing, otherwise the epic of *Gilgamesh* would end with Enkidu on top of a ziggurat, clutching Shamhat in his paws while the citizens of Uruk stood around waiting for someone to invent the biplane.

In Enkidu's tale, as in Kong's, Beauty does not kill the Beast. What she does do is arouse his curiosity about things alien to his experience (in Enkidu's case she arouses a lot more than his curiosity, but that's where it starts). She distracts him from his previous way of dealing with things, which was through simple brute force. Above all, she makes it impossible for him to return to his former world. And, having changed his life irrevocably, she leaves him to his own devices. How well or how badly this ends now depends entirely on him. Enkidu makes a go of his new existence; Kong can't. In this, Kong is even more like Samson than Enkidu: The big, strong, hairy guy's experience with Beauty distracts him, weakens him enough to enable his capture by lesser men, and results in a captivity that he ends by a massive act of destruction that results in his own death.

So far it looks like we've reached the following conclusions:

1. *King Kong* really isn't "Beauty and the Beast," even though it's got a Beast and a Beauty. (I've decided to be merciful and spare you the analogy to Apple Jacks™ cereal, which, as the commercials so emphatically state, contains no apples. No jacks either, but they don't mention that.)

2. *King Kong* inarguably does end badly for its Beast. By comparison, its Beauty gets off lightly, though her scream-stressed vocal cords will never be the same.

3. Beauty and the Beast itself does not end badly.

4. Yes, it does.

Apologies to the tidy-minded, but as long as I'm dealing with the theme of "Beauty and the Beast—Must It Always End Badly?" in good conscience I can't end this essay without pointing out one rather toxic point about the source story: It may not end badly for the characters, but for some members of the audience, the story's implied message has much damage to answer for.

In "Beauty and the Beast," the Beast's curse is broken and he is returned to his original, handsome, human form. He is usually a prince. Beauty marries him, becomes royal, and continues to live in wealth and comfort. (Psyche really hits the Beauty and the Beast jackpot: A handsome husband, wealth, comfort, and immortality!) And how does Beauty achieve all this? By using the magical power of Love to change a being that everyone else sees as a monster.

As in: "I know he hits me, but if I only Love him

enough, I can change him."

As in: "My family tells me that I have to get away from him because the last time he hit me I wound up in the hospital, but they don't know him the way I know him, and when my Love finally changes him they'll see that they were wrong."

As in: "He's still hitting me and now he hits the kids, too, but it's really my fault because if I only Loved him enough he'd change."

And that, my friends, is one Beauty and the Beast story that always ends badly.

POSTSCRIPT

Received Wisdom is what often happens when someone tells us something they want us to accept without question and is usually phrased in such a way as to make us feel like misfits, monsters, traitors, ignoramuses, or naughty, naughty children if we should ever dare to consider challenging their contention. I don't know about you, but when I hear sentences that begin "Everyone knows that . . ." or "Normal people never . . ." or "A real American would . . ." I tend to reach for a big box of Mama Esther's Instant Sez You, which goes very well as a side dish with a helping of properly aged You Wish.

The case for insinuating that Kong wants to make Ann his literal bride rather than his midnight snack is based on a number of subtle and not-so-subtle actions on the part of the animated ape, specifically the scene where he carefully peels away some of her clothes, gently strokes her unconscious body, and then sniffs his fingers.

"The Bravest
Girl I Ever Knew . . ."

Howard Waldrop

F ROM MOVIE FAN MAGAZINE, April 1952:

A Note From *Movie Fan*'s Editor:

Everybody knows the story, or thinks they do. The most famous find in movie history, before Lana Turner's discovery at Schwab's drugstore. A movie producer, desperate for a leading lady, finds exactly the right girl stealing apples from a vendor at the depth of the Depression. Seven months later she's the most famous woman in the world.

Her career blazed across the screen for exactly one year. Then, like the later Louise Brooks, she left, with no regrets. The usual wisdom is life and Hollywood broke her heart.

But the story is not that simple (Hollywood stories never are) and for the first time, we at *Movie Fan* are going to set the record straight, removing all the glamour and tinsel. The true story is both more plebian and much stranger than all the legend and fiction written about her. Our writer, Miss Ellencamp, has spent the last year assiduously combing through studio records, newspaper articles, and publicity handouts; a truly huge mass of materials, building a true picture of the meteoric star, a piece we call simply:

ANN

by Margot Luisa Ellencamp

First off, Ann Darrow was Canadian, born in the community of Dollarton on Vancouver Bay in 1920. Her father, "Big" Bill Darrow, formerly a logger, was killed with half of his battalion at Beaumont-Hamel; her mother, Angelina, was taken off by the Spanish Influenza in 1918.

Secondly (as those who've seen her last two films know), she was brunette. For her first and most famous role, the producer Carl Denham insisted she be blond, to play up the dark vs. light, Beauty and the Beast theme. (Ann and Charley—the cook—spent much of the voyage to Skull Island getting exactly the right shade of blond, and the right amount of curl, with the many home permanent formulas, still in their infancy, that Denham had picked up in a beauty shop supply store on the way back to the ship with his newly found leading lady, just before they sailed.)

Third, as those who've seen all three films know, she could do more than just scream—even in Denham's *Kong* she does a lot more than that—it's just the screaming that most people remember.

When Denham asked her, "Did you ever do any acting?" she said, "Extra work out on Long Island. The Studio's closed now." Well, that was Paramount. At the time in which the movie was set, the Astoria studio had just suffered a disastrous fire and the decision had been made to move all production to the West Coast.

That ended Paramount's ability to do something the other studios couldn't—to use Broadway talent without that talent having to take the five-day train trip west and live in California while making their films.

The "extra work" Ann Darrow had done had

been in several of Paramount's East Coast productions. The Marx Brothers had made both *Cocoanuts* and *Animal Crackers* at Paramount's Astoria studio in the daytime while appearing in *I'll Say She Is!* at night. (It ran on Broadway for two years.) If you look closely (as I did) you can see that Ann is one of the crowd of girls on the beach just before the Irving Berlin "Monkey-Doodle-Do" musical number in *Cocoanuts*, and is one of the guests at the unveiling of the painting in *Animal Crackers*. She was 19 and 20 when she did those. She's only on for a few seconds in each, and don't be looking for a blonde.

Like all Hollywood stories, even her extra work has been glamorized and embellished. Stories circulated that three of the four Marx Brothers were so smitten by her beauty, they tried various campaigns and stratagems to lure her into love affairs.* Most writers think this was a figment of some publicist's imagination, retroactively fired by the thoughts of Ann's beauty and the Marxes' notorious behavior.

The Depression hit Ann as hard as it did anyone else; she'd had a few walk-on parts in a couple of revues written by writer-friends of hers, but those jobs, like the extra work, dried up. At the time Denham found her, she was living in a $6.00 a week rooming house at the edge of the Village, and according to friends, having to borrow part of that amount most weeks.

Then Denham offered her the "fame and adventure and the thrill of a lifetime and [the] long sea voyage leaving at six o'clock in the morning," and the rest is just like in *Kong*. Little known is that all the scenes in *Kong* detailing Ann and Jack's adventures from the time

---

* But of what single woman on a Marx Bros. movie set was this not true? (With the possible exception of Margaret Dumont.) The best quote was Archie Lee Johnson's: "In the movies, Harpo acted out his libido. On movie sets, Chico acted on his libido."

Driscoll left Denham on the other side of the ravine were recreations—about the last thing Denham still had money for after Kong fell off the building—he saw the movie as a way to recoup some of his losses from the disaster that was Kong-as-a-Broadway-attraction.

What was recreated for the film were the early fight with the *Tyrannosaurus*, the scenes of Kong with Ann in his lair, the scenes of Jack and Ann's escape from Kong, and a few of the scenes of Kong breaking the gate in the wall to get at the native village in his search for Ann.**

The rest was pieced together from scenes taken aboard ship and on Skull Island, and newsreels and Denham's own films of Kong as exhibition and of his New York rampage.

In the studio, they got a well-known animator to re-create scenes. The effects were so wonderful and life-like it was hard to tell where the real Kong left off and the 18-inch-high model/actor took his place. But the effects were hurried, which accounts for Kong's variations in size. Assume when you see *Kong* that everything when the camera is not near Denham is a re-creation done in the few weeks between the death of the real Kong in March, and the release of the movie in June.

What mattered to Ann was that she and Jack Driscoll, the man she loved, worked together in the studio a few weeks, filling in the gaps in the story.

** True to Denham's prediction, the cameraman ran. After filming Kong shaking the sailors off the log, and getting that horrifying pan-shot down into the ravine, the cameraman went with Denham back to the Wall. Denham was filming while Kong was trying to break the gate, then went to help in the futile attempt to stop Kong from breaking through. The guy dropped the camera and bolted for the shoreline; Denham shot most of the destruction of the village and the camera-man, now out by the boats, got the shots of Kong's gassing.

KONG UNBOUND

Kong as a living exhibit premiered two days before FDR took office as president, and it made an enormous amount of money that first night, even though FDR had already announced the five-day bank holiday in which all banks throughout the nation would be closed. People turned out to see Kong at top ticket prices, no matter what.

The same thing happened when the film came out—it was an enormous hit. Denham had been right all along about "being a millionaire and sharing it with you, boys" and in this case, girl. At least, he would have been right had not Denham's expenses and litigations eaten up all the money from the exhibition and movie.

But by the time the movie premiered, Denham and Englehorn were on their way back to Skull Island, to find the treasure that would eventually save Denham, and with another leading lady.

People ask, why didn't he just take Ann back with him? At the time of his greatest financial troubles, the one valuable asset he did have was Ann Darrow's personal contract. She was the most famous woman and actress in the world at the time. Denham had loaned her out to MGM for a huge sum of money for their next superproduction.

Of course she did it—she owed everything to Carl Denham—but little did she realize she would have to do it with a sorrowing and broken heart.

She and Jack were to be married two weeks after the premiere of *Kong*, the movie. One night while Ann was off making a personal appearance at a charity event, Jack ran into a bunch of sailors he'd shipped out with before he became Captain Englehorn's first mate, and they went off to some speakeasy and drank some bad liquor. How bad? Four of the sailors died, Jack among them.

The newspapers that week said that Ann was inconsolable—first Denham and the ship had gone back to the island, she was on loan out to MGM, and now Jack was dead. That was the state of things when she took the Zephyr out to California in the summer of 1933, to star in *The Return of Tarzan*, where she played Queen La of Opar, opposite Johnny Weissmuller and Maureen O'Sullivan, who reprised their roles from *Tarzan, the Ape Man* of 1932.

Some of her broken heart is still up there on the screen—especially in the scenes of longing for Tarzan, and her immortal words: "It was La and Tarzan before this woman came. We were happy. Let us be happy again. Rule with me, over my kingdom!"

Cedric Gibbons's set design for the collapsed Opar (the Ophir of the Bible)—the half-broken dome, remnants of former buildings, ruined gardens, crumbled and vine-covered statues—all got across a feeling of a vanished civilization, older and larger than the one on Skull Island. The inhabitants—La's subjects—shambling half-ape men, beautiful women—chanted and danced at the thought their Queen was to marry the Lord of the Jungle.

Ann threw herself into her work, all the while fending off Weissmuller's "busy, busy hands," as she called them once in an interview. ("He was like a six-foot upright octopus," she said.) Her screen time in the film is thirty out of ninety-six minutes, but they were memorable and intense minutes. The famous still of her (cut from the movie) half-crouched on her throne, backed by the two crossed twenty-foot-long ivory tusks, still sells for high prices to collectors of movie memorabilia. More so even than the Elephants' Graveyard sequence in the first movie, what most people remember is the scene with La and Tarzan standing on the broken balcony, looking over the vine-covered remnants of the former great city while the moon rises behind the two bodiless legs (broken off just at hip level) of the statue of the Ape-god of the ruined city. (Cedric Gibbons again . . .)

MGM rushed her into her next (and what proved to be last) film. It's her most atypical, and the one she liked best. It was in the middle of filming *Take My Heart Please* that the first news came out of the Indian Ocean that Denham was on his way back.

Ann Darrow got the role of a lifetime (and the cast of a lifetime to act with) in *Take My Heart Please*. During the filming of the offbeat movie, some publicist had put up a sign, supposedly from her, on her dressing room door: "Please, no more gorillas." It sounds like publicity, as Ann never denigrated Kong's role in her life in any published interview.

In the movie Ann is a low-tier stage actress who lives in a rooming house much like the ones she'd lived in only eighteen months before. She and her best friend, Zuxxy ("the x's are silent"), are hired by a producer to play (offstage) the parts of the producer's and assistant producer's wives. This is in order to counteract the suspicions of the society mother of a rising starlet—whom they want to hire—about bachelor producers of Broadway shows.

The usual complications ensue: one screwy complication leads to the lies that set up the next one. Ann's character and Zuxxy end up with the (wrong) right people, and there's a tremendous chase with a hook-and-ladder fire truck and trolley car.

For Zuxxy, Eve Arden was on loan-out from Paramount (in return, Loretta Young spent two weeks at Paramount in a South Seas movie no one ever saw). The producer was played by Leon Ames, the associate producer by Franchot Tone—who ends up with Ann's character while Arden ends up with Ames—the society dame by Margaret Dumont, this time in a not-very-comic role, and she was very good in it. There are bits by Edgar Kennedy, Raymond Walburn, and Franklin Pangborn. Grady Sutton is the young starlet's brother, sort of a thinking man's suspicious weasel: the more he looks, the more he sees about the false situation.

It had the only screenplay ever worked on at one time or another by the young John Huston, the not-so-young F. Scott Fitzgerald, and Dorothy Parker aided by her husband Alan Campbell.

People who saw it at the time or in rereleases think it's a wonderful film, full of the kinds of things people used to go to the movies for. Ann was never better: she's a terrific physical comedienne, and the byplay between her and Eve Arden is just magic.

It was one of only twelve films MGM released that year that only broke even at the box office. No one knows why. It's a much better movie than 90 percent of the hits the studio had that year.

In December, just after *The Return of Tarzan* was released, she got a telegram from Hawaii.

GEE KID LOOKS LIKE YOURE A HIT. WILL CATCH THE FLICK IN HONOLULU TOMORROW. RETURNING TO THE STATES NEXT WEEK. DONT WORRY ABOUT ME–THINGS ARE GREAT. OUR MONEY WORRIES ARE OVER. STAY THE WAY YOU ARE AND BE SWELL.

DENHAM

It was with much surprise that Ann was given the 1934 Academy Award for Best Supporting Actress, in a strong field, for her role in *The Return of Tarzan*. (Gibbons won the first-ever-given Academy Award for

KONG UNBOUND

his art direction.) At the ceremony, Eve Arden had a telegram from Ann that said:

EVE IF I WIN JUST SAY THANK YOU VERY MUCH AND SIT DOWN.

ANN

So Eve said, "Thank you very much and sit down."

That same month, *Take My Heart Please* opened to some great reviews and disappointing box office.

By then, Ann was 6000 miles away.

FROM THE ONLY INTERVIEW PAUL YOUNG* EVER GAVE— IN 1941—TO AN AP STRINGER WHO HAD WALKED THE 50 MILES FROM THE NEAREST RAILROAD STATION IN HOPES OF GETTING A STORY FROM HIM.

PY: I fell in love with that girl the first time I laid eyes on her. Not the googly-eyed movie love, either. I said, "Paul, this is the one for you." That was late in '33, and I was leaving this rubber-and-peanut plantation for the States on business anyway, and I set about winning her heart, after all that Kong stuff, and the sad business about Driscoll, and Denham's troubles and whatnot. (I once said: no one has to worry about Carl Denham.)

Anyway, I knew people who knew people, and I found myself at a party somewhere up in the LA hills and there she was, and brother, I wasn't in the least bit disappointed. I had shaved off my mustache for the trip: she was shorter than she looks on-screen, and reached up and poked the dip under my nose and asked, "How do you shave in there?" and I said something Hollywood, with embarrassment, like "For you, I'll cover it back up," or something.

---

* Despite what some sources state: he was not, nor related to, the famous bamboo fly rod maker of the same name and era.

176

Three months later we were on our way back here, as happily married as two people have ever been in the history of the world.

FROM: *THE NINTH WONDER OF THE WORLD:*
MY LIFE BY CARL DENHAM, 1946.

She came into my office after she finished that last picture. She looked around, eyeing all the sharp new stuff I had.

"It's true, then," she said. "I don't have to worry about you any more, do I, Mr. Denham?" (She never called me anything but Mr. Denham in all the time I knew her.)

"Don't worry about me ever again, Ann," I said. "I'm rolling in it. Anything you need? Anything at all! You don't know how much it meant to me, those first few destitute months back on Skull Island, knowing you were here, giving it your all, becoming a star."

"Well, yes, there is one thing," she said. "I've fallen in love with a wonderful man-He's, he's not like Jack at all-but there's no fakery about him, either. He wants me to be his wife."

"That's just great, Ann," I said. "If you're sure that's what you want."

"I'm as sure of it as I've ever been about any-thing." And she reached across my desk and took my hand—the only time she ever did that, either. "It's what I want. I want to ask you to release me from my contract. My future husband will pay whatever amount you think—"

"Pay? Pay! There's not enough money in the whole world to pay what your contract's worth, kid," I said.

She looked crestfallen.

I reached in my desk and took out her personal contract, signed like what seemed long ages ago on a rusty old ship. I tore it in half and handed her both pieces.

"This isn't something you buy and sell. This is something you give away for love." Then I slapped myself in the face. "What am I saying? The price for this is you two owe me a dinner so I can meet this guy who's taking you away from all this. I want to size him up."

"You name it," she said. "We'd love to."

"Tonight. The Coconut Grove. Eight sharp."

"We'll be there."

And then she leaned over and kissed me on the forehead.

"I've always wanted to do that," she said, and tousled my thinning locks. "That, too."

"Banana oil!" I said. "Get outta here before I change my mind!"

She left.

That night as I said goodbye to them outside the club, I thought sure she would be okay for the rest of her life (well, she was, but you know what I mean . . .). I shook hands with Paul—he had working hands, not the ones of a sissy—and said, "Take care of my little girl. I mean it."

"I surely will," he said. "I love her more than anything. I'm the luckiest guy in the world."

"If I had a heart," I said, "I would probably love her, too."

They got in the cab and waved. They looked so happy.

It was the last time I saw her alive.

Poor kid.

FROM THE 1941 INTERVIEW WITH PAUL YOUNG.

PY: I asked her when we first got back here if she didn't miss all that.

"Not really," she said. "Though sometimes I think what a wonderful thing it would have been to make more movies with Eve. She's just so great.

"But look around, Paul. It's just like you said. It's cool at night, and not as hot and muggy as somebody would think. The world can go by out there somewhere and you'd never even know it was there."

She loved this place. It was like my whole life led me to buy this plantation, just so it would be there for her when she needed it. It made me proud to have done that. That had been the major accomplishment of my life.

FROM: *THE NINTH WONDER OF THE WORLD:*
MY LIFE BY CARL DENHAM, 1946.

I wrote her a letter about a year later. I put it in here to show what I was still thinking at the time . . .

April 20, 1935
Dear Ann (and Paul),

I can't believe it's been a year—I've been so busy I just looked up and a whole year was gone. I got to see your last picture a few months ago—you and it were swell; so was everybody else in it, and you're right—that Eve Arden is a pistol! Sorry the picture tanked. But it's still there for everybody to see, from now til the end of time. They can't take that away from you.

What with the two pictures I made this year, and what's left of the Skull Island treasure, I look to be sitting pretty for a long long time—but I've got to admit, I'm getting a little too stiff to be running around jungles and throwing gas bombs and such.

People keep bringing me plays and movie scripts they say you'd be great in, and trying to get me to get you back over here, but I tell them, "Don't get your boxers in a twist–I know she's happy AND she knows the door's always open if she ever changes her mind. Meanwhile, write your stuff for Carole Lombard and Jean Arthur—though neither has Ann's range."

I just want to say again how much knowing you has meant to me—we gave 'em some socko stuff, didn't we kid? I hope you're tremendously happy, and my best to Paul.

Your Pal,
Carl Denham

FROM THE INTERVIEW WITH PAUL YOUNG.

PY: She woke me up the night of the day we'd gotten back from Madoni, where she'd seen the doctor and knew she was going to have a baby. She was upset.

"For the first time in a year," she said, "I dreamed about Kong, and it wasn't a nightmare, like all the other times in the past. We were on top of Skull Mountain, outside the cave, where the *pterodactyl* picked me up. But the only ones in the sky were far, far away. Kong was sitting, leaning forward, his hands out in front of him, his legs were dangling over the abyss. We were just sitting. I didn't say anything. It was like he knew what was going to happen. Like Denham said—he was a tough egg but he'd already cracked up and gone sappy. Like he'd already accepted anything and everything that was going to happen. Because of me.

"Paul, no matter what the future holds, I want you to know it's—well, it's not necessarily for the best, always, but it will be what's supposed to happen. I'll be okay if I know you're going to do one of two things for me. If I have a boy, I want you to name him—don't be upset, please—Jack Denham Young and give him this." She'd been shopping in Madoni, where there's not very much shopping to be had, but they'd just got in stuff from Nairobi–where it came in from British-controlled Africa, I don't know—she handed me a baseball glove. "I know there aren't any teams out here, but teach him how to play like he was a boy in America."

"Ann," I said. "Why are you talking like this? You can teach him how to play. You've got a better arm than me!"

"And if it's a girl," she said, and handed me a crazy-looking doll, "I want you to name her Jill Eve Young and give her this, whose name, I just decided, is Genevieve. Can you promise me you'll do those things?"

"Of course!" I said. "Of course. But don't be talking like this. You're going to be fine. We'll have as many kids as you want; we'll make our own baseball team."

She put her finger up to my lip. I'd grown my mustache back by then.

"Just do whichever of those things you need to do and I'll be happy. Well, happier. Dreaming of Kong that way made me realize the world goes on forever."

"Well, sure it does," I said. Then she went back to sleep, and I remember just standing there watching over her for a long time.

That was six years ago. [This interview was from 1941.] There isn't an hour that goes by that I don't think about her and miss her. (I'll take you out to her grave when you're through interviewing me.) But of course I have Jill there to remember her by, even with all the trouble she's caused me, trading my best flashlight for Joe out there. Look at them playing. I don't think Joe's got all his growth yet—he's going to be a real handful before he gets through.

I just wish Ann would be here to see all this. Sometimes I'm sorry I ever brought her here, but then again, I wouldn't trade what we had for anything. Sometimes I think she was just visiting us here on Earth, and her life here was like a dream, rounded with a gorilla on each end.

You want to come down by the river with me now? It's really very peaceful there.

It was her favorite spot.

King Kong –
My Favorite Nightmare

Frank M. Robinson

I WAS RAISED in a boys' orphanage from about three until I was nine years old. It was the middle of the GreatDepression and we ate garbage picked up by the orphanage truck that went around to the equivalent of grocery store dumpsters in search of anything still edible. But shed no tears—there were compensations. My mother was one of the matrons and my two older brothers were there as well so I wasn't totally bereft of family. Plus we had a summer camp—Camp Hardy on Little Blue Lake, not far from Holland, Michigan. Close by was a Boy Scout encampment, whose manager regularly asked us to search for Scouts lost in the woods (great for our *esprit de corps*).

I never considered myself deprived or even poor—I had a lot of young friends and the orphanage (supported by the Lutheran Church) found plenty to keep us occupied and entertained. What I remember most fondly was that every Saturday afternoon when it wasn't raining or snowing, they'd line us up and march us to the local theater for a double feature, a serial, three or four cartoons, and a free candy bar. The films were courtesy of the theater; I suspect the candy bars were more than a few days old and were courtesy of the local candy stores. (One of the few nice things about the Depression was that everybody chipped in to help each other.)

I first saw *Frankenstein* there and later, *King Kong*, and it's a toss-up which gave me the worst nightmares. I suspect *Frankenstein*—I was a few years younger then—but *King Kong* was no slouch. Both were released in the years before the Hays Office's Production Code was enforced, and there was no such thing as PG-13. I also doubt that many film directors worried about the reactions of a bunch of little kids sitting in a darkened theater watching a huge, ferocious ape chew on people like they were chicken drumsticks and not only squish natives into the mud but twist his foot to make sure they were dead. And even at a tender age we wondered about the love affair between the monster ape and the heroine. When Kong's curiosity gets the better of him and he strips off some of Fay Wray's clothing and then smells his fingertips, the universal reaction among us kids was "ewww." And there was more than one late-night discussion in which the older boys decided bigger could not possibly always be better. For my part, I discovered that one thin blanket wasn't nearly enough to hide under when the nightmares came.

But the good parts of *King Kong* were remarkably good. The long mysterious buildup to Skull Island, Kong and his fights with the *Tyrannosaurus* and *Pterodactyl* . . . hot stuff! Nothing equaled them until *Jurassic Park* hit the screens. Willis O'Brien's detailed reconstructions of dinosaurs were absolutely convincing and none of us minded their somewhat jerky movements. King Kong fought with jabs and upper cuts and moves that would have credited a champion boxer or wrestler. Sure enough, I discovered years later that Merian C. Cooper, the director (along with Ernest B. Schoedsack), and Willis O'Brien had once been boxers and wrestlers. Kong's fight moves occurred naturally to them.

King Kong was, for a long time, my favorite movie and even now rates way up there. I've often wondered about the appeal of the film and its longevity. Bits and pieces of research over the years have caused me to come

7 9##

up with one conclusion: Neither Cooper nor Schoedsack ever attended a film school or could boast of a Master's in Cinema or knew anything about CGI. They had set out to make the greatest adventure film of all time, one that would please themselves, not some focus group in Tulsa. And they were uniquely qualified—both of them were honest-to-God adventurers. Cooper was an idea man, Schoedsack a photographer, and they quickly became a working team. Their first venture was *Grass*, a documentary about the migration of 50,000 Bakhtiyari tribesmen in Persia (Iran). The film was enormously successful on the lecture circuit and Jesse Lasky bought it for general release by Paramount. When Lasky asked Cooper and Schoedsack to do a follow-up, they produced *Chang*, a documentary about elephants in Siam (Thailand). It won an early Academy Award for "Artistic Quality of Production." (*Grass* and *Chang* are available on DVD.

I recently screened *Grass* on laser disc and was disappointed—the reproduction was terrible. The first half of the film was dull—too many shots of Marguerite Harrison, the third partner in the project. The last half, lousy repro and all, was far superior. Watching the Bakhtiyari cross rivers and mountain ranges and break trail over snow-covered mountains, while barefoot, was riveting.)

Cooper and Schoedsack later worked for David Selznick at Paramount and went to Africa to film backgrounds for the silent version of *The Four Feathers*. When Selznick left Paramount to go to RKO, he hired Cooper as a production assistant. Cooper went through the backlog of studio projects and found *Creation*—unfinished— about the crew of a submarine blown off course that ends up on a South American island populated by prehistoric beasts. (This was in 1931-anybody who thinks the storyline resembles that of Burroughs' much earlier *The Land*

That Time Forgot is exactly right. Hollywood haircuts existed even back then.)

Cooper studied Willis O'Brien's recreations of dinosaurs—O'Brien had also crafted the dinosaurs in 1925's *The Lost World*—and felt O'Brien had the key to making a film he'd thought of for a long time. As a kid, he'd read a book about giant apes that raided native villages and carried off young maidens, and while in Africa he had become fascinated with the life of a tribe of baboons. O'Brien's prehistoric monsters blown up to fill a theater screen were exactly what he was looking for.

Things moved very quickly after that. Selznick— though he personally didn't care for it—saw the commercial possibilities and green-lighted the project. Willis O'Brien was signed, as were Armstrong, Fay Wray, and Noble Johnson (the native chief). All three were working on *The Most Dangerous Game*, directed by Schoedsack. *King Kong* was shot simultaneously with it and used some of the same jungle sets. Armstrong was perfect as Denham, as was Fay Wray as Ann Darrow—once Cooper gave her a blond wig. Bruce Cabot (not his real name— he was born a French-Canadian) was a bit player in films and pieced out his income acting as doorman for a Hollywood nightclub. Cooper picked him as the hero and gave him the munificent salary of seventy-five dollars a week. Cooper's mantra for making the film was "distance, drama, danger." *Kong* had all the elements early on but Cooper always wanted a "chariot race," a la Ben Hur—the one element that would bring the audience out of their seats (or nail them there). He found his chariot race while in New York when he glanced up and saw a plane flying close to New York's Life Insurance Building, then the tallest in the city. It was no stretch at all for Cooper to visualize his great ape on top of a tall building batting at the planes that were trying to shoot him down.

KONG UNBOUND

The actual production of the film was primitive-no budget of millions, no hundreds of computer technicians—but complicated for the time, being a mixture of live action, stop-motion, and rear projection, all combined in the optical printer. There were six models of Kong (see Dick Lupoff's excellent reminiscence in this book) and bits and pieces of the actual giant ape. An enormous head, fully operational with the aid of compressed air, a huge foot, and, of course, the hand that tenderly holds Fay Wray. The six miniatures were fully articulated and covered with rabbit fur. One unintended consequence of smart thinking was that every time the model was manipulated, the fur would be crushed down. Seen on screen, it looks as if the wind is rustling through the fur. The producers later claimed it was Kong's muscles rippling . . .

Max Steiner got the assignment to do the score and, according to critics, wrote a type of score that had never been done before. But I was eight years old when I saw it and young kids don't go to movies to listen to the music (they don't nowadays, either, despite the kudos lavished on John Williams for his scores of the *Star Wars* films). What impressed me much more were the horrendous growls and roars of Kong, courtesy of a sound technician who visited the San Diego zoo and recorded the sounds of the lions at feeding time, then lowered the results by an octave.

The movie finished production in February of 1933 and cost $695,000 to make.

Everything didn't come up roses for *King Kong*. Cooper personally cut one scene after a screening—the one where the sailors are shaken off the log by Kong, fall into a ravine, and are eaten by giant spiders. There were other cuts made when the movie was rereleased over the years. When it came to future rereleases, the new and beady-eyed Hays Office was on the job.

Cooper had attempted to do the near impossible at the beginning—to turn a monster gorilla who kills human beings in various terrifying ways into a sympathetic villain, the victim of an impossible love affair, and one for whom the audience, at the end, feels a certain sympathy.

Unintended consequences again—the Hays Office and the various cuts it demanded made it much easier for the audience to shed a silent tear over the monster. Oddly, this didn't hurt box office at all and in various rereleases, *King Kong* topped the charts.

Shortly after its initial release, Selznick left the studio for the greener pastures of MGM. His parting gift to RKO was changing the title of *Kong* (formerly *The Beast*, *The Eighth Wonder*, *The Eighth Wonder of the World* and then simply *Kong*) to *King Kong*.

King Kong, the movie that Selznick didn't particularly care for, has been credited with saving RKO.

I've often wondered about the success of *King Kong* and why it gripped the imagination of so many moviegoers. For a movie of the period, it was certainly meticulously made. In the portrayal of the huge Kong and the various dinosaurs, it was unique. Nobody had seen anything like it. You had attractive actors like Fay Wray, Robert Armstrong, and Bruce Cabot. But the real appeal of the movie lies elsewhere.

It's in the story and how it's told.

Cooper was exactly right when he refused to start the movie with Kong on the stage and Carl Denham introducing him with the whole beginning of the film told in flashbacks, as Selznick had wanted. Flashback stories are always hard to do, but Cooper's decision went beyond that. He chose a linear story form, easy to follow, and one that in the beginning relies heavily on anticipatory suspense. We don't know where we're going—neither does any member of the crew—but Carl Denham is carrying along a load of gas bombs and he has to have a use in mind, right? One of the best scenes in the movie is when Denham has Ann Darrow scream and Jack Driscoll (Bruce Cabot) says, "I wonder what he thinks she's going to see?"

They arrive at Skull Island and interrupt a group of natives—some of them dancing in ape suits while a native girl is being prepared as the bride of Kong. The chief sees Fay Wray and wants to buy her. Denham refuses and the crew returns to the ship. The natives then abduct Ann Darrow, the crew of the ship discover that she's missing, and Denham, Jack Driscoll, and various crew members grab rifles and go to the village to get her back.

It's too late. She's been strapped between two pillars just outside the huge gates (easily the best set in the movie), the natives ring the gong for Kong, and the ape comes and takes Ann Darrow away. Driscoll, Denham, and company arrive just in time to see this. They open the gates and stream out into the jungle to hunt Kong and rescue Ann Darrow.

From there until Jack and Ann reappear outside the gates is one long chase, filled with fights between Kong and various dinosaurs, sailors being eaten, and other gory highlights to be loved by kids everywhere and of any age. But Denham seems curiously unmoved by the slaughter of his own men. His mind is on what a great attraction Kong Kong will make in New York and he's got the bait for the beast to follow—Ann Darrow.

Kong shows up and batters down the gates (Why were the gates made so huge? Because it makes for a terrific scene, that's why). Kong demolishes the native village in scenes that are almost shot-for-shot the same as in

Chang, when the elephants stampede and trample the village. Denham tosses a gas bomb at Kong (he could have used a few before and perhaps saved some of his men), knocks out Kong, and in the next scene the giant ape is onstage in a huge theater. Ann Darrow and Driscoll come onstage, newsmen take dozens of pictures in a storm of popping flashbulbs, Kong thinks they're attacking Ann and breaks his bonds. He knocks down the side of the theater, wrecks the Third Avenue El (Cooper had a grudge against it—when he was living in New York, it used to keep him awake at night), finds Ann and eventually climbs the Empire State Building where he's shot down by two pilots—played by Cooper and Schoedsack. And then we have Carl Denham's memorable last line: "It was beauty killed the beast."

The movie is one of the best cinematic thrillers of all time, one exceedingly well told. There were attempts to duplicate its success—namely the De Laurentis remake back in 1976, starring Jeff Bridges and Jessica Lange and with Kong climbing the Twin Towers at the end. Leonard Maltin gave it one-and-a-half stars but he was being generous. Then there was *Mighty Joe Young*, directed by Schoedsack, with story by Cooper and script by Ruth Rose, starring Terry Moore, Ben Johnson, Robert Armstrong (once again) and featuring a somewhat smaller and more friendly ape. Willis O'Brien and Ray Harryhausen did the special effects. It rated three stars with Maltin and the movie deserved it. It wasn't *King Kong* and Terry Moore was no Fay Wray, but one can't have everything.

The biggest misfire of all was *Son of Kong*. Directed, again, by Schoedsack (executive produced by Cooper, script by Ruth Rose) and starring Robert Armstrong. O'Brien does the special effects and in a sense even Fay Wray is present—they used her recorded screams from the original. The movie was released in 1933, some months after the original. The honchos at RKO were anxious for a moneymaking sequel and naturally wanted a "bigger, better" picture. They also decided to save money by cutting the budget and making the film shorter. Gone was the buildup, gone was the pacing, gone was the suspenseful storyline. And the smaller Kid Kong comes with white fur and big soulful eyes, and is a Good Guy. He looks like an aging Ewok and saves all concerned at one time or another. In this case, the closest approach to Cooper's "chariot race" is when there's an earthquake and the island sinks into the ocean with little Kong holding Armstrong above the waves until a boat can rescue him.

Just incidentally, there's Papa Kong and little Kong but no Mama Kong. (Room for another sequel there, right?) Some things never change—if the first one is a smash, let's make a sequel . . . only it's seldom as good. (*The Bride of Frankenstein* and *The Empire Strikes Back* are among the few exceptions.)

King Kong did quite well in rerelease and in 1984, Criterion released a copy on laser disc with running commentary by film historian Ron Havers plus a video documentary. Sequences deleted in 1938 were restored using clips from a 16 mm print. In 1988 Turner Home Entertainment found a pristine 35 mm print and later released it, as well as *Son of Kong*, as a double disc laser set. A year later Turner released a colorized version of *King Kong* on laser. Interesting, but it couldn't help but be a disappointment. There are few gradations in color—all the skin tones are the same, all the trees in the jungle are the same shades of green and brown, and so on. (Don't say I didn't warn you.) *King Kong* was shot in black and white and, like color, black and white has its own demands and requirements. It is available on VHS.

However, as of this writing it's not available on DVD though it undoubtedly will be.

After the release of *King Kong*, some of the principals went on to greater glory. Merian C. Cooper became a heavyweight in Hollywood, producing such films as *Little Women* (Executive producer), *Flying Down to Rio* (ditto), *The Last Days of Pompeii*, *Dr. Cyclops*, *Rio Grande*, and *This Is Cinerama*. (According to Leonard Maltin, Cooper ended his days managing a small motel in Southern California.)

Robert Armstrong had roles of varying importance in more than a hundred films. (Armstrong and Cooper died within 24 hours of each other in 1973.) Bruce Cabot also carved out a substantial career in Hollywood, appearing in a number of films starring his buddy John Wayne.

Fay Wray appeared in relatively few films after *Kong*. She retired in 1942 (the first time) and resurfaced later for a few more films and television roles. But *King Kong* had marked her for life as the Queen of Scream.

Willis O'Brien, of course, became the acknowledged master of stop-motion, especially when it involved dinosaurs.

In one sense, Max Steiner was the most illustrious of them all, contributing music and songs to more than 500 films, including *The Charge of the Light Brigade*, *A Star Is Born*, *The Dawn Patrol*, *Johnny Belinda*, and *Key Largo*.

As for myself, there are days when I desperately wish I were eight years old again and watching *King Kong* for the first time. I'd even make peace with my nightmares and consider them as personal sequels to one of the greatest adventure films ever made.

Dating Kong: The Stop-Motion Animated Rape Fantasy

Pat Cadigan

BEFORE WE go any further (even just as far as first base), let's get the whole definition thing out of the way. Rape is a loaded word and I've been through this argument before. So, last time and never again—don't write me, don't e-mail me, don't call me, because I won't dance: Rape fantasy has nothing to do with the horror that is felony rape. Women no more dream of being battered and violated against their will than rich men fantasize about being robbed at gunpoint and then beaten to death. Rape is a reprehensible crime.

Rape fantasy is completely different. Rape fantasy, to paraphrase the late, great Marion Zimmer Bradley, is when Brad Pitt has managed to talk his way into your house and now he won't take no for an answer. He wants you, he needs you, he must have you, he will have you.[1] If you've got a problem with that, don't read this.

So. Fay Wray, the golden woman, is chosen out of every other woman in America–hell, in the world–to go to an exotic, dangerous island and come face to face with raw, unchained libido. Some call that a movie; I call it the first date. What I mean is, the first date ever.

That sound you hear is a multitude of women chuckling to themselves and nodding. Young womanhood's rite of passage is alive and well and sweating up palms and underarms everywhere year after year. Doesn't matter if that first date is someone you've seen every day of your life because your mothers shared a cab home from the hospital after giving birth, or if you sat side by side from kindergarten to high school graduation—hell, not even if he's the kid you got caught playing doctor with in the garage. The first-ever date makes you the golden woman in unknown and dangerous territory, about to come face to face with something so big that nothing will ever be the same afterwards.

It's my guess, however, that few women if any think of *King Kong* on their first-ever dates, especially these days. The late-night TV *Creature Feature* in its original form is gone forever. With the advent of videotapes, DVDs, and programmable hard-disk units capturing one thing or another out of 500 cable and/or satellite channels (not to mention downloading movies directly to computer), the relationship between people and their movies has been reformatted.

But the relationship between people and their monsters from the id—to borrow a phrase from a different cinematic icon—is mostly unchanged. Whether we travel to an exotic, dangerous island somewhere off the coast of Nowhere or take off for another star system light-years away, we're taking everything that makes us human with us. This includes ancient myths, fairy tales, and *King Kong*. And we've got our hands full carrying this stuff, because none of our baggage ever gets checked.

King Kong the original movie is, by today's standards, no technical marvel. Paradoxically, this is exactly what makes it a technical marvel. Never mind the way the giant monkey's fur is constantly twitching in all directions because no one brushed the fur after it was repositioned. That twitching fur only added to the monster's utter power and made him scarier than anything we had ever seen. King Kong was even more frightening than Frankenstein's monster or the Phantom of the Opera, both of whom wanted pretty much the same thing—i.e., a date. Next to Kong, however, they were little more than ninety-eight-pound weaklings. Kong was not merely capable of kicking sand in their faces—he could squash them like bugs! If a date with Frankenstein's monster or the Phantom was unthinkable, a date with Kong was impossible.

Not a simple matter of forbidden desire but impossible desire. Kong was too inhuman, too out of control, too uncivilized and uncivilizable, yes, but most of all, he was too big. Too big. Even if by some miracle you could tame him, train him, and get him a total body wax, he would still be too big. There's only one thing you can do with a monster that's too big and that's kill it.

'Twas beauty killed the beast.

Do we have to take all the blame for that? Well, no, not quite. We really wouldn't have had to do that if you guys hadn't gone looking for the trouble in the first place by asking us to go out with you.

Yes, now the truth can be told. King Kong isn't the unchained male libido in action.

It's ours.

Most people will argue that Kong is a decidedly male symbol of raw, untamed libido. Well, it's a decidedly male mask. Fay Wray, terrified and screaming for help, is the classic damsel in distress, abducted on Skull Island and then stranded at the top of the (then) tallest building in the world, needing rescue by the combined efforts and firepower of the police and the armed forces (all men, many of them with daughters).

But those are adult concepts and the delicious, unknown terrors/delights of the first date are not for adults—these are for adolescents not long past the onset of puberty, which itself occurs only a handful of years after the end of the polymorphous perverse stage of human development (i.e., that time of life when you're most likely to get caught playing doctor in the garage).

Adolescent sexuality, driven as it is by fluctuating hormonal levels, is a bumpy ride for all concerned. The libido, just starting to flex its muscles and get acquainted with its own power, is not interested in things like sensitivity, etiquette, or consequences. But neither is it completely without consciousness—while there is a lot of raw instinct at work, human intelligence is also present. The combination of primitive libido and human intelligence is why we have lovers' lanes and motels (although these are things that almost always come after the first-ever date).

The first quintessentially female Fay Wray experience occurs during the journey to Skull Island, when movie director Carl Denham gives Ann Darrow[2] (whom he has rescued from a life of apple-stealing) a sort of screen test. While filming her, he talks her into imagining some ineffable menace descending upon her, getting her so worked up and terrified that she lets out the very first of those classic screams.[3]

But why is she screaming? Not because of something that is happening to her, and not in the face of a visible danger. She's screaming because Carl Denham scared the bejesus out of her without even being specific about what she had to fear, i.e., the unknown.[4]

Well, when you are anticipating/dreading your first date, you aren't adept at distinguishing real dangers from imaginary ones, which is how we all end up following Carl Denham off the boat and onto Skull Island, if you see what I mean. The man who got our heroine all hysterical over nothing (visible) now courts obvious disaster by spying on a village performing a mysterious ceremony/first-date ritual around one of the village women. That the villagers will discover Denham and the rest of the party is inevitable; also inevitable is the chief's insistence that "the golden woman" take the place of the village woman. At this point, no one knows exactly what this ritual is for but even the most naïve of the naïve could figure out that this isn't the senior prom as we know it. Denham whisks Fay back to the supposed safety of the boat, where gallant Jack Driscoll stammers a proclamation of love.

Subsequent events have often been written up as the actions of the typical dumb-ass movie heroine, deliberately putting herself in danger. Instead of locking herself safely in her room after a chaste good-night kiss from Jack Driscoll, our girl decides to treat her insomnia with a little fresh air on deck alone in the middle of the night. There's nothing dumb-ass about this. Earlier, she was screaming over nothing. Now she wants to see what all the screaming is about and by this time, she has experienced enough to know that it ain't Driscoll. And sure enough, she gets carried away, first by the villagers and then by Kong.[5]

At this point, a whole new world opens up. It's not just Kong beyond the high wall on Skull Island but a whole prehistoric menagerie of dangerous creatures, including rampaging dinosaurs. Lives are lost, some to the dinosaurs, some to Kong, and throughout all of it, Fay is screaming her head off, definitely terrified and somewhat traumatized but ultimately unharmed. Of course. No matter how badly things go on that first date, you never actually die of embarrassment.

Nor do you really want to be rescued from the grip of your own wakening libido. Not until Kong wears himself out fighting a dinosaur do the agents of civilized humanity overwhelm him, take him prisoner, and "rescue" Fay.

Now, in the context of all that has gone before, am I saying that men are the civilizing influence that (at least temporarily) tames our libido and brings it back under our control? Hell, no. The dynamic here is between Fay and Kong. Kong is subdued, because Fay allows it (by humans acting on Fay's behalf). If Kong is Fay's libido—our libido—then Fay knows subconsciously that she could order him to lay waste to her would-be rescuers. Instead, she allows herself to be rescued and her libido is overpowered . . . for the moment.[6]

What follows is a classic civilized-human mistake. The practical thing to do would be to get the hell off Skull Island and set a course for home, dropping the map overboard on the way. But Carl Denham doesn't feel that escaping with his life is of enough value—he wants the monster to display to the folks back home. Kong's capture comes at the expense of more lives, but even after seeing the monster break through the wall that has always contained him in the past, Denham still believes that he can keep the beast restrained just because he wants to.

If you think the great ape has it tough, trussed up for exhibition to anyone with the price of a ticket, that's nothing compared to what a sex symbol has to face.

The paradox of the sex symbol is something that I've always found fascinating and, at the same time, incomprehensible. Society really loves its sex symbols, society worships them—until they actually have sex. In one notorious instance, a Miss America was stripped (you should pardon the expression) of her crown when sexually explicit photos became public. Somehow, I doubt that the woman in question lost her title simply because the photos involved another woman. I don't think things would have played out any differently even if she had been all by herself in the nude. It's one thing for someone to be blessed with a physical appearance that is sexually attractive but it's quite another for that person to have sexual feelings. And the idea that she would act on them as well! Call the police, Mrs. Grundy, our decency and morals are in danger!

As if mere police would be enough.

In the movie, we see King Kong breaking his bonds in a protective fury, thinking that Fay is in physical danger from the Jazz Age paparazzi.[7] And yes, you can make the case that this is very male behavior—possessiveness, territoriality, all that. I submit that it can also be seen as the female libido deciding it's had enough of the constraints forced on it. Separated from its more acceptable chaste aspect—Fay—it rampages through the concrete and steel jungle until it finds her, making the divided self whole again.[8]

Unfortunately, there is no place in that world for a civilized woman with an unchained libido. Kong deals with large vehicles, buildings, and elevated trains the same way as he dealt with dinosaurs and giant snakes back on Skull Island. Then, with Fay in hand, he heads for the highest point he can find—i.e., the Empire State Building. The police really aren't enough. Carl Denham thinks it's all over but Fay's civilized boyfriend Jack Driscoll suggests calling out the air force, saying, "If he should put Ann down, and they could fly close enough to pick him off without hitting her . . ."

If he should put her down . . . ?

Maybe it's just me but that's one hell of a big if. In fact, it seems to me that it isn't really an if in Jack Driscoll's mind, or for that matter, anyone else's. Everyone seems to assume that Kong will set Fay down somewhere safe so he can be picked off without any of the aircraft fire hitting her. Or perhaps it's just polite society at work again—i.e., they all know that there is a possibility that Kong won't set her down, or if he does, she won't be safely out of the line of fire, but it's really too awful a prospect to say aloud. Better just to proceed, maintain a positive attitude, and pray everything works out. If it does, that's swell, and Jack and Fay can go ahead with the wedding. And if it doesn't—well, poor Fay, what a shame, but a thing like that couldn't be allowed to run loose and destroy everything we hold dear.

As it happens, everything does work out for Fay, Jack, and civilization in general, but not for Kong. He may have prevailed over giant snakes, T. rexes, *pteranodons*, and *pterodactyls*, but he's no match for a bunch of Fokkers.[9] Riddled with bullets, he bids a sad, fond farewell to Fay before taking what was at the time the longest death plunge anywhere in the world (including, presumably, Skull Island), while all of New York looks on.

I ask you, how do you top a date like that? Well, you can't—there is only one first time, after all.

Of course, this hasn't stopped anyone from trying. But I think it is worth pointing out that only two sequels have been attempted and both were way less than successful. The first, *The Son of Kong*, came after the original and focused on Carl Denham, the impresario who caused all the trouble by bringing Kong to New York in the first place; the less said about the second, *King Kong Lives*, the better.[10]

I think it is also important to point out that there has been no attempt at all to speculate about Fay's post-*Kong* life. The assumption at the end of the original movie was probably that after Jack Driscoll helped her down from the Empire State Building, they had a quiet wedding and went off to live happily ever after in the most conventional way possible. Although I would have thought that would be somewhat easier said than done. Would Fay be dealing with post-traumatic stress, or the letdown of conventional, unexciting, Kong-less life in the suburbs, say, where a chain-link or picket fence is enough to keep both the family dog and her libido from running loose and wreaking havoc?[11]

KONG UNBOUND

We'll never know, of course. The story has never been about Fay or her turbulent relationship with the great ape, but about the force that is Kong and only that. And this is why *King Kong* has continued to captivate us for over seven decades—it is one of the few examples of a story in any medium built around the primal aspect itself, rather than, say, the human struggle against succumbing to it. The men fighting Kong are not in conflict as to how they feel about him. And as for Fay, nobody ever stops to ask her what her feelings are. They all assume that she is screaming for help. It's a reasonable assumption but no one ever stops to think that maybe there's a lot more to it than that.

Once Fay is determined to be safe, she actually drops out of the story altogether. Since she has nothing more to scream about, her part is finished. She can now go home with Jack Driscoll while the rest of the world ponders with fear and fascination the corpse of the great ape in the street.

The truth is, I can't picture Fay Wray's character ever being able to settle only for life with Jack Driscoll or even Carl Denham. On the other hand, she can't live on Skull Island, either—there's no shopping. The only satisfactory ever-after would be for her to commute between the two, and even that comes with a certain amount of letdown. Managing our wild, uncivilized aspect is nowhere near as exciting as letting it have its way.

Of course, this does beg the question: what choice do any of us have?

Well, besides cultivating a rich fantasy life, we can always go to the movies.

Footnotes
1. Actually, I think the example MZB used was Robert Redford. I've swapped the name out for a contemporary (as of this writing) male.

Those of you disposed more favorably toward a different male, a different sex, or a different species, may perform your own swap.

2. Ann Darrow is the name of Fay Wray's character in the film, but come on—if you were a post-pubescent drama queen, which name would you go by: Fay Wray or Ann Darrow? Yeah, me, too.

3. Could that be suggestive? Gee, ya think?

4. In the first half of the twentieth century, this was often what passed for sex education in America, particularly in Catholic schools.

5. At this point, you've probably noticed that I've ignored Jack Driscoll, Fay's nominal love interest. I'm going to continue to do so. Driscoll is not the good boy opposing Kong, the bad boy. This isn't about good boys and bad boys.

6. So if King Kong is, for my purposes, the female libido on a rampage, why do I keep referring to it as "he" and "him"? Because just as there's a little estrogen in all men, there's a little testosterone in all females. Deal with it.

7. Today's paparazzi think Sean Penn is tough. Ha. There were giants in those days . . . literally.

8. Hey, there are doctoral dissertations in gender studies with even wilder premises.

9. This joke in slightly adapted form is stolen from Harlan Ellison and the late William Rotsler.

10. There have been other monster movies, such as *King Kong vs. Godzilla*, *King Kong Escapes*, and *King Kong Appears in Edo*, but these really have nothing to do with the original iconic figure. Or Fay's libido. Or anyone's.

11. *Valley of the Dolls* isn't quite right and *Desperate Housewives* won't appear overtly until after the turn of the century/millennium.

KING KONG:
THE UNANSWERED
QUESTIONS

DAVID GERROLD

THE FIRST seventeen times I saw *King Kong*, I didn't worry too much about backstory. I just wanted to see the great ape fighting the giant dinosaurs. It's a terrific adventure and it's a classic fairy tale of the twentieth century—and if I were a literary deconstructionist, which I most assuredly am not, I might even say that it's a metaphor that symbolizes the eternal battle between chaos and order, between man and nature, between beauty and the beast. Nah, at best, it's an allegory about doomed love—about being too big and too hairy and so socially inept that even beautiful movie stars don't want to go out with you.

But as much as I loved this marvelous escape from reality, part of me—the eternal analyzer—always insists on asking questions, what I call "refrigerator door" questions. It works like this: You go to the movies and you deliberately suspend disbelief so you can fall into the wide-screen, multichannel immersion of the grand adventure unfolding before you. Afterward, as you sit with friends at Starbucks, eating and drinking overpriced confections that bear only a passing relationship to coffee and cake; afterward, still enraptured by the postcoital bliss of the experience, you continue to believe you've seen a great movie. It isn't until you finally get home, when you open the refrigerator door, looking for a snack—is there any pizza left, or fried chicken?—that it finally hits you; you were conned. "Hey, if E.T. could fly away at the end of the picture to save himself and Elliott, why didn't he fly at the beginning of the picture?"

Um . . . he didn't have a bicycle?

No. Because if he had flown away at the beginning, there wouldn't have been a movie.

That's a refrigerator door question. It stops you cold in your tracks, and you stand there pondering it while the salad wilts, the ice cream melts, and the Jell-O starts to sag.

So look, if Anakin Skywalker really was that powerfully tuned into the Force, why didn't he recognize Senator Palpatine as Darth Sidius? Because if he did, there wouldn't have been a movie.

Right.

But there's another kind of refrigerator door question too. How was Indiana Jones able to stay on the deck of the submarine all the way across the ocean—especially without food and water? For that one, we have to assume that the submarine never submerged, that it made the whole trip on the surface—and that the trip didn't take more than a day or so. But as easily as the filmmakers skip over that question, so do we—we willingly make the assumption so that we can stay immersed in the story. It is a deliberate deferral of skepticism. Yeah, I know. It's the movies—but why wasn't he severely sunburnt, at least?

So now that we've established context, that we're willing to accept the circumstances of the story, let's leave the refrigerator at home and head off to Skull Island. Max O'Hara clearly knows what to expect. A canoe-load of natives got swept out to sea by a storm; they were picked up by a passing tramp steamer. Conveniently, someone onboard knew enough of their language to draw a map and hear the tale of Kong, some kind of giant ape. And apparently, they weren't the first boatload of natives to escape the island, because the legend is common enough in the region that even Captain Englehorn is familiar with the name Kong.

But how did the natives get to the island in the first place? And where did Kong come from in the grand evolutionary scheme of things?

Consider:

The dinosaurs on the island have clearly been there since the Jurassic era. We don't know how they survived the mass extinction that occurred when a comet slammed into the Yucatan 65 million years ago, but never mind that; the scientific evidence for that particular event only came to light in the past two decades. In 1933, it was assumed that the dinosaurs died off because their babies were too heavy for the stork to deliver. We will also ignore the fact that isolated on this single island, all these various creatures did not seem to evolve beyond their ancient antecedents. Nor did the limited amount of resources to be found on this island stunt their growth. (Although the opposite evolutionary case can be made for gigantism.) Et cetera, et cetera.

Let's just accept that the dinosaurs on Skull Island are the real deal, one way or the other. Despite the serious evolutionary pressures of an island existence, they are still recognizably the same creatures as their distant predecessors.

But their existence still raises some fairly obvious ecological issues. How many dinosaurs live on this island? Does the island generate enough biomass to support the herds of herbivores necessary to support a family of predatory T. rexes? For that matter, how many T. rexes live here? Are there enough to keep the stegasaurs and apatosaurs in check, so that they don't denude the island's foliage? Or did Kong kill the only one? The last one? Uh-oh . . .

The ecology of any island is a fragile system. A

continental ecology has much more resilience, a much greater ability to withstand events like hurricanes, volcanic eruptions, and other chaotic surprises. An island, however . . . well, there are a lot of unanswered questions here. We still end up coming back to the essential one— even if we don't consider the evolutionary issues: how have these dinosaurs managed to sustain themselves for 65 million years?

It's a leap of faith, and we need to make that leap of faith for the story to work. But even after we make that particular leap, the existence of Kong is the greater mystery. How does a 25-foot ape evolve in an ecology dominated by predatory proto-reptiles? For that matter, where's the rest of Kong's family? Apes travel in troops, don't they?

We know from the sequel, *Son of Kong*, that Kong must have had a mate. Where was she all this time? Where did she come from? Where did she go? Why didn't we see her in the first picture—and if Kong had a wife (and presumably an even more-terrifying mother-in-law), then why the hell was he sneaking off to Skull Mountain for a quickie with Ann Darrow? We know from the visual evidence that he thought she smelled good, he kept sniffing her undies, but we also know that apes are generally monogamous—is Kong experiencing lust in his heart? Is he committing virtual adultery with Ms. Darrow?

But for the sake of this discussion, let's stick solely to what we can observe in the first picture, and ignore the issue of Kong's issue. Let's assume he's single, possibly the ape equivalent of a nerd, unable to get a date on Saturday night, unless she's chained to a pedestal outside the native village. But even in that case, we still have to ask, where are the rest of the giant apes? If they're not living up in the eye of Skull

Mountain, have they already been eaten by the dinosaurs below? Is Kong the last of his kind? If so, does he qualify as an endangered species? It would certainly explain his crankiness as well as his hunger for female companionship. And if Kong is the last of his kind, then Carl Denham and crew are eco-criminals, aren't they? Knowing that they're destroying a fragile island ecology, it's hard to feel sympathy for them when they fall into the spider pit, isn't it?

But even after we ignore all these questions, so we can accept the existence of dinosaurs and giant apes on Skull Island, the continuing presence of the natives has to be questioned. Are these people stupid, or what?

It's fairly obvious how the natives must have arrived at Skull Island. The entire South Sea area was originally colonized by waves of migrants who started out from the eastern coast of Asia at least ten thousand years ago; island after island—Tahiti, Hawaii, Fiji, and so on. So the question isn't how the natives got to Skull Island; the question is how they survived.

At some point in the past, let's say a thousand years ago, some exploratory canoes landed here—on an island filled with predatory dinosaurs and the ancestors of a 25-foot gorilla. Assuming that these folks were stupid enough to stay—or so desperate that they thought this was a better alternative than putting back out to sea—how do they survive long enough to build a village and a thousand-foot wall to separate themselves from the monsters on the island? Was building the wall really easier than getting back in their canoes and paddling away as fast as possible? What was so important that it justified staying? Or maybe the smart ones fled and the folks still on the island are the descendants of the people too stupid to leave?

How did these people develop such a weird relationship with Kong anyway? He lives way the hell on the other side of the island, up on Skull Mountain. For that matter, why does he live up there? Most apes prefer forests. And why does Kong like to eat native girls? Obviously, he considers them a treat—the ringing of a giant gong is his dinner bell. And for that matter, where did the giant gong come from? These natives don't seem to have a lot of metallurgical skills, do they? And we don't find gongs anywhere else in the South Seas, so it's unlikely that they brought it with them. They had to manufacture it locally—how?

And what about those natives? They are apparently sacrificing a beautiful young maiden to Kong on a regular basis. Once a month? That's 12 girls a year. Now maybe they have an overabundance of beautiful young maidens on their side of the wall, enough so that they can hold regular sacrifices at every full moon, but it seems to me that's a good way to deplete the population in a very short time—and do significant long-term damage to the gene pool. If only beautiful girls get sacrificed, pretty soon the only ones left to have babies will be ugly girls, and in a very short time, a matter of twenty generations or so, everyone on the island will be ugly and there will be no more beautiful maidens for Kong anywhere. Or does he even care about physical beauty? We're talking down-the-hatch, sweety.

Maybe the sacrifices are limited to once a year? Every year, we give Kong a new bride and he leaves us alone for the next twelve months. Except, judging by the way Kong treats the rest of the natives, it's unlikely that his brides last a whole year.

Regardless of the timing of the sacrifices, it's apparent that the locals have some very mixed feelings about their relationship with their deity. They respect Kong, obviously. They fear Kong, obviously. They sacrifice maidens to appease him, obviously—but the way they scramble up to the top of the wall to watch him with Ann Darrow... well, there's a certain amount of morbidly curious, prurient interest going on here as well. Possibly because they don't have freeways, they have no place to slow down to gawk at every roadside accident. This is their local celebration of violence and brutality.

So I'm betting that the virginal (another assumption on my part) sacrifices are the local equivalent of football or soccer or any other violent sporting event. It's the Roman circus, without Romans, lions, or Christians. It's great fun for everyone—except the virgin, of course. (That the whole South Sea Island region is not healthy for virgins has long been known. Tourists are now advised that they must bring their own virgins to throw into local volcanoes.)

Moving on . . .

How does Carl Denham get Kong back to New York? The crew builds a raft, they float Kong out to the ship, they use a crane to lift him off the raft and lower him into the cargo hold. Then what? What do they feed him? And how much? Who cleans up after him? Does somebody go in with a shovel to clean up the giant gorilla turds? A new somebody every day? Or do they just hose the waste away? That's probably the safest way to handle the mess. But what does Kong think about all this?

We know that Kong has a temper. We know that he will break down walls to get to Ann Darrow—is he really going to sit docilely in the bottom of the ship's hold? Or is he going to get really, really, really pissed off?

None of these questions are ever really addressed—we just cut quickly to a glittering sign that advertises "King Kong, The Eighth Wonder of the World." The assumption here is that somehow all these separate issues have been resolved. At least well enough to get us all to Broadway. Just like the business of Indiana Jones's submarine ride, Kong's long sea journey is also skipped over in the blithe assumption that you're so eager to get to the next part of the story that you won't stop to ask, "Hey, wait a minute—what about E.T.'s bicycle?"

But clearly, Kong's captors have treated him well on the journey—although he was only 18 feet high on Skull Island, by the time he gets to Manhattan, he's had a growth spurt; he's now 25 feet high. But that all happened offscreen, because we don't see a lot of evidence that he's being treated like a king.

Let's step away from Kong for a moment and talk about another giant ape. . . Mighty Joe Young. Mr. Joseph Young, not quite as big as Kong, but with a much more appealing personality, leaves Africa for a career in show business. Because this was before the formation of People for the Ethical Treatment of Animals, Joe is kept in a small cage backstage at the nightclub where he performs. From his point of view, he's not in Hollywood to experience the bright lights and the big city—he's in prison. To say that he's not happy is an understatement; but he's got a big heart, spiritually as well as physically. And so we open our hearts to his plight and cheer his escape. Unlike Kong, Joe does not tear up the town, he rescues orphans from a burning building. Even more reason to admire his great spirit. (God knows what the orphan thinks about this particular rescue—if you had just climbed out the window of a burning building, would you regard the sudden appearance of a giant ape as an agent of salvation? Yeah, right. People have died of fright in far saner circumstances.)

Back to Kong. We don't see Kong backstage in his dressing room at the Broadway theater; but if you've ever been backstage at a Broadway theater, then you know there's not a lot of room backstage—certainly not enough to house a giant 25-foot gorilla. Oh hell, there's barely enough room for the average diva. Although more than one producer has fantasized about putting his divas in cages instead of installing them in dressing rooms— gorillas probably look easier to manage, which may go a long way explaining Carl Denham's obsessive need to bring Kong to Manhattan.

Never mind. The point is that once we get back to New York, we see no respect for Kong's personal welfare. No one seems to care about the giant ape's well-being. We see no cage, no food, no water, and certainly no facilities for cleaning up after him. Just how much urine can his bladder hold anyway? Backstage must smell horrible! Possibly even the first three rows of the theater as well. (Have you ever seen what an angry chimpanzee can do with a handful of feces?)

What we see is Kong strapped helplessly to a cross; his arms and legs manacled, he's trapped in a grotesque parody of Christ's torment. Well, yes. This is a fairy tale, a metaphor, a movie. We're not interested in the nuts and bolts. We don't care why E.T. didn't fly away and why Anakin Skywalker is such an ignorant lout. We're in a hurry to get to the good stuff. We want to see Kong smashing an elevated train or climbing the Empire State Building. We're not worried about who shovels the gorilla shit, so we don't ask how they move Kong back and forth from cage to stage and back again to cage. Obviously Carl Denham hasn't thought about it. He's designed his show to fail. No wonder nobody wants to invest in his adventures anymore.

Of course, Kong breaks free. There are no engineers in Manhattan smart enough or foresighted enough to stress-test the steel manacles and ensure that they would be strong enough to withstand the strength of an enraged giant ape. No—just like Jurassic Park was designed to fail (that's another rant), Kong's escape is equally inevitable.

In 1933, there were probably five or six million people in the greater New York area. Nevertheless, Kong is able to find Ann Darrow with little or no difficulty. Okay, he steps on a few cars, bites the head off a cop or two, yanks a woman out of bed and drops her to her death twenty stories below, but those are just youthful indiscretions, no worse than the hijinks of the average congressman. But Kong must have one incredible sense of smell to find Ann Darrow so easily in the heart of midtown Manhattan, just a few blocks from Broadway—especially with all those odiferous delicatessens and pungent hot dog stands in the neighborhood.

To be fair to Kong, he probably does have an incredible sense of smell—after all, he's got a bigger nose than Pinocchio testifying under oath. And while Kong has Ann Darrow up on Skull Mountain, he does spend a lot of time sniffing her lingerie. Is Kong a panty fetishist? Hmm, maybe that's the source of his obsession.

Or maybe, Kong is female—that would go a long way toward explaining the existence of the Son of Kong in the sequel of the same name. But if that's the case, then Kong isn't King, she's Queen—a lesbian, the ultimate bull dyke. (See how one fact can change your whole point of view? Don't make assumptions.)

Meanwhile, after retrieving Ann Darrow from Jack Driscoll (who obviously isn't man enough to protect her from a giant rampaging gorilla), Kong heads toward the Empire State Building, the highest point on the island. Now, here's the real refrigerator door question to think about. All those others were just warm-ups. How does Kong climb the side of the building with Ann Darrow in one hand? Think about it . . . If he has her in one hand, then he can't grip the building with that hand, can he? If he lets go with his other hand so he can reach higher, that's right—he falls down. But we clearly see him climbing. Did he hold Ann Darrow between his teeth? Did he put her on top of his head or on one of his broad shoulders? We don't see that. When they arrive at the top, she's still in his hand. Hmm. It's E.T.'s bicycle all over again.

But it is here, at the top of the Empire State Building that the movie works its real magic—the transmogrification of Kong from beast into tragically doomed hero.

For most of the picture, Kong has been the enemy—something to fear. He's been obsessed with Ann Darrow; he only broke free of his chains when he thought she was being attacked; then he raged through the streets of Manhattan in search of her. But abruptly, now, here, at the top of the Empire State Building, mortally wounded by the airplanes, we see the great beast demonstrate his true feelings. He doesn't want Ann Darrow hurt. He checks to see that she is safe, then tragically falls to his death.

Does he hit anything? Or anyone? It's a safe bet that he does. The streets of New York are narrow and always crowded. There's no need for New Yorkers to gather in a crowd, they're already in one. Drop a 25-foot gorilla from the sky anywhere in Manhattan and you're likely to take out 30 or 40 people. Probably more with the splatter.

And finally, who removes Kong's dead body? And how do they do it? This is going to require cranes, bulldozers, and teams of guys operating chain saws. And how long is it going to take? I'm assuming that Kong smelled pretty ripe when he was alive—how bad is he going to smell three days after he's dead? What's that going to do to the property values in the neighborhood of Thirty-fourth Street?

And if Carl Denham is still obsessed with his dreams of Broadway, he isn't going to let anyone dispose of Kong's body so easily. He's going to hire a small army of taxidermists and have Kong stuffed and put on display somewhere.

Finally, it's time for the killer question. What about the lawyers? If you thought the dinosaurs on Skull Island were rapacious, you haven't seen a pack of Manhattan raptors in action. We're talking very bad news. There will be subpoenas for everyone and anyone. The city will sue Denham, Denham will sue the people who made the manacles that failed, the elevated train company will sue Denham, Denham will sue the makers of his gas bombs, the theater owners will sue Denham, Denham will countersue the theater owners, the owners of the Empire State Building will sue for the bullet damage, Ann Darrow will sue for emotional distress, the families of those who died will sue Denham and the city, the owners of every piece of property that got smashed or squashed will sue Denham and the city, the insurance companies will sue everyone just to be safe. The courts will be asked to rule the whole event an act of God, so as to let everybody off the hook. The legal proceedings will last until December 7, 1941, when everyone's attention will be distracted by other matters.

Now do you see why I'm the wrong person to take to the movies?

Kong Long
to King Kong

Philip J. Currie

WHEN *KING KONG* was conceived, there was considerable public interest in dinosaurs. Dinosaurs had been discovered scientifically more than a century earlier, but the first thirty years of the twentieth century had been a golden age for new discoveries. The rich fossil fields of the Red Deer River of Alberta had been opened up by Barnum Brown, who had also discovered the first specimens of *Tyrannosaurus rex*. Many of the dinosaur skeletons from the North American West, and others collected by the enormously successful expeditions to the Gobi Desert led by Roy Chapman Andrews, were displayed in the American Museum of Natural History in New York. Because of the high visitation at that museum, the dinosaurs exhibited there have become some of the most famous and well-known. It is no surprise that all of the dinosaurs in *King Kong* are ones that have long been on display in New York.

Under the guidance of the chief technician, Willis H. O'Brien, models of *Brontosaurus*, *Stegosaurus*, and *Tyrannosaurus rex* were done by sculptor Marcel Delgado, who was influenced by the work of Charles Knight. Two other dinosaurs from the halls of the American Museum of Natural History, *Styracosaurus* and *Triceratops*, never made it in the final version of the movie, although they did appear subsequently in *The Son of Kong*.

There are many unlikely scenarios concerning the dinosaurs in *King Kong*, including the premise that dinosaurs are still alive on some remote island. In this case, it was an uncharted island somewhere southwest of Sumatra. Although animals and plants that were long thought to have been extinct are sometimes discovered alive in remote corners of the earth, they generally are small and relatively easy to miss. One classic example was the discovery that coelacanths, a type of fish remotely related to the earliest air-breathing land animals, had not perished in the Cretaceous as had long been believed. They had survived in deep water off the coasts of Madagascar and the Seychelles.

However, it is much more difficult to hide a large, air-breathing animal like a dinosaur. Generally, the larger an animal is, the larger an area it needs to support a healthy population with sufficient food and other resources. This is the reason that large animals like elephants generally do not inhabit islands. When large animals invade regions of limited areas, natural selection goes to work to produce smaller species (such as the now extinct dwarf elephants of Japan and certain Mediterranean islands). Furthermore, the larger an animal is, the harder it is to hide from modern man. Not all dinosaurs were large, but if Carl Denham's expedition had discovered only small dinosaurs on Kong's island, it would not have had the same dramatic impact in the movie.

Stegosaurus is the first dinosaur encountered by Denham's search party after Kong abducts Ann Darrow. Although this is a large dinosaur with a length of about 20 feet (six meters), the individual portrayed in the film is much larger than that. The head alone appeared to have been as large as Carl Denham, so the animal must have been at least three times larger than the biggest stegosaur known! Stegosaurus and its relatives were plant-eating dinosaurs, and undoubtedly were never as aggressive as portrayed in the film.

KONG UNBOUND

The aggression shown by the stegosaur was mild compared with the next encounter the search party had with a dinosaur. As they rafted across a swamp, a long-necked sauropod rose out of the water to attack them. Delgado and O'Brien did a good job of reconstructing and animating the dinosaur from information available at the time.

Consequently, there is no problem identifying the sauropod as the famous "thunder-lizard" *Brontosaurus* (the correct scientific name is *Apatosaurus*). A dead giveaway is the shape of the head, which at that time was believed to be quite broad because of a scientific mistake. The skull that was originally associated with the skeleton of this dinosaur actually belonged to a different kind of sauropod called *Camarasaurus*. It has only been in recent years that museums have removed the incorrect skulls and replaced them with the correct ones. Several aspects of the sauropod scene in the original movie stretch the viewers' credulity. The dinosaur is enormous, yet somehow slips underneath the raft to overturn it; the problem is that the water is shallow enough for the seamen to use poles for pushing the raft across the swamp!

Sauropods were a successful and diverse group of dinosaurs, but all of them were plant-eaters with relatively weak teeth. The sauropod in *King Kong* turns over the boat, kills two of the men in the water, and follows the rest onto shore. There it plucks a third man out of a tree, and kills him too. At one point, the dinosaur snarls, curling its lip to reveal a handsome set of teeth! Although there is controversy to this day concerning whether or not dinosaurs had lips, it is still unlikely that they had the kind of musculature found in mammalian cheeks that would have allowed them to snarl! Finally, when the search party first encountered the sauropod, it was completely submerged in the waters of the swamp. At one point in time, many paleontologists believed that sauropods supported their massive weights by staying in the water. Some even imagined that they used their necks as snorkels when they were submerged, and raised their heads above water only when they needed to breathe. We now have lots of evidence to show that sauropods were mostly, if not entirely, terrestrial animals. They definitely could not walk on the bottom of a river or lake with only their heads above water. To do so would mean that their bodies would have to counteract a staggering amount of water pressure, and they would not have been able to inflate their lungs to breathe.

For me, one of the most memorable dinosaur fight scenes in any movie is the encounter between Kong and a giant theropod dinosaur. In the movie script and the novelization by Lovelace, it was referred to simply as a large carnivorous dinosaur. O'Brien himself referred to the dinosaur as *Allosaurus*. However, the model was clearly derived from a *Tyrannosaurus rex* painting by Charles Knight, in which the eye socket was positioned incorrectly and there were three fingers on each hand (Glut and Brett-Surman, 1997). Ann Darrow was being stored in a tree while Kong wandered off to take care of a few troublesome seamen by sending them to their deaths in a deep gorge. Kong returned when he heard Ann's signature screams that were stimulated by the approach of the dinosaur. The tyrannosaur was based on what we thought this dinosaur looked like in the early part of the twentieth century.

The first *Tyrannosaurus rex* skeletons discovered were incomplete and did not include the hands. It was therefore assumed (by both paleontologists and O'Brien) that this animal had three fingers like *Allosaurus*. It was only with the discovery of a good skeleton of the closely related *Gorgosaurus* that it was realized the tyrannosaurs had only two fingers. The first restorations of bipedal dinosaurs, including the one in *King Kong*, showed them upright with their tails dragging on the ground to form a well-supported tripod. Analysis of anatomy and footprints has since shown that *Tyrannosaurus rex*, like other bipedal dinosaurs, walked with its body held horizontally. It used its tail, which was held high off the ground, as a counterbalance.

At the beginning of the twentieth century, most dinosaurs were depicted as giant scaly reptiles, even though skin impressions had already been discovered for the herbivorous duck-billed and horned dinosaurs. Specimens found in recent years in North America and Asia show that tyrannosaurs actually had relatively smooth skin that most closely resembles the thick hide on some types of modern rhinos. Furthermore, there is even evidence to show that some species of tyrannosaurs were covered by feathers! Somehow, I do not think a down-covered T. rex would have created the same terrifying impression when the movie was released.

One thing that was a little odd about the T. rex in *King Kong* was the relatively wimpy nature of the jaws and teeth. By the time *Tyrannosaurus rex* was named 100 years ago (in 1905), it was already known that it had enormous teeth, the largest crowns of which protruded more than six inches beyond the gum line. Although serrated front and back, they do not resemble steak knives because they are much too thick. This is because the teeth were adapted for biting through flesh AND bone. Bones of *Triceratops* have been found in Montana with deep punctures left by T. rex teeth. By studying the depth of tooth penetration, scientists have calculated that Tyrannosaurus rex had the most powerful bite known for any animal, living or extinct. Given the awesome strength of those jaws, it is unlikely that Kong could have killed his adversary by prying open the jaws and breaking its neck.

Two other reptiles appear in the original *King Kong* but neither are dinosaurs. The first is a giant lizard that crawls up a vine, presumably to try and eat Jack Driscoll when he is hiding from Kong on a ledge below the top of the canyon. Lizards are more distantly related to dinosaurs than crocodiles and birds. They can become very large, however. The Komodo dragon is a living species from the East Indies that can grow even larger than the one that Jack Driscoll killed. Because Cooper had originally intended to use Komodo dragons in the film, this is likely the identity of the animal that was climbing up to Driscoll.

The second unknown reptile attacked Kong in his cavern, and looks like a boa constrictor or python as it tries to strangle its intended victim. The giant serpentine monster in the film has legs, however, and may have been inspired by a marine reptile that lived in Europe more than 200 million years ago. *Tanystopheus* is an impossible-looking animal with a neck longer than its abdomen and tail. Its long neck was composed of relatively few vertebrae, however, and it would have had neither the flexibility nor the strength to constrict Kong. Furthermore, as a marine animal it is unlikely to have lived in a pool of freshwater inside a cave on Kong's island.

The supposed origin of Kong himself is of course a complete mystery. He is clearly an ape, rather than a monkey or a caveman. The only ape in the East Indies, however, is the orangutan, although Kong more closely resembles a gorilla. One can assume that he was the last of his kind, perhaps a descendant of *Gigantopithecus*. One can speculate that his ancestors grew gigantic in response to competition with the relic populations of dinosaurs on the island. If he lived alone, he must have been very ancient indeed. The natives clearly had taken a long time to build the wall and gate that separated them from Kong and the dinosaurs. Further evidence that Kong was a very old animal is that the natives had developed a ritual of apparent antiquity for dealing with Kong. The native choice of a name for the giant ape was curious in that "kong" means "strong" in China, where dinosaurs are referred to as "kong long" (strong dragons).

Kong himself represents the fascination that humanity has with size. It is generally size that attracts us to dinosaurs first. This is evident from the questions children ask when I give lectures on dinosaurs: "Which is the biggest dinosaur?" "How long was *Diplodocus?*" "How much did T. rex weigh?" and so on. Size-related questions are the most common ones that children ask as they try to define the boundaries of their world. We are still fascinated as adults by the limits of size for living plants and animals, but our horizons expand to take in other aspects of their biology as well. Nevertheless, there are limitations. For example, when dinosaur eggs and embryos were discovered, both by the American Museum expedition to the Gobi Desert in the 1920s, and by our more recent discoveries in southern Alberta, it stimulated unprecedented interest in dinosaurs—at least until it became evident that dinosaurs laid relatively small eggs, and the babies themselves were less than two feet long. As museum exhibits go, baby dinosaurs attract very few spectators in comparison with the large skeletons of the adults.

Another aspect of our fascination with dinosaurs is their apparent ferocity, which is in part related to size. Ounce for ounce, a shrew is much more ferocious and voracious than a tiger, but is unlikely to strike fear in our hearts. Cooper, who had an interest in gorillas and Komodo dragons, certainly recognized this in making Kong into a super-sized gorilla, fifty times as strong as a man.

Willis O'Brien used stop-motion animation to animate the dinosaurs of *King Kong*, as he had done in the original adaptation of A. Conan Doyle's *The Lost World*. But the animation in *King Kong* set new standards that at the time the film was released were realistic enough to terrify the audience. It would be many years before Ray Harryhausen, a fan and apprentice of Willis O'Brien (they worked together on *Mighty Joe Young*), would take animation of dinosaurs to new levels of realism with films like *The Valley of Gwangi* (1969) and the remake of *One Million Years B.C.* (1967). As audiences became more sophisticated, dinosaur animation generally continued to improve. The initiation of modern accepted standards of animation came with the release of Spielberg's *Jurassic Park* in 1993.

I had been a professional hunter and researcher on dinosaurs for almost two decades when *Jurassic Park* was released. I had given hundreds of lectures and media interviews up to that time, and was always struck by the fact that my efforts had made barely a dent in the public perception of dinosaurian biology. I was constantly being asked things about dinosaurs that had been proven wrong long before I started my career. Public knowledge changed overnight with the release of *Jurassic Park*, however, and I realized for the first time what an enormous impact Hollywood has on public education. And it is not restricted to the public perception, because even scientists can be prejudiced by concepts they grew up with. Michael Crichton had done his research well in writing *Jurassic Park*, and presented a modern, up-to-date view of our understanding of dinosaurs. Although the movie differs in details from the book, Steven Spielberg was concerned enough about the accuracy to bring on Dr. John Horner (Museum of the Rockies) as a consultant for this and subsequent sequels.

Most of the new ideas concerning dinosaurs that were introduced in *Jurassic Park* were subtle, but the public picked up on them nevertheless. Overnight, the questions we were being asked as paleontologists were no longer related to the dinosaurs that had been presented in *King Kong*. The questions now encompassed modern research that suggested dinosaurs were warm-blooded animals related to birds. It will be interesting to see if the timeless story of *King Kong* holds up in the new version, whether the animation sets new standards, and how it will affect and intrude upon the publics knowledge of dinosaurs.

Reference

Glut, D. F., and Brett-Surman, M. K. 1997. "Dinosaurs and the Media." Pp. 675–697 in *The Complete Dinosaur*, edited by J. O. Farlow and M. K. Brett-Surman. Indiana University Press, Bloomington.

King Kong:
A Kid's Tale

Joe DeVito

" **I** AIN'T GOIN'!"

It was the spring of 1963, in New York City, and the Alligator was waiting for him. That's what the boy called his godfather's Citroen station wagon. It idled hungrily behind a fully-loaded moving truck, and he knew why: it was waiting to take his family away from their home on West 43rd Street for the last time.

The mover's meter was ticking, but no one was going anywhere until the reluctant six-year-old could be packed into the car with his other five siblings. That wasn't going to be easy—he was wrapped around the railing of the front stoop like an octopus.

His older brother, Vito, knew the one thing that would work. But it was a drastic measure, so he kept silent and watched as every possible coercive action was taken. From the promise of ice cream to the threat of physical pain, none of them made a dent. The kid was tough and held his ground ferociously.

Finally, the older brother gave in. He couldn't stand the thought of hearing screaming in his ear the whole trip. "Hold it!" he yelled. "Listen, you nut, if you let go of the railing and get in the car right now, I'll cut all the King Kong pictures out of my monster magazines and you can have them."

Suddenly, a dead silence fell, followed by an incredulous, "Really?"

"Yeah, but it will cost you 25 cents." The magazines, after all, were his prized collection, and he did not want the deal to be a total loss.

There was no hesitation. "Okay."

The standoff came to an abrupt end and the family finally moved to the "country": the town of Berkeley Heights, New Jersey.

I wish I still had those pictures from my brother's *Famous Monsters of Filmland* magazines. To this day, forty-two years later, *King Kong* has the power to transport me to another world. What is it about the fantasies of childhood that can be so enduring? Perhaps it is because they carry us back to a time where only good thoughts are remembered. True. For me it is also because they can be so real. *King Kong* is still real to me. More than any other film I have ever seen, it has engendered a perpetual sense of wonder. Yet, after almost 500 viewings, I still have not seen it in the format it was actually made for-a full-sized movie screen. Hopefully, that sacrilege will be remedied one day. How I envy those who were there for its opening. It must have been mind-bendingly spectacular-particularly back in 1933.

The impact of the original *King Kong* must have been something to experience firsthand. At a time when audiences were just getting used to people talking on film-the technology itself was only about twenty years old—*King Kong* took them to a place they never even dreamed of. In a way, my small world was really not much different. I had no understanding of the historical uniqueness of *Kong*, its myriad "firsts" as a storytelling and technical tour de force. I was just a boy who hungered for the fantastic. I knew nothing of the amazing intangibles that converged in *King Kong* to create a world icon worthy of the ages. I only knew what I felt, that I was seeing something that went beyond my wildest imaginings.

In later years I learned the film's backstory and marveled all the more. There were so many intangibles

KONG UNBOUND

that aligned to create a film of such lasting originality, things that go beyond the creative desire in and of itself and have their origin in historical serendipity. To begin, there was the joining of a charismatic dynamo like Merian C. Cooper with another artistic pioneer of extraordinary abilities named Willis O'Brien, not to mention a host of other incredible personalities. The film introduced some, and perfected many other, extraordinary animation and film techniques; Kong's climactic scene atop the Empire State Building (which had just been built) was a juxtaposition of elements that is reserved for only the rarest confluence of cultural and archetypal imagery. I believe Max Steiner's was the first full musical film score; and on and on. There is no arguing the fact that *King Kong* has left an appropriately large footprint on the world's collective imagination.

Almost seventy-five years after its initial release, *King Kong* still has the power to rattle my imagination. CGI be what it may, and other technical advancements in movie effects notwithstanding, there is something about Kong that is alive in my mind as no other movie monster ever was. I feel there is a charm to stop-motion animation that computer-generated characters are hard pressed to equal. What I immediately connected with in the movie was Kong's personality. Tellingly, the great stop-motion movie monsters of Willis O'Brien, and Ray Harryhausen after him, were essentially the product of individuals. Because of this there is a clearly definable character instilled by direct contact with the creature that is tough to match by a team of people working together through computer screens.

Current special effects are often so hyper-real that they can actually make it harder to suspend disbelief. It's odd: the more real something looks, the more believable it would seem to be. But that is not always so when you know it is not real. The less perfect puppets and slightly jerky action of stop-motion can engage the imagination more effectively by enabling the viewer to subtly project his own sense of reality onto what he is seeing.

Much of this can be debated since there are no such absolutes, as proven by some extraordinary new effects movies, and techniques will be improving all the time. To be sure, an infinite number of reasons contribute to an individual intimately bonding with a film, or any work of art. Perhaps the most powerful intoxicant is sheer nostalgia: nothing can top an initial experience and the memories associated with it. Whatever the reasons, when it comes to movies of imagination, I still think the original *King Kong* has no equal.

For me, the stage was set for my enthrallment with *Kong* in a very predictable way: my love of dinosaurs. As a boy, I was lucky to live not far from the American Museum of Natural History. For anyone who has ever been there, there is no need to explain what that adventure must have been like for a kid with an overactive imagination. Walking through the Hall of Dinosaurs was an experience to inspire the wildest daydreams. The paleoart of the museum—and the world—had been shaped by the pioneering painting and sculpting of Charles R. Knight at the turn of the twentieth century and beyond.

By the time my small footprints began stalking the paved jungle of the city decades later, a whole new slew of dinosaur related images had arrived. These were spearheaded by Rudolf Zallinger's Mesozoic mural that appeared both on the cover and in a lavish interior spread in *Life* magazine in the early 1950s. These images were all part of the coffee table book *The World We Live In*, published shortly after the magazine story. That was followed by his fabulous Golden Book, *Dinosaurs*, in 1960. Other dinosaur-related things that stand out in my mind from that time are *The How and Why Wonder Book of Dinosaurs* and the Marx plastic dinosaur set, all of which I loved dearly (perhaps greatest of all, although I did not see them until a few years later, were the multiple large-format volumes of Czech artist Zdenek Burian).

All in all it was dinosaur heaven for any kid so inclined. By age four, in 1961, I had become a certified dinosaur fanatic. I drew constantly and copied the pictures from the pages of my favorite books. It was a time of pure fascination. Every detail mattered, and correct names were important. I actually knew how to spell *Tyrannosaurus rex* before I could spell my own name. I remember being serenely content in my world of dinosaurs, which was augmented by a fascination for other giant creatures such as whales, giant squid, and sharks. I guess I was predisposed toward such things. Was there ever a boy who hasn't been?

But then one day my older brother sat me down to watch *King Kong*, and my self-created prehistoric world was abruptly turned inside out. I do not have a specific memory of the event, only an overriding feeling of sheer wonder as I struggled to grasp what I was seeing—the raw power of it overwhelmed me. I don't remember any details other than what I saw on our family's black-and-white TV. It is entirely possible that the initial experience erased other mundane trivialities from my mind. I needed every brain cell to absorb the far more important reality of what was unfolding before my eyes.

No longer were dinosaurs imprisoned on the page of a book, frozen in a drawing, or lurking dreamlike in my mind. They now moved and breathed. Everything was so perfectly realized that I immediately accepted Kong's existence as a fact, even though I'm sure I was told it was "only a movie." There was nothing about Kong that contradicted my common sense—I knew animals could grow that big, I'd seen their bones! And he was so convincingly portrayed, his personality was so tangible, that in spite of what I must have been told, I wanted to believe. King Kong was so real to me that from then on when I visited the Museum of Natural History, I roamed the halls hoping to see a magnificently mounted exhibit of Kong's bones. Where else would he be?

What added to the magic was that it was all so fleeting. Unlike a DVD or VCR viewer today, I was unable to freeze the picture, or play the movie again at will. When it was over, I had to wait. And wait. Until it aired again. This was excruciating, but it only heightened the excitement. Nothing is so desirable as that which you want desperately, yet can't have. I don't think this inability to view *King Kong* at will could be overstated as a reason for the allure and fascination the film has fostered in the imaginations of generations of people, particularly kids.

From that time on, the beeping RKO radio tower at the beginning of a film was the source of genuine panic every time I heard it. I would scream *"King Kong* is on!" and fly toward the TV set. How often I was shattered to realize that the beeping sound was most times the prelude to a different movie—but so great was my desire to see the King (Elvis was of absolutely no consequence) that despite my experience to the contrary, it never quite sank in that the beeping sound could belong to any other movie. In time I accepted Kong as a fiction, but the reality of the movie's fantasy remained unique.

So far as I can remember, there were only two real antidotes to my Kong addiction. The first was *The Million Dollar Movie*. Anyone who lived on the East Coast in the 1960's would remember that *The Million Dollar Movie* showed the same movie twice a day, at 9 A.M. and 3 P.M., for seven straight days. Outside of owning a print of the film, it was the closest viewers could ever come to getting all they could of *King Kong*. I saw it fourteen times in one week—twice—not an easy feat for a kid who is supposed to be in school.

The second way was seeing pictures of Kong in Forry Ackerman's *Famous Monsters of Filmland* magazine. This offered the possibility of viewing various stills at will. But even that presented a problem in the beginning since I was very young and my parents would not let me buy them, which is where my older brother came in. Being artistically inclined himself, he could empathize now and again and let me page through his copies. That is, when he wasn't trying to kill me for rifling through his desk drawers when he wasn't home, looking for his stash of monster magazines on my own.

Around 1963, the movie *King Kong vs. Godzilla* came out. While I loved it as a kid, even then I knew it was not in the same universe as the original *Kong* and the two (along with all subsequent men-in-monkey-suit Kong or gorilla movies) always remained separate in my mind. By the mid-sixties Aurora had released their monster model kits, King Kong included, and the box art by Jim Bama alone was worth the price of admission. These were followed by a King Kong trading card set that had the most comprehensive group of Kong images from the original movie that I had ever seen to that date—albeit with comical captions superimposed on them. The intoxicating scent of trading cards and bubble gum is one that I still remember. By that time I had also begun collecting monster magazines of my own. These things all combined to feed my fascination with King Kong for years.

When word got out that *King Kong* was being remade in the mid-seventies, I was thrilled—along with countless others, I'm sure. There was all kinds of hype, from an actual 50-foot robot being constructed for the film to a mass call for extras that were needed for the final scene at the foot of the World Trade Towers (for which I was present). But for connoisseurs of the original film, I think the sight of Kong's broken body embedded in the fractured sidewalk at the end of the remake was a perfect metaphor for any hope they may have had for the movie itself.

Thankfully, all was not lost. In the mid to late seventies, I remember seeing for the first time a book called *The Making of King Kong*, by Orville Goldner and George Turner. Another great compilation released around the same time was *The Girl in the Hairy Paw*, edited by Ronald Gottesman. There was also a great tome on the work of Ray Harryhausen called *From the Land Beyond Beyond* by Jeff Rovin, which prominently mentioned *King Kong* as well, followed by Ray Harryhausen's *Film Fantasy Scrapbook*. And then a few years later there was a marvelous homage to the work of Willis O'Brien in *Cinefex* magazine. These were the kinds of books and magazines I had been waiting all my life to see. They could not have come at a better time for me. After a couple of years of wandering aimlessly, I had finally made up my mind—I was going to become an artist.

I can't remember how early they started, but all along the way I had dreams of King Kong in scenes that I never saw before (I still do). Sometimes they were terrifying. Other times they were incredibly evocative as though I were a spectator watching primordial history unfold. I would go to sleep the next night hoping to dream more of the same, vainly searching for a way to make them repeat at will. Unfortunately, that rarely happened. Ideas began to form, but more than ten years would pass before I had a clue of what to do with them.

Things first started to come together when I entered New York's Parsons School of Design in 1979. I began to dabble in all forms of illustration, particularly oil painting. I studied comparative anatomy, took writing classes, and made contacts. I spent three intense years there before getting my first professional job the day after I graduated in 1981. Over the next ten years I worked innumerable hours, illustrating mainly science fiction, fantasy, and horror novels before I showed my paintings for the first time in 1991 at a prominent East Coast science fiction convention called Lunacon. It was there that a man named Barry Klugerman first saw my artwork and introduced himself. Within weeks, if not days, he had proposed the possibility of doing a project together: illustrating a coffee table book of King Kong. However, there was no financing and plans were uncertain at best. That didn't matter. What did was that I knew it was time for me to branch out and Kong was back in play.

Amazingly, unrelated circumstances fell into place shortly thereafter to create another unexpected development. After years of illustrating other people's stories, I finally got the opportunity to write and illustrate my own story. With King Kong already on the front burner, I immediately searched for a way to work him into my plans. The answer was obvious: write a story to answer all of the questions about Kong that I had been pondering for over three decades. This, both Barry and I knew, was definitely the path to take.

Although it was a lifetime in the making, it seemed my Kong addiction had found its purpose overnight. I set sail for Skull Island in an attempt to uncover its mysteries: What happened to Kong's body? How could any civilization build such a wall on an island populated by giant monsters? What happened to cause them to slip back—if indeed the natives living behind the wall were their descendants? If the wall was supposed to keep Kong out, why did it have doors big enough to let him in? And what was Kong—a freak giant gorilla or part of a unique species? How did dinosaurs survive on the island? The questions went on and on.

The first step was to create a dynamic that enabled me to not only get back to Skull Island, but have a good reason for a compelling story to tell once I got there. Getting back to the island was easy. After a chance discovery of his father's hidden map, Denham's son, Vincent (who is now a paleontologist in New York's Museum of Natural History), finds his way there with the help of an older Jack Driscoll. On the surface Vincent wants to find evidence of living dinosaurs and clues to Kong's existence. He would then return as the most famous paleontologist of all time. But underneath he is struggling greatly with the bitterness of losing both his father and his mother, who was unable to fend off the legal avalanche left in her husband's wake. He has in effect cut himself off from the world and needs to make sense of his chaotic life before it is too late.

The hard part was connecting everything that took place on the island, both past and present, with Vincent's internal dynamic in a way that provided the framework on which to build the backstory of King Kong himself, particularly of how the young Kong became a King.

The answer came to me one day while driving on the New Jersey Turnpike (I had taken to not listening to music while I drove to create more time to think). I suddenly realized that the barrier Vincent had built inside himself was no different than the wall on the island was to the natives. Vincent was hiding in fear behind an emotional barrier just as the natives on the island were trembling behind a physical one. Both were slowly dying inside. What's more, the wall figured forebodingly in the fate of Kong himself. I immediately realized I needed to transform the "w"all into the "W"all and in effect make it a character in its own right. Suddenly all the pieces fell into place and the stage was set to build an entire island dynamic, both past and present, that could intertwine the fate of all concerned.

After numerous scenarios, the final plotline took this form: Vincent is captured when he arrives on the island and finds himself in the care of an enigmatic island elder who calls herself "Storyteller." He slowly comes to realize that answers to his questions—and his life—hang on the outcome of her compelling tale of the events that took place almost a century before his father took Kong from the island. It involves the quest of two Skull Islanders, Ishara and Kublai, who attempt to break the thralldom of the Wall and find a way to save their culture from a horrible fate. Casting a shadow over their plight is the irresistible rise of an orphaned young giant who is destined to become the prehistoric island's legendary beast-god, King Kong. Along the way, we ultimately discover many mysteries surrounding both Kong and his island, the unexpected result of Carl Denham's intervention, and the fate of Vincent.

After several years I finally had enough story and presentation art and it was time to track down who had what rights and see if my project was doable. This led to beginning a relationship with the family of Merian C. Cooper, first through their lawyer, the late Charles FitzSimons, and then directly with Merian Cooper's son, Col. Richard Cooper. Their kindness and encouragement in helping me pursue my book and the family's willingness to give their imprimatur helped to affirm that I was on the right track. But the road was a long and winding one. Because of the tangled legalities surrounding Kong, it soon became clear that the better course was to connect my book to the 1932 novel, rather than the 1933 film.

The novel was published in November or December of 1932, several months before the original movie debuted in March of 1933. Although the two are essentially identical in plot and characters, some differences do exist: In the novel Englehorn's ship is called the *Wanderer*, as opposed to the *Venture*; a character called Lumpy in the novel was replaced by Charlie the cook in the movie; the famous spider scene that was cut out of the movie remains in the novel, as well as the appearance of two triceratops that chase the men onto the fallen tree (which is why in the movie all the men are running like crazy onto the log and are frantically looking behind them). Also, in the book Kong is chained in a steel cage in a stadium when in NYC, as opposed to standing atop a steel scaffold in a theater, and the scene where he impolitely takes out his frustrations on the subway car does not exist in the book.

There were additional benefits to basing my story on the novel as well. I could plausibly overlook the *Son of Kong* movie, which, by the way, was a movie I loved. As a kid who craved to see and know more about King Kong, it was the only glimpse I ever got. But it was played for laughs and left something to be desired as a true follow-up to the original. Later on, when I read that it was rushed into production and that most involved were not really happy with the movie, it confirmed what I always felt in that regard. In the end the film revealed so little and forever buried so much. I needed an island to go back to.

A quarter century after the original novel was published, always a good milestone, enabled me to start my story in 1957. By that time a lot of historical events had taken place since Kong's rampage through New York City: the Depression, WWII, the Korean War, and the Cold War, to name a few. All the intervening upheavals were good reasons to believe that a fast and concerted

KONG UNBOUND

cover-up of the evidence after Kong's death along with the disappearance of Carl Denham could cause the whole event to slip away into myth and legend.

Additionally, besides being the year I was born (which may not mean much to anyone but me), 1957 was very symbolic for another reason. It was the year Sputnik was launched, which ushered in the age of satellite technology. Before long the entire surface of our planet would be catalogued like a phone book—a useful result of technological advancement, but a sad loss of charm and mystery just the same. The year 1957 represented the swan song of the long sea voyage to an uncharted island. All of these reasons combined to make it the perfect year to begin my story.

With the big picture in place, I was finally able to delve completely into the origins of Kong and his island in both words and pictures. From a creative point of view the endeavor presented many challenges. Over a period of years I accumulated an untold number of sketches and text. There were details and suggestions made by others from time to time, but my core story remained the same.

My lifelong love of dinosaurs came fully into play in many ways, particularly in the creation of Kong's adversary, a super-saurian 65 million years in advance of the dinosaurs we are familiar with. I invented weird types of architecture; I developed the underpinnings of the island civilization past and present; I eventually had to conceive an entire backstory to the backstory as well (much of which could only be hinted at) in order to tie the various elements together.

Although I have always written and loved storytelling, I had concentrated on art as a profession and the odds were against my achieving a seamless level of polish in both disciplines as a first-time author, particularly since my story was such an intricate one with multiple time

244

lines. Rather than take on such a task alone, I was grateful to be introduced to Brad Strickland, an accomplished author or co-author of over 60 books. I asked him to cowrite with me. Brad provided the framework and steady direction of a highly experienced writer to make sure that things stayed on pace and developed correctly.

We worked very closely together and developed a true collaboration, spending countless hours writing and rewriting each other's pages. Little by little Kong's world all became as real and familiar as the world I saw outside my window. I particularly remember working on a scene with pterosaurs one morning. At noon I took a walk to the river (or "crick" as they say in PA) that flows past my backyard. Just as I arrived, an immense great blue heron flew past me at eye level, not fifteen feet away. Its bill was enormous and the wingspan could only be guessed at. I saw the ancient-looking folds surrounding its eye as the disc shifted to get a fix on me. For an instant, I could have sworn a *Pterodactyl* gazed at me through that orb across seventy million years. I worked on the paintings concurrently with the writing, and for several more months besides–almost two years in total for the images—before the project was complete.

It was in the late fall of 2004, almost fourteen years after my first notes were written, that I finally held the finished book in my hands. I still have a hard time convincing myself it has been realized. It was such a personal exploration, one which actually began when I was four years old, that it never truly dawned on me until the book was almost finished that so many others would see the end result. It suddenly hit home that millions of other Kong fans have their personal view of *King Kong* as well. What if they did not like what I did? I consoled myself with the thought that I did my best. At worst, I hoped the effort showed. At best, I hoped they would love it. Thanks to Mike Richardson and DH Press, time would tell.

In some ways my journey began the same way as my move from New York City a lifetime ago—clinging to a railing. In this case it took the form of a thriving career as an illustrator and sculptor. Just as traveling into the unknown so many years earlier brought me to a time and place that I never dreamed, filled with friends and experiences that I carry with me to this day, I hoped this book held the same promise. So I let go. Once again the lure was *King Kong*.

When things were going smoothly, was it worth it to take on the emotional, financial, and physical strain on a hope and a prayer (there was no guarantee my book would ever be published) to go in search of a mysterious island that might never exist? I don't think I really had a choice; I could not have lived with the "What if?"

Just as it unfolded all those years ago, the trip was filled with unexpected surprises and many new friends. I became acquainted with the Cooper family, childhood icons such as Ray Harryhausen (who was even kind enough to write the foreword for my book), Ray Bradbury, Jim Bama, Bob Burns, and so many others in many different fields. Those experiences alone made it all worthwhile.

The first time I saw *King Kong*, it altered the landscape of my imagination. That is one of the things that makes Art in all its forms so special. It enables everyone, regardless of differences or time, to communicate in the common language of ideas, symbols, and imagination, where all things are possible. In this case, it is the remote prehistoric home of the beast-god of Skull Island. Could it be real? To quote a famous showman, "I am here tonight to tell you a strange story. So strange a story that no one will believe it. But, ladies and gentlemen, seeing is believing."

I believe.

Rooting Against the King

Alan Dean Foster

ADORED *KING KONG*. Still do. Probably seen it a hundred times or more. Watching it as a child, the film reinforced and inspired many life-long dreams that as I matured I was eventually able to fulfill. I learned a lot from repeated viewings of it—but Kong himself was for me another matter entirely.

Loved the movie, disliked the big guy.

To what can be attributed this deviance from the general norm? Might my attitude be a consequence of early DVS (Darth Vader syndrome)? Also known as a perverse desire to cheer for the bad guys? Could this malady be a consequence result of watching *Gunga Din* too many times while coming to the realization that the evil guru was smarter and had a more valid rationale for his actions than did imperialist hero-soldiers Cary Grant, Victor McLaglen, and Douglas Fairbanks Jr.? Was this what prevented me as a kid from not only failing to acknowledge Kong as "the eighth wonder of the world!" but relegating him to a backup role in the film where everyone else proclaimed him to be the lead and center of attention? I didn't recognize the cause when I was ten, or even fifteen, but I do now.

It was all the fault of science. Science twisted my view of the great ape. From a very early age, a love of science compelled me to view *Kong* the film not as a mis-shapen love story (certainly not at the age of ten—maybe a little more so at fifteen), but as an excursion into a number of wondrous scientific realms, from paleontology to ethnology, botany to anthropology, geology to geography. For me, every viewing of *Kong* meant a trip not to the absurdist kingdom of Hollywood melodrama, but to the sharply sculpted and geographically fascinating Skull Island, the marvels of the Mesozoic, the wonders of the rain forest, and the exotic delights of every faraway place ever glimpsed in an old, tattered travel catalog. Unlike other film buffs, my trade magazine of choice was and has always been not *Variety* or *Hollywood Reporter*, but *National Geographic*.

Compared to a lot of kids in my school and neighborhood (mostly the ones I knew who didn't read), I never fantasized myself as Kong, trampling natives or tearing down elevated trains. I wasn't into the delights of preadolescent rampant violence. Rather than Kong, I identified with the fabulous life stories of the film's producers, Merian Cooper and Ernest Schoedsack. Those were the simians whose astounding adventures I wanted to emulate. I would even have happily settled for swapping places with the gaunt but knowledgeable Captain Englehorn, whose life apparently consisted of crossing the oceans of the world while plying the fevered coasts of distant, exotic islands. Those were the characters in the film I identified with—not the mindless, raging, primitive Kong.

I wanted to be William Beebe, plumbing the deepest depths of the ocean, or Roy Chapman Andrews, unearthing the first nests of dinosaur eggs in sandstorm-swept Mongolia. I never had the slightest desire to be the boastful, fame-obsessed Carl Denham, forever placing his own men in danger in hopes of satisfying his own egotistical needs.

From the very first viewing I can ever remember seeing, of a scratched and truncated version of the film on an early independent Los Angeles television channel back in the 50s, I found myself rooting for the dinosaurs, not Kong. For the natives, not Kong. I wanted to be on that tramp steamer, the *Venture*, the purpose of whose voyage so closely resembled an Americanized version of my favorite novel, Arthur Conan Doyle's *The Lost World*. I wanted to see active, breathing, "real-life" examples of all the plastic dinos I had so assiduously collected throughout my childhood. And as the film progressed—wonder of wonders, there they were! Tramping through swamp and forest in all their profound, immense, saurian glory. For a young dinosaur lover like myself, it was seventh heaven.

And then this big monkey—,okay, okay, big ape—shows up.

Why? Where'd he come from? It was many years before I resigned myself to the inevitable conclusion. He had sprung full-grown, like Topsy, from something known as a Plot Point. This nondiscriminatory incubator can give birth to anything, anytime, as needed. Like the genie of the lamp.

Only in my logical young world, giant apes had to have giant ape parents. Young as I was, I could never get past the reality of Kong's inexplicably solitary existence. Where were his giant, smelly relations? The problem of the great hermit ape never left me free to lose myself in the rest of the picture. And this long before David Quammen's *The Song of the Dodo. Pace* science.

After it makes its way beyond the great gate, we are invited to watch the *Venture's* landing party shoot down a charging *Stegosaurus*. Subsequently, they are menaced, attacked, and scattered by a rampaging *Brontosaurus* (now renamed *Apatosaurus*, in the sorriest rechristening of an extinct creature since rightist Republicans declared Sen. Joe McCarthy nothing more than a well-meaning but misguided patriot). Ann Darrow nearly has herself plucked by a foraging *Pteranodon*. Kong fights off a snake-lizard thing that closely resembles an over-sized *Kentrosaurus*. There was also a scene showing a browsing *Styracosaurus* (ceratopsian kin to the much bet-ter-known *Triceratops* of *Jurassic Park* fame) that was, alas, cut from the film.

What is truly fascinating from a scientific stand-point is how this Hollywood production turns out in ret-rospect to be far more accurate in its depiction of dinosaur activity than were the pictures constructed by the pale-ontologists of the time. In this, *King Kong* is one with the dinosaur sequence in Walt Disney's *Fantasia*, whose fran-tic, active dinos also went against the scientific grain.

Back in the 30s and 40s, and up until relatively recent times, all large dinosaurs were generally believed by the scientific community to be torpid, slow-moving, rather lethargic creatures. Sauropods like *Brontosaurus* (a name I'll use here because that's how it's identified in the film) were thought to live in dense swamps where their massive bodies could be partially supported by water (this environment, at least, Kong follows). Big predators such as *Tyrannosaurus* were not thought of as being much swifter than what they ate. They wouldn't have to be, if all they had to catch up to was ponderous, slow-moving prey.

Paleontological research over the last twenty to thirty years, incorporating analysis of everything from dinosaur histology to the stride lengths implicit in fos-silized footprints, indicates that large plant-eating dinos were active creatures capable of considerable speed. As we have learned, just because a critter is big and bulky doesn't mean it can't move fast (see: elephants, rhinos, hippos). As for those bipedal ferocities who preyed on them, they were at the very least competent sprinters while smaller ones such as *Deinonychus* and *Velociraptor* were quite likely downright feline in their reaction times. Flying reptiles such as *Pteranodon* didn't merely glide: they flapped their wings, if only to get off the ground.

Just as they were depicted in Kong. For a change, Hollywood trumps Harvard. Impossible giant apes aside, the science of Kong proves prophetic in ways its makers never dreamed of. Those were the depictions and revelations I loved in the film—not nonsensical drivel about giant apes ascending skyscrapers.

For many years, however, it did bother me that supposedly harmless herbivores like *Stegosaurus* and *Brontosaurus* would engage in unprovoked attacks on a cluster of comparatively tiny humans wending their cautious way through Skull Island's jungle. But just as our knowledge of dinosaurian anatomy expanded greatly since the 30s, so too did our understanding of saurian behavior.

That attacking *Stegosaurus*? Perhaps reacting to the presence of alien creatures within its marked territory. Or maybe protecting a nest full of eggs located somewhere close by. The *Brontosaurus* that attacks and sinks the raft carrying the men from the *Venture*? Maybe it was in musth. In elephants, musth is "an annual period of heightened aggressiveness and sexual activity during which violent frenzies occur." If a similar condition afflicted male sauropods, that would have made for a whole lot 'o'stampin' goin' on, even to the point of possibly taking offense at the presence of inoffensive intruders as small as humans. Oh, and the animal that kills more people every year in Africa than any other? Lions? Leopards? Poisonous snakes?

It's our pudgy friend the slightly silly-looking, plant-eating hippopotamus.

So now we come, as we must, to every male kid's favorite dinosaur—the great and noble *Tyrannosaurus rex*.

Watching the film, those of us who had taken the time to read our young-adult paleontology texts knew that no way nohow would some big ape be able to take down our hero (ours, not RKO's), far less without suffering so much as a scratch. For those of us who were bookworms (the scientific term for "pre-geek"), the celebrated fight sequence never works. We sit there watching the scene while muttering "Ah, baloney!" (or something similarly suitably evocative). One bite from a *Tyrannosaurus*'s immensely powerful jaws lined with their serrated six-inch teeth would have sheared off more than monkey fur. A bite to the monkey-throat would have been fatal. Allowed to bet on this battle between giants, not one kid I knew would have put his candy money on the ape. Not many zoologists, either, I'd reckon.

But in Hollywood, the good guy wins even when the bad guy is bigger, stronger, smarter, and more athletic.

The last straw for my young self raptly watching this titanic contest came when Kong suddenly resorted to wrestling holds. Time, time! The fix is in. Since when do gorillas, of any size, have access to techniques from *WWF Smackdown?* In order for Kong to win, the filmmakers had to resort to an obvious, blatant cheat. As a young viewer, I felt cheated by this subterfuge, too.

Alas, poor rex—we children knew him, Merian; a dinosaur of infinite jest, of most excellent fancy. Maybe you could fool the adult moviegoing public of 1933 with your fight, but I bet you couldn't fool the scientifically inclined ten-year-olds of that or any other year.

Thank goodness the elaborate filmed sequence at the bottom of the gorge, where the unfortunate sailors land after being rolled off the log bridge by Kong, was cut from the finished film. As Cooper said, "It stopped the picture." With its giant spiders and such, it would have stopped my overly literal scientific mind as well, bringing any last, lingering suspension of disbelief to an abrupt halt. As already mentioned, the existence of something like Kong himself was difficult enough to try and accept.

It was not just the dinosaurs whose images excited and delighted me as I devoured rerun after rerun of *Kong*. My burgeoning interest in science was aroused by far more than just these hyperkinetic resurrections. As a child, the closest I had ever come to wandering through a real rain forest was when my mother would take me for an afternoon's stroll to the enclosed botanical gardens in New York (the family doctor having insisted the extra oxygen and humidity would be good for my weak lungs). Those lush surroundings form one of my most enduring memories from the ages of three and four.

Ever since, I looked forward to one day tramping through real jungle, battling giant insects (a highly overrated activity) while observing colorful and exotic wildlife (never overrated). I have been fortunate enough to do so. But while soaking up my surroundings in the Amazon or Asia, I never forgot that the lush interior of Skull Island was my very first rain forest—even if much of it was composed of shredded rubber and molded clay, transplanted moss and clever matte paintings. All the elaborate and accurate detail that Kong's set decorators and miniature builders put into their work helped prepare me for when I eventually encountered the real thing in Asia and South America.

Just as *Kong* helped to nurture my first interests in paleontology and zoology, botany and geology, it also made me aware of issues in sociology and ethnology. Not only did the film champion and solidify a then-unaccepted view of dinosaurs, its sorely put-upon natives constituted one of the subtlest and most subversive attacks on Hollywood's and the nation's view of its non-Caucasian citizens of any movie from that era.

Their origin was clearly intended to be African. "Way west of Sumatra" indeed, Skull Island must lie, for an Indian Ocean island to be inhabited by other than folk of Asian extraction. This despite the knowledgeable Captain Englehorn's description of "kong" as a term "Malay in extraction." Even as a kid, I knew that the inhabitants of Malaysia did not look like those from Malawi. Or even parts of L.A.

Be that as it may, it is worthy of noting—and as a child growing up in a virtually all-white section of the San Fernando Valley, I noticed-that unlike their counterparts in the typical 30s and 40s Hollywood films I eagerly inhaled from late-night Los Angeles TV, the natives of Skull Island were allowed a modicum of dignity. No one watching *Kong*, even in 1933, would ever mistake nor compare Noble Johnson's portrayal as the native chief for a Pacific riff on Stepin Fetchit. Watching his portrayal, it could not escape my very young mind that perhaps civilization might have existed beyond the bounds of my up-until-then wholly Eurocentric view of history. Long before I knew of the ruins of Great Zimbabwe, I knew instinctively not to buy Englehorn's awestruck attempt to explain the origin of the great wall by declaiming, "It could almost be Egyptian!"

While I doubt that this consequence was in the minds of producers Cooper and Schoedsack when they were filming it, the scene where Kong attacks the great gate and Carl Denham urges the natives to join them in trying to hold back the ape's assault was the first instance I can recall seeing in a film (certainly in an old one) of blacks and whites working together toward a common goal (the threat of joint extinction being a wonderfully unifying force). I also cannot keep from wondering if it occasionally struck filmgoers in the 30s, subconsciously or otherwise, that while all the white sailors from the *Venture* were fleeing for the lives, it was a group of natives armed with little more than spears who ascended flimsy bamboo platforms to stand and fight. What other Hollywood film of that time shows black men fighting for their homes and families?

As to the natives' kidnapping of Ann and offering her up as a sacrifice, well, in a court today they'd plead self-defense in the face of Kong. (Not to mention the need to preserve their cultural identity and traditions.) Remember, until the *Venture*'s ape-hunting trespassers showed up, the tribe was ready to offer one of its own daughters in the service of the cause.

A little research reveals that maybe we shouldn't be so surprised at this very atypical, un-30s portrayal of the villagers. Unlike their cosseted tinseltown counterparts, for whom leaving Los Angeles (other than to visit New York or Europe) was an excursion into the wilderness, Cooper and Schoedsack had spent a good portion of their younger lives overseas, living and interacting with native peoples while making historically important films such as *Grass* and *Chang*. Having lived and worked in the Third World, participating in grueling migrations in search of forage or watching local people deal with man-eating tigers and other travails, how could they succumb to the commercial portrayals of such folk in their Hollywood film? Movie buffs always yearn to go back in time to watch Willis O'Brien animating Kong and the dinosaurs. Myself, I'd like to have been present while Cooper and Schoedsack were giving directions to the human inhabitants of Skull Island.

And as a cinematic/historic aside: sadly, the brief appearance of the great athlete Jim Thorpe as a native dancer on Skull Island was not deemed worthy of greater notice or exposure.

In the same sociological vein as the film's treatment of the villagers, and perhaps drawn from life, is the film's portrayal of the *Venture*'s Chinese cook, Charlie (Victor Wong). True, his pidgin English is sometimes played for light laughs, but the laughter is not at the expense of Charlie's essential humanity. Unlike so many "oriental" film portrayals of the 30s, he's not stuck in the film for sinister purpose or comic relief—he's a full-fledged member of the ship's crew. It made a distinct impression on me when, seeing the film as a child, I saw that it was Charlie who had the presence of mind to note the nocturnal visit of the islanders to the ship and sound the alarm—as opposed to one of his Caucasian counterparts asleep in their bunks.

The consequences of my repeated childhood viewings of *Kong* were profound and long-lasting. Admiration for the commanding presence of the native chief. Admiration for Charlie, who had more presence of mind than any of the dozing fools on the ship. Admiration, awe, and a never-fading interest in all those wonderful dinosaurs, who were after all only minding their own business and defending their respective territories against human intrusion and the hairy ringer who had been dropped in their midst. Admiration for and a desire to visit jungles and understand their magnificence, and a fascination with the lure of unknown lands, are enthusiasms that have stuck with me to this day.

Nor was I alone in my passions. After a session of watching *Kong* with friends, we would engage in animated discussions of whether a T. rex could really defeat a giant ape, how the film's dinosaurian portrayals clashed with those of famous paleontological reconstructors such as Burian and Colbert (not to mention Disney), and just

KONG UNBOUND

what Indian Ocean/South Pacific tribes the native inhabitants of Skull Island were actually related to (I always opted that they were the descendants of blown-off-course sailors heralding from the Solomons or Fiji).

Kong was never a monster movie to me and my closest friends. It was a grand paleontological and anthropological study underpinned by one of the greatest film scores ever written, stuck with the misfortune of having been saddled with a silly and completely unbelievable love story. Why was Denham so obsessed with bringing back a giant ape? Try as we might, my friends and I couldn't understand it. Didn't he, like Professors Challenger and Summerlee of Doyle's *Lost World*, see that bringing back a dinosaur or two would have been a bigger financial draw than bringing back an oversized gorilla, not to mention the excitement from a scientific viewpoint? Apes, even absurdly big ones, were not extinct. My friends and I wanted our dinosaurs.

Much later, Spielberg gave them back to us. *Jurassic Park* frightened and enthralled millions, with nary a monkey in sight (well, Jeff Goldblum does sport an impressive coiffure. . .). Why was it so successful? Because we believe in dinosaurs because they existed. They come down to us through the labors of science, not from the rubbing of a magic lamp. Colossal apes do not exist, and never did, except in Hollywood.

As to the classification of *Kong* as a horror movie, it never was for us. How could my friends and I be scared by something whose relatives we could see sitting and snoozing at the local zoo or begging for handouts? A T. rex, now, that was a different story . . .

My movie-viewing companions and I would never get a chill from watching a goofy-looking monkey. An ape is an ape, no matter how big the movies make him. Nor did we sympathize with Kong's "character" in the way Cooper and Schoedsack intended. How can you sympathize with a creature that slaughters everyone in its path in order to keep a new toy? That's a creation that reminds me more of Donald Trump (we'll skip the too-easy hair comparisons) than it does Tom Cruise in heroic mode. I mean, in the course of one movie, how many people did Kong stomp, munch, log-roll, and fling to their deaths from the granite cliffs of Manhattan? What did the commuters on that elevated train ever do to him?

Me, I was cheering for the guys in the planes (where we will presumably glimpse Peter Jackson at the end of his version of *Kong*, in keeping with the view we got of Cooper and Schoedsack, aloft, in the original film). At least the Alien was motivated by a desire to reproduce, Frankenstein by a quest for his missing humanity, Dracula for nourishment and company, and the Wolf Man—well, now there's a hairy character from the 1940s who was deserving of an audience's sympathy.

On the other hand, *Son of Kong* featured an ape I could at least partially empathize with. But then, he was a kid, too. And what of Mrs. Kong, who we must assume is still pining away back on Skull Island? Maybe we'll be introduced to her through Mr. Jackson. I'll bet she didn't feel sorry for the King, though. (Feel sorry for Kong? If I have to grieve for a King, give me Elvis.)

Stick with the dinosaurs, folks. They were real monsters. I'd rather lose myself in the science of *Kong*. Like Doyle's expeditioners, the story's human characters would have fared better had they done so, too.

On Kong

A Conversation among William Joyce, Maurice Sendak, and Michael Chabon

'VE ADMIRED Maurice Sendak since I was a child.
Please forgive me, "admired" is such a decorous, adult
word, so let me rephrase that . . . I've devoured with
relish, wild abandon, and unbridled joy the work of
Maurice Sendak since I was a child.

I've felt the same way about the work of Michael
Chabon since I first read his novel, *The Amazing
Adventures of Kavalier and Clay.*

Over the years I've made their acquaintance.
Becoming friends with my favorite writer from childhood
and my favorite as an adult is such a rare treat.

"Friend" is a splendid word, but the likes of Mr.
Sendak and Mr. Chabon deserve a more expansive
description, one redolent of the pleasures of being their
familiar, so I will refer to them as "friends" and "co-
conspirators."

I don't know if that's entirely accurate but I
like the snarky sound of it and if you were to look at
our various fictions you might be able to detect enough
thematic strands to say we were at least woven from
something like the same cloth.

King Kong is one of those strands that have
shaped, to various degrees, the stories we tell.

We chatted about the old fellow recently from
our different time zones and points of view. The following
is a record of that pleasurable communication.

—William Joyce

Joyce: Look let's talk about Mr. Kong.

Sendak: Well, I'm even older than him.

Chabon: But not by a lot are you?

Sendak: No. But since I was a kid brother—and other people were fortunate who had younger brothers, I would always make believe that the Empire State Building was my kid brother.

Joyce: That's a big kid brother.

Sendak: Well, you know, I don't have a small ego.

Chabon: So I think the building went up in 1932.

Sendak: And I think *Kong* was the first time the building was in a movie. I can't quite recover emotions like that, except I've always adored the building like it was family. Like maybe it was just the pleasure of knowing I came before something.

Joyce: So did you go to the building as a kid?

Sendak: No. If you lived in Brooklyn, the Empire State Building in New York City was the same as if you went to King Kong Land. It seemed as far away as Skull Island.

Sendak: So then when the movie came out and both these images are combined; this giant sex-crazed gorilla and that extremely big penislike building. Well, it's so hard to explain things that make *King Kong* powerful, it's so intrinsically, as I'm sure it is with you guys, bound up with so much primal passion, fear, sexual anxiety. God knows all those things are in *Kong*. And the majesty and the horror; I know I loved him. I loved him and suffered terribly every time he was killed.

Joyce: It was the first great tragedy of my life. I was inconsolable. Within days I also saw *Old Yeller* and *Shane*. So I was pretty much a wreck. But *Kong* hurt the worst. And since it was on TV and I was like five, I thought it was true like the news, so my parents had to explain what fiction was so I'd quit whining. But that made things worse. I believed in Kong—if he wasn't true then there were no wicked witches, Easter Bunny, no Santa. Nothing but grown-ups who I've distrusted ever since.

Chabon: I don't remember the first time I saw *Kong*, but I did show my kids. At first they were like "it's so fake" but within minutes they were completely into it.

Joyce: Yeah. It's still powerful. But the older I get the more essential the "fakeness" of *Kong* is to me. I mean it gives us more of a leap of faith to make. It somehow makes the once-upon-a-timeness stronger.

Chabon: Well it's that way with all the Harryhausen stuff, too; that weird, jerky, stop-motion thing that sets the monsters apart from the everyday, from reality. It separates them from us. It gives them the power of enchantment.

Joyce: And it seems, I dunno, to make it more accessible at least to a kid. I mean I could actually imagine myself sort of getting the same effect with my toys. And I wonder, even though kids now sort of demand a more convincing reality . . .

WILLIAM JOYCE, MAURICE SENDAK, AND MICHAEL CHABON

Chabon: . . . that something isn't getting lost.

Joyce: Bingo!

Sendak: The sight of him as the train is coming down the tracks was one of the most frightening images of my entire childhood.

Chabon: Uh-hum.

Joyce: You see him peek up over the tracks like an impossibly big "jack-in-the-box."

Sendak: The train and the little music—tah, tah, tah, tah. I just have to hear that. It just brings up the most panicky feeling in me.

Joyce: Well, you know, it just, it's something out of such a fever dream. It's better than anything you actually could think up.

Sendak: And somebody thought it up.

Joyce: Yeah, and then they got it on the screen.

Chabon: But it feels like it just always existed, I mean at least for me. I mean it's amazing to hear, to even think that the Empire State Building was once brand new. And that they worked it into the movie so quickly and that it was this new thing that he was climbing up to the top of. Because you know by the time I saw the movie, it was like he was climbing up to the top of a mountain or something that had always been there.

Sendak: Well, you know if you think of it in those terms it is so completely a New York filmland thing that they would use this brand new building for a commercial movie and you have this fantastically phallic commercial. A symbol of money, wealth, power, manhood, strength.

Joyce: America.

Chabon: Empire.

Sendak: And then you show the primitive aspect of our nature, a giant, impossibly big gorilla from a land of fucking cannibals. And then the girl—in his hand where he could innocently flip her breasts.

Joyce: Calm down, Maurice.

Sendak: I'm getting too excited.

Joyce: And mixed in with that how powerful Kong is . . . initially, you know, it's like you wish you were that. So powerful that no one, at least on Skull Island, could push you around.

Sendak: He was the beginning of the world.

Chabon: Right. And he's worshipped as a god.

Joyce: Yeah, and he kicks everybody else's ass. I mean that thing with him and the T. rex.

Chabon: Yeah.

Joyce: Kong is littler than the T. rex but he outsmarts

him. He has got these great moves. He breaks the rex's neck and does that amazing roar of triumph.

Chabon: Yeah.

Joyce: It was the same feeling I had when I watched *Tarzan* as a kid, when Tarzan would win he would throw his head back and do that insane yodel.

Sendak: Yeah.

Chabon: Uh-hum.

Joyce: But there's something innocent about Kong too. I mean he snaps the T. rex's neck and then plays with the jaw, like a little kid. It's a great, grim little joke. I wanted to be able to do that.

Chabon: Yeah, yeah.

Sendak: I wanted to do it to my mother.

Chabon: (Laughter)

Joyce: OK, well I think we all have childhood issues with our parents.

Sendak: But you know, it's a weird fantasy—I never understood it. I still don't.

Joyce: Well, that's probably what keeps it so strong.

Chabon: Yeah.

Sendak: Well, that's why we go back and we see it over

and over and over again though the mystery keeps expanding rather than being explained, I'm glad of that.

Joyce: I know.

Sendak: I would hate to think there really is an explanation to all of this.

Chabon: Right.

Sendak: That's what makes the perfect fantasy and the perfect nightmare. The filmmakers hit a nail, right on the head, that we didn't know existed.

Joyce: You know what scene freaked my kids out when they first saw it more than anything else?

Joyce: The one where he gets the wrong girl. I mean she's in her bed and this giant Peeping Tom shows up. She's unaware. He reaches in, drags the bed you know to the window, takes her, looks at her, she's freaking out, but he's holding her upside down and he drops her head first. And it just seemed even worse than the other ones that he had stomped on or bitten or thrown away. You know, it's like so horrible, it's funny.

Sendak: I think it told you immediately that this was savage energy run amuck. And that it is Kong's desire to kill arbitrarily. It's like the movie began to turn against him, that we should not really feel sorry for him because this is what he was capable of doing. The movie underestimated our own lust for killing and watching creatures die.

Chabon: Right.

WILLIAM JOYCE, MAURICE SENDAK, AND MICHAEL CHABON

Sendak: I had no sympathy with the airplane guys, none.

Joyce: Me neither. They were nothing.

Chabon: Nothing.

Sendak: I wanted to see those planes crack out with a blaze.

Joyce: I was on Kong's side from the beginning.

Sendak: I think everybody was.

Chabon: Of course.

Sendak: I really think everybody fell in love with him.

Joyce: The obvious question is "If he's such a savage why do we love him?"

Chabon: You can't help but pity him. You know, he is in a world not of his own making and maybe that's another thing that we identify with when we watch him is, you know, he got dragged to this place. He never asked to go there.

Joyce: Right. Just like first grade.

Sendak: Exactly.

Chabon: Or the world. I think from the minute you see him in chains on that stage, you love him. And it's just kind of an endless series of humiliations after that. I just always felt so awful when they start to shoot him from the airplanes—just seeing him bloodied like that.

Joyce: Well, it seems unfair. And it's a strange thing. I've
thought a lot about his rage, Kong's rage. Why that
appealed to me so much as a kid. It's like your own childhood rage, but amplified. Blown-up to an extremely satisfying proportion; you're a little guy and all these giant
grown-ups are telling you what to do and trying to tame
you and civilize you and push you around. So I loved
Kong's wrong-sizedness, you know. He was too big, I was
too small, and he didn't take it. You know he went, "All
right, God dammit! You're going to push me around, let
me show you what I can do."

Sendak: And then society shows you what they could do.
To warn you that any digression from norm. "I'm not
doing the proper thing; I'm not being a good little boy."
Don't you dare, don't you dare try that shit with us. We'll
break your ass, and just because you just got your first
hard-on and you came a droplet in the bath.

Joyce: Yeah. As a five-year-old it was a real wake-up call
when they killed his ass at the end of the movie.

Sendak: Well, I think, Bill, I think you got something by
the tail. What we've been talking around is simply that
this is a child's ultimate fantasy of power.

Joyce: So do you really think, Maurice, and Michael, do
y'all think that beauty killed that beast?

Chabon: I never bought that part of it. Whenever I would
try to think about the story in terms of "Beauty and the
Beast" it just didn't fit that mold. Because to me, in
"Beauty and the Beast" the beast is in control in so many
ways and he sets the terms of the relationship with the

girl and she has to abide by the rules of his house, and it seems like such a very different situation. But the thing about *King Kong* is that it feels like the story that fits into so many other stories. It feels so mythical in so many ways. But then, when you actually sit down and try to think of what other kinds of stories that it's related to, it seems completely unique.

Joyce: It's so daft. So primal.

Sendak: I think it is the primal situation of power and young life and sexual desire, which you don't understand as a kid and probably scares you to death.

Joyce: "It was beauty killed the beast" always reminded me of the "no place like home" part of *The Wizard of Oz*. I mean you don't believe that shit at the end about there's no place like home.

Sendak: I always thought that.

Chabon: I hate that message.

Joyce: But you know when *The Wizard of Oz* was re-released in theaters a few years ago and I went to see it. When it came to the end, to the part I've always scorned, the "there's no place like home" part. But seeing it up on the screen, for the first time I thought, maybe Dorothy doesn't believe it either but she's got to come up with something. To get by with.

Sendak: She's much wiser then. It's not like she hates her aunt and uncle, she realizes they're limited. She's an artist. She's a creative young girl. They don't have her vision and they're afraid of the dark side of things. So,

OK, you don't stop loving them because they're limited. All parents to us seem limited so "No place like home" is a kind of, to me, a kind of irony. Her effort to make the grown-ups feel better.

Joyce: I mean the farm is in ruins. Elmira Gulch for all we know is even more powerful, so Toto's gonna' be roadkill. So it's a lie she's trying to convince herself of. Auntie Em and the farm, as cruddy as they are, that's all she's got.

Sendak: And then she's sitting in bed: "You want to hear what happene, Auntie? You want to?" "No honey. No honey. You just lie back."

Joyce: Yeah. Right.

Sendak: In other words, grown-ups don't want to hear the horrors of childhood.

Joyce: No, they really don't, and most children realize that.

Sendak: It doesn't make you stop loving your auntie or your mommy, you just come to that realization that it is limited but there is no other place like home.

Joyce: Well, you have to admit, there is no girl like Fay Wray.

Chabon: I mean, I guess there are [other] stories about women being ravished by monsters or carried off by animals or beasts and so on.

Joyce: Well, in "Beauty and the Beast" it's the beauty of sexual power.

Sendak: As big as you are, as grotesquely killer-like as you are and you can destroy the world and climb the Empire State Building, sexual passion will bring you down.

Chabon: I don't know. I was told it can.

Sendak: But it's all in her.

Chabon: With beauty?

Sendak: That beautiful tiny little form.

Joyce: And she said no.

Sendak: Exactly. The one thing he can't deal with, he doesn't have any experience to lean back on.

Joyce: But how could he? I mean that's what's so curious. As a kid it seemed to me like there was only one Kong. It was like he hatched rather than was born.

Chabon: Right.

Sendak: Well, you know it's not so unlike the first *Tarzan*. Yes, we know how Tarzan got to the jungle, but we don't believe he got to the jungle the way they told us; maybe, like you say; maybe he hatched from a magic egg or something.

Joyce: What kind of thing lays a Tarzan egg?

Sendak: But Tarzan is a beautiful hero again brought down by beauty. Instead of sticking to his business of killing snakes and snapping animals' heads off, he lets this girl mop the floor with him.

Chabon: Yeah. But really, was it really beauty that killed the beast? I mean, wasn't it, the airplanes?

Joyce: I dunno. I dunno.

Chabon: Yeah?

Joyce: Well, they put him in those chains and it took him—what?—two seconds to get out of that? He knocked down a train on the El. He knocked down at least one of those planes rather matter-of-factly.

Sendak: But if he hadn't been smitten by her. After all she was just another sacrifice to him. I mean how different was she than the other girls he'd grabbed and eaten?

Joyce: Well, as Carl Denham said, "Blondes are kind of scarce around here."

Sendak: There you go, the first Marilyn Monroe.

Joyce: With that little slip . . .

Sendak: That little slip—mamma mia.

Joyce: I mean, the other girls had coconut bras and I just don't think that was alluring.

Sendak: But, it's his weakness. In *Samson and Delilah*, man is brought down by woman.

Chabon: *Samson and Delilah*. That's part of it, you're right.

Sendak: Yeah.

Chabon: That is definitely part of it.

Joyce: So what: Is it planes? Is it the girl? What killed Kong?

(Long pause.)

Joyce: It was the blonde.

Chabon: " 'Twas peroxide that killed the beast."

Sendak: It was Hollywood that killed the beast.

(Another pause.)

Sendak: If he had just eaten her.

Joyce: Instead of sniffing her.

Sendak: Then he would have gone on forever.

ABOUT THE AUTHORS

ABOUT THE AUTHORS

RAY HARRYHAUSEN was dazzled as a child by the special-effects work of Willis O'Brien in films like *King Kong*. As an adult he became a master—and legend—in the field of stop-motion animation. His first film, *Mighty Joe Young*, even teamed him with his mentor O'Brien. Harryhausen's work on the many horror, fantasy, and science fiction films from the 50s to the 80s has left an indelible mark on moviegoers of all ages. He is best known for his work on the dinosaurs in *One Million Years B.C.*, battling skeleton armies in *Jason and the Argonauts*, and a multitude of 50s creature features from *The Beast from 20,000 Fathoms* to the classic *20 Million Miles to Earth*. Harryhausen's unique hands-on touch provided an aura of personality, charm, and even menace to the creatures he animated.

RAY BRADBURY, American novelist, short story writer, essayist, playwright, screenwriter, and poet, was born in Waukegan, Illinois. He became a full-time writer in 1943, and contributed numerous short stories to periodicals before publishing a collection of them, *Dark Carnival*, in 1947. This was followed by *The Martian Chronicles* in 1950, *The Illustrated Man*, and *Fahrenheit 451*. Other works include *The October Country*, *Dandelion Wine*, *A Medicine for Melancholy*, *Something Wicked This Way Comes*, and *I Sing the Body Electric!* He published more than 30 books, close to 600 short stories, and numerous poems, essays, and plays. His short stories have appeared in more than 1,000 school curriculum "recommended reading" anthologies. Bradbury's work has been included in four *Best American Short Story* collections. He has been awarded the O. Henry Memorial Award, the Benjamin Franklin Award, the World Fantasy Award for Lifetime Achievement, the Grand Master Award from the Science Fiction Writers of America, and the PEN Center USA West Lifetime Achievement Award, among others.

KAREN HABER is the author of eight novels including *Star Trek Voyager: Bless the Beasts*, co-author of *Science of the X-Men*, and editor of the Hugo-nominated essay collection celebrating J. R. R. Tolkien, *Meditations on Middle Earth*. Her short fiction has appeared in *Asimov's Science Fiction* magazine, the *Magazine of Fantasy and Science Fiction*, and many anthologies. She reviews art books for *Locus* magazine and profiles artists for *Locus* publications including *Realms of Fantasy*. With her spouse, Robert Silverberg, she has co-*edited Best Science Fiction of 2001*, and the popular "Universe" anthology series. She and Jonathan Strahan have continued the "Best of" series with *Best Science Fiction of 2003*, *Best Science Fiction of 2004*, and *Best Fantasy of 2004*. Her newest science-fiction novel, *Crossing Infinity*, a tale of gender confusions, will be published in November 2005.

RICHARD A. LUPOFF has led a long and varied career writing mysteries, fantasy, mainstream, and science fiction. He has also been a soldier, a college professor, a short-order cook, a filmmaker, and a Hollywood bit player. Among Lupoff's books are: *The Classic Car Killer*, *The Comic Book Killer*, *Edgar Rice Burroughs: Master of Adventure*, *The Great American Paperback*, *The Comic-Book Book*, *Lovecraft's Book*, and *Sword of the Demon: A Novel*.

CHRISTOPHER PRIEST was born in Cheshire, England. He began writing soon after leaving school and has been a full-time freelance writer since 1968. He has published 11 novels, three short story collections, and a number of other books, including critical works, biographies, novelizations, and children's non-fiction. His most recent novel, *The Separation*, won both the Arthur C. Clarke Award and the BSFA Award. In 1996 Priest won the James Tait Black Memorial Prize for his novel *The Prestige*. In 2001 he was awarded the Prix Utopia (France) for lifetime achievement. His novels include: *Indoctrinaire*, *Fugue for a Darkening Island*, *Inverted World*, *The Space Machine*, *A Dream of Wessex*, *The Affirmation*, *The Glamour*, *The Quiet Woman*, *The Prestige*, and *The Extremes* (1999). He is married to the writer Leigh Kennedy. They live in Hastings, England, with their twin children, Elizabeth and Simon. You can visit his web site at: www.christopher-priest.co.uk.

ROBERT SILVERBERG was born in New York City and educated at Columbia University, and has been a resident of the San Francisco Bay Area for many years. His first book, *Revolt on Alpha C*, was published in 1955. He has won four Hugo awards (1956, 1969, 1987, 1990) and five Nebulas (1970, 1972, 1972 again, 1975, 1986) as well as most of the other significant science fiction honors. In 2004 he was designated a Grand Master by the Science Fiction Writers of America. He is the author of over a hundred books and an uncounted number of short stories. Among Silverberg's best-known titles are: *Dying Inside*, *The Book of Skulls*, *Nightwings*, *Thorns*, *Up the Line*, *Lord Valentine's Castle*, *The Man in the Maze*, *Downward to the Earth*, *The World Inside*, *Shadrach in the Furnace*, *At Winter's End*, *Born with the Dead*. His most recent book is *Roma Eterna*.

JACK WILLIAMSON was born in 1908 and arrived in New Mexico via covered wagon at the age of seven, where his family homesteaded land that they still manage today. He first became aware of the new field of "scientifiction" in his late teens, and decided that writing these new adventures would be even better than reading them. He sold his first story to *Amazing Stories* in 1928, and quickly became one of the most popular writers in the genre, a distinction he still holds today. Named a Science Fiction Writers of America Grand Master in 1976, he has won numerous awards for his writing, including both Hugos and Nebulas. His latest novel, *The Stonehenge Gate*, was published this year, as was his newly updated autobiography, *Wonder's Child*. Despite having traveled the world several times, he still lives and works in Portales, New Mexico.

HARRY HARRISON sold his first short story in 1950—when a sore throat and fever made his hand too shaky to complete artwork he had been selling to science fiction magazines. A writer was born—and has been publishing for 55 years. In his anthology, *50 in 50*, containing one story from every year between 1950 and 2002, is "The Streets of Ashkelon," which has been anthologized 43 times. His novels include *The Stainless Steel Rat* series, the *West of Eden* trilogy, and *Make Room! Make Room!*, which was adapted for the film *Soylent Green*. A winner of the Nebula Award and the Prix Jules Verne, he makes his home in Ireland.

WILLIAM STOUT has been a professional illustrator for over thirty years. Beginning as a cartoonist, he worked on such newspaper comic strips as *Tarzan of the Apes*. He was the first American contributor to *Heavy Metal* magazine. His subsequent work in comic books garnered the field's two top awards, the Eisner and the Harvey. Stout has loved all things Oz since he first saw the MGM film, and owns a complete collection of the original Oz books. Stout worked in 1999 as the lead designer for Kansas City's "Wonderful World of Oz" theme park. In early 2004 Stout was the designer for *The Muppets' Wizard of Oz* movie. Stout has recently won awards for his illustrations and artwork that appeared in *Abu & the 7 Marvels* (which won awards for Best Young Adult Book) and *Hiding the Elephant—How Magicians Invented the Impossible and Learned to Disappear*, which was a *Los Angeles Times* bestseller.

PAUL DI FILIPPO has been writing professionally since his first sale in 1977. Among his best-known titles are *The Steampunk Trilogy* and *Ribofunk*. He recently penned a special e-issue miniseries of the popular comic book series, *Top 10: Beyond the Farthest Precinct*, for America's Best Comics. He lives in Providence, Rhode Island, with two cats—Queen Mab and Penny Century—and a chocolate cocker spaniel named Brownie, who carries on the legacy of parti-colored cocker Ginger, who, after serving as vice president of Paul's fiction factory, recently died after fourteen years of unstinting loyal comradeship. His mate, Deborah Newton, serves as Fay Wray to his King Kong.

ESTHER M. FRIESNER is the Nebula Award-winning author

of 31 novels and over 100 short stories, in addition to being the editor of seven popular anthologies. Her works have been published in the United States, the United Kingdom, Japan, Germany, Russia, France, and Italy. Besides winning two Nebula Awards in succession for Best Short Story (1995 and 1996), she was a Nebula finalist three times and a Hugo finalist once. She received the Skylark Award from NESFA and the award for Most Promising New Fantasy Writer of 1986 from *Romantic Times*. Her latest publications include a short story collection, *Death and the Librarian and Other Stories*, and *Turn the Other Chick*, fifth in the popular *Chicks in Chainmail* series that she created and edits.

HOWARD WALDROP, who was born in Mississippi and now lives in Austin, Texas, is one of the most iconoclastic writers working today. His highly original books include the novels *Them Bones* and *A Dozen Tough Jobs*, and the collections *Howard Who?*, *All About Strange Monsters of the Recent Past*, *Night of the Cooters*, and *Going Home Again*. He won the Nebula and World Fantasy Awards for his novelette "The Ugly Chickens," and has been short-listed for both awards many times.

FRANK M. ROBINSON is a science fiction and suspense writer whose bibliography includes a collaboration with the late Tom Scortia on *The Glass Inferno*, filmed as *The Towering Inferno*, "a gaggle of techno-thrillers," and the novels *The Dark Beyond the Stars*, *Waiting*, and most recently, *The Donor*. He has also written the coffee table book *Pulp Culture*, and *Science Fiction of the 20th Century*. He lives in San Francisco.

PAT CADIGAN is the author of fifteen books, two of which, *Synners* and *Fools*, have won the Arthur C. Clarke Award. She lives in North London with her husband, the Original Chris Fowler, her son Rob Fenner, and the Queen of the Cats. Several years ago, she and Rob took a stuffed monkey up to the observation deck of the Empire State Building. However, since they took the elevator, no one really noticed.

DAVID GERROLD writes: David Gerrold is an imaginary companion. Please do not encourage him.

PHILIP J. CURRIE is a Curator of Dinosaurs at the Royal Tyrrell Museum of Palaeontology in Drumheller, Canada. He has published 100 scientific articles, 85 popular articles, and 11 books, focusing on the growth and variation of extinct reptiles, the anatomy and relationships of carnivorous dinosaurs, and the origin of birds. Fieldwork connected with his research has been concentrated in Alberta, Argentina, British Columbia, China, the Arctic, and Antarctica. Since 1986, he has supervised or co-supervised 31 MSc and PhD students at the University of Calgary, the University of Saskatchewan, and the University of Copenhagen. He has given hundreds of popular and scientific lectures on dinosaurs all over the world, and is often interviewed by the press.

JOE DEVITO was born in New York City. He graduated with honors from Parsons School of Design in 1981, studied at the Art Students League in New York City, and has taken several workshops in human and animal anatomy with John Zahourek. His love of learning and his strong artistic inclinations have led to a long career as an illustrator and sculptor. Over the last twenty years Joe has illustrated hundreds of book covers specializing in science fiction, fantasy, adventure, horror, and dinosaurs. His credits include covers for Piers Anthony, Terry Bisson, Robert Bloch, Jonathan Carroll, Robert Heinlein, and Katherine Kurtz, and illustrations for the last seven *Doc Savage* books. An avid writer as well, Joe has recently created and illustrated his first book, *KONG: King of Skull Island*, which he co-wrote with Brad Strickland. Joe can be contacted at both www.jdevito.com and www.kongskullisland.com.

ALAN DEAN FOSTER is a prolific writer of science fiction, fantasy and movie novelizations. He is best known for his science-fiction novels set in the Humanx Commonwealth—an interstellar union of races including humankind and the insectoid Thranx. In the area of fantasy, his best-known work is the

KONG UNBOUND

Spellsinger series. In addition, it has recently become known that he wrote the original novelization of *Star Wars*, which had been credited to George Lucas.

Printed in the United States
By Bookmasters